# Johnny Doesn't Drink Champagne

**Also by Cody Young**

*American Smile*

*Scandal At the Farmhouse (a novella)*

*The Lady and the Locksmith (a novella)*

**Coming soon**

***Johnny and the Vampires of Versailles***

**For more information about Cody Young please visit:**

**www.codyyoungblog.blogspot.com**

# Johnny Doesn't Drink Champagne

**Cody Young**

**Golden Bay Press, Auckland, N.Z.**

© 2011 Golden Bay Press
All rights reserved.

ISBN 978-0-473-19403-1

Printed in the United States of America

Cover Design: © Golden Bay Press
Cover photo: © Joseph | Dreamstime.com

## Acknowledgements

Without the love and support of my husband, I wouldn't be writing love stories at all. Thank you, Andrew, for making this and many other dreams come true.

Warm thanks to my writing buddies, especially Amanda Antonio, for all her help and advice. Heartfelt thanks to my mother, Joy, and my mother-in-law, Barbara, who both thought I should write a vampire novel. Here it is.

# Chapter One

It's always been my dream to go to London, and now, at last, I'm here.

Well – almost. I'm at Heathrow airport and it's packed with all kinds of people. I'm standing near the baggage claim waiting for the giant tartan wheelie bag my grandmother insisted on lending me for the trip. Seriously uncool, I know. I look down at my feet, standing for the first time on English soil. Or English carpet tiles, at least. My sneakers are new and chafing a little – that ten hour flight from Chicago was a killer.

It's late – nearly midnight. I look around for the rest of my group. Twenty-eight teenagers on a high school trip to London, all from the same small town in the Midwest. Can't be too hard to spot. I was last off the plane because I left my coat under the seat and had to go back. I gaze across a sea of unfamiliar faces, and I wonder if any of them made the journey for the same reason I did. I see tourists, backpackers and airline pilots. Young women in headscarves and old men with walking sticks. Moms with screaming babies and guys with big ice-hockey bags. Tall skinny girls who look like runway models and men in long robes, jabbering away in languages I've never heard before. But then, the noise seems to fade away – as if someone has turned the volume right down. A chill goes through me. I turn, as if I know he's there, though I swear I have no idea why.

That's when I see him.

In one endless moment that lasts less than a fraction of a second, he is imprinted on my mind. He could have stepped out of the pages of a magazine. My memory takes a dozen photographs, yearning to remember the heart-searing beauty of his face. An entirely masculine beauty that only now I understand. Yes, perfection exists – because *he* exists. His jacket is dark and austere – perfectly cut. The word 'Armani' comes to my lips like the words of a whispered incantation. Silently, I form the syllables, but I'm unable to make a sound. He moves through the crowd, heading my way. I can't quit staring. No man alive deserves to be blessed – or cursed – with looks like his.

He moves as if cameras flashed around him, lighting up the perfect angles of his face. His hair is dark, longer than average, swept into a sleek side part. In my mind, I caress it. I run my fingers through the strands, and yes – it is as smooth as silk. I shiver. I shake my head to dispel the decadent images that cloud my mind. I long for him to look my way – and yet I fear it too. For if he looked into my eyes, I feel sure I would see disinterest or disappointment in his. A blue jeans girl with a soap-and-water beauty routine; I wouldn't get more than a glance. My faded shirt with butterflies on the front isn't likely to impress a man who wears Armani.

But as I stand there, he turns his head, and his eyes meet mine. My heart cries out in agony of the sweetest kind. He has fiercely intelligent eyes, darker than my own – much darker. The eyes of a French nobleman, or an Italian movie star, glittering as they turn to meet my helpless, hopeless stare. His face is more youthful than I first thought. He could not be more than twenty, or twenty-one. But I'm a schoolgirl, and I have no business eyeing up strangers in unfamiliar airports in the middle of the night.

I know I will die if he smiles at me. He looks like a man who smiles often. For the paparazzi. And yet tonight, he is alone.

He is so close. I fight a wild impulse to reach out and touch his sleeve. I long to feel the texture of the charcoal wool beneath my trembling fingers. I clench my hands into fists and fight with all the mental strength I possess, and I do not move from the spot. I realize I'm in his way, but my feet won't move. They will not obey my desperate command to step out of his way and let him pass.

His brows arch in enquiry as if to ask why I stand – spellbound – in front of him. A hint of a smile plays upon his lips. He knows. He knows the reason for my stunned, involuntary stare. I swallow in mortified embarrassment. But still I let my eyes feast on him.

My face flames and my tongue tries to remember how to speak. 'Forgive me,' I murmur and step aside.

The smile dies on his face, and a look of surprise replaces it – if I am not mistaken. There is another emotion too, there in the depths of his glittering dark eyes, and it scares me.

Anger? No. Surely not. My helpless adoration wouldn't make him angry.

Fear? It could not be. Guys who look like that don't feel fear.

Recognition? Yes. Recognition. But that's not possible. I would definitely remember if I'd met *him* before.

To my undying surprise, he reaches out. He reaches out and touches me! He grips my arm and his grip is tight and unrelenting. I gaze down and see his strong male hand, gripping hold of my arm. I can feel his strength through the soft cotton fabric of my shirt.

"What did you say?" he demands. His accent isn't French, or Italian. It's English.

I gulp. "I think I said 'forgive me' – because I was in your way and I… "

"Say it again." His eyes glint with that dangerous emotion I saw just a moment ago.

I am shaking now. He is a stranger. He is, without a doubt, the most beautiful young man I have ever set eyes on. Yes. But at this moment, he is behaving like a crazy person. Even in my dazed and delusional state I can see that. I glance around wildly, and I wonder how I came to be separated from my group. I must shake free of him and find the others. Brody and Lydia and everyone else. Mrs. Bertorelli. I'd even be glad to see her, just now.

"You know, I gotta go." I look down at his fingers on my arm.

His grip doesn't falter. "Say it again!"

It seems best to humor him, so I smile a weak, idiotic smile. "Forgive me."

"It's you. Madeleine." He speaks with real astonishment in his voice and he expects me to know him.

"No. No. I'm Madison. I'm sorry." The words are out of my mouth before I realize how dumb it was to tell the guy my real name.

"Madeleine! I know it's you!" He sounds quite angry now.

It bothers me that he picked a name so similar to my own, but surely this must be a coincidence?

I shake my head. "I'm not Madeleine."

He frowns. He studies my face, searching for signs of recognition.

"You're not Madeleine?" His dark eyes seem almost soulful for a moment.

"No. Sorry."

He lets go my arm, and the confident, movie star manner evaporates. I stare into his troubled dark eyes and glimpse something I did not expect to see. Tenderness. Confusion. Sadness. Somewhere inside this know-it-all, seen-it-all, super-cool guy, there is a boy, not much older than myself. But then, he narrows his eyes.

"My mistake," he says, in a voice laced with anger and suspicion. He inclines his head, giving me a curt, old-fashioned bow. "I apologize."

I try to smile, but the whole conversation has been rather unsettling. He seems to expect more, so I give it my best shot. "No problem. Could have happened to anybody."

"Jet lag," he says tersely.

I realize that I have succeeded in putting *him* off balance. Quite a turnaround from just a moment ago. I nod in hearty agreement, though one surreptitious glance at his Calvin Klein face reveals no sign of exhaustion. No lines, no shadows under the eyes, nothing. Just smooth, perfect skin, and glittering dark eyes. He's as crisp and fresh as that starchy white shirt he's wearing. Probably travels First Class all the time.

I tear my gaze away and try to concentrate on the matter in hand: finding my bag. I study the luggage carousel like my life depends on it. I fix my attention on the row of black and navy bags passing by, giving each one serious consideration as if it might turn tartan and shout 'surprise!'. But all the time I feel his presence – just a few feet away. I try to remain focused on waiting for my bag, but now and again I steal a sidelong glance at him, and I strongly suspect him of doing the same.

Out of the corner of my eye, I see him get something out of his pocket. I risk taking another look. It's a little piece of paper, old and yellow. He stares at it, scowls, and then he crumples it up in his fist. I watch as he lets it slip from his fingers and fall to the ground. Quite deliberately.

A loud American voice startles me. "Madison! There you are!"

Mrs. Bertorelli. Cross with me. Worried about me.

I can see from her face that she's tired and I've put her through the wringer. She's a short woman, a New Yorker, with a wide face and a double chin. She wears her hair in one of those styles that has 'a lot of volume' and she must have sprayed it to hell and back so it didn't deflate while she was on the plane. With hair like that she wouldn't even need a neck pillow. The color is basically purple, though I'm sure it must have said something like 'burnished mahogany' on the box. She's waving her fat little hands at me, to get my attention. Her rings are glinting in the artificial light. She wears a lot of rings, on all but the third finger of her left hand.

"Madison, honey. Where have you been?"

"Oh. Hi… Sorry!" I don't say the fatal words 'forgive me' this time.

"We've been looking all over for you! Everyone else has gone to find the bus."

"I had to go back for my coat, Mrs. B. I left it on the plane. One of the fight attendants went in and got it for me."

"I see," she says, and she reaches out and touches the jacket with her short stubby fingers, as if to make sure I'm not faking. "I guess you can't go round London in September without a jacket," she says grudgingly.

"It's still August, Mrs. B." I remind her gently.

"You know perfectly well what I mean. Put it on. It's cold outside tonight. Thank goodness I've found you. I thought I was one down before we even made it to the hostel."

I haul on my jacket, obediently. "Sorry I scared you, Mrs. B."

"Oh my gosh, Maddie. Is that your bag?"

I turn and see the giant tartan eyesore being swept away on the conveyor belt. It's already out of my reach, and so I try pushing my way through the crowd to see if I can rescue it, apologizing all the way. I catch frustrating glimpses of it as I try to shove my way through to try to grab hold of its old plastic handle. I can see I'm not going to get it. It's heading serenely towards the black rubber strips concealing the entrance to that unknown, unnamed area out back. The place where all the lonely unclaimed bags end up. I suppose I'm in for a long, long, wait while it does another lap of honor around the entire system. Or worse – they might pull it off the conveyor and send it to Lost Property.

I sigh. Mrs. B isn't going to be thrilled about this.

Then I see him again – the man in the immaculate charcoal suit. He appears through a gap in the crowd and suddenly he's right there – reaching out his hand to grab my bag. I see his outstretched arm and his pale, elegant fingers, rescuing my runaway bag, just before it disappears out of sight. He lifts it up and off the conveyor, and then he checks the label. I watch him tweaking open the tag and taking a look.

I frown. Now he knows where I'm staying. I bite my lip.

He looks up and catches my eye. He looks kind of angry – in a sultry, stormy sort of way – but he moves towards me, and holds out the offending tartan bag.

"I believe this is yours, Miss Lambourne."

I take hold of the handle, and my fingers graze against his as we do the exchange. I look up, feeling grateful and a little guilty. "Thank you."

"Not at all." His tone is light and casual. His eyes are not.

"My teacher's waiting for me." I say, desperate to get away, but mesmerized by him all the same. I'm drowning in his dark eyes. Yearning to feel the glancing touch of his hand again. Knowing I never will.

"Of course," he says. Very British. Very proper.

He turns away and releases me from his spell. I can breathe again, and I remember my manners. "Thank you. Thank you so much!"

He spares me one last, intoxicating glance. "Fare thee well, sweet lady."

His strange turn of phrase leaves me struggling to make sense of him, again. I stare as he disappears into the crowd. Fare thee well. What archaic words they are, and used so lightly, so naturally, as if he spoke like that all the time. I feel a tiny surge of pleasure, and I can't suppress a smile. Sweet lady. He called me sweet lady! Though I have to say his voice was a little gruff and bitter when he said it. But he said it, all the same.

Again, it's Mrs. Bertorelli who breaks into my little daydream with her harsh New York whine. "Now wasn't he your guardian angel, huh? He came along just in the nick of time."

I smile weakly and struggle with my bag. The ancient mechanism that allows the handle to extend seems to be jammed. At this rate I will have to drag it like a dead animal out of the airport, instead of wheeling it gracefully away like everyone else.

"Didn't kill him to help out a pretty girl, of course." Mrs. B says, with a laugh.

I bite back a swear word that comes to my lips, and tug at the handle of my horrible bag. At last it gives. The handle extends and I straighten up. I can wheel it along – slowly and with a repetitive bump every few inches. One of the wheels must have gotten squashed out of shape or something. It's like towing a little drunk guy along by the hand. A little drunk guy in a huge tartan overcoat.

"Move it along, Maddie! I wanna be on the bus, honey. My feet are killing me. I need to take the weight off and I still have to get all those kids settled into the hostel. If that bus has gone without us I am going to be so mad!"

"I'm doing my best, Mrs. B." I try to sound cheerful and upbeat, but it's late and I'm tired too. The crowd has thinned out a little, and we start walking towards the door that leads to passport control. I see something pale on the floor up ahead of me – a scrap of paper, discarded like an old candy wrapper. People are walking right over it, treading it into the carpet, but I am drawn to it like a magnet. I feel certain that I know what it is and I want to go see if I'm right. I watch people passing by and dread that one of them will notice it first and take it before I can get there – but of course, they don't. To them it's just a piece of litter.

I veer away from Mrs. Bertorelli and I go and check it out. Staring down, I see that the paper is thick and yellowed with age. It's folded and crumpled and it's been trodden on, but I'm guessing there's writing inside. I bend down and pick it up.

"Maddie!"

"Shoelace," I insist, stuffing the ball of paper into my pocket. I make a pantomime of adjusting my shoe. Then I hurry after her and we make our way out towards the long queue for the checkpoint.

Outside, in the parking lot, I can see the bus waiting for us, with everyone else on board. The driver is standing outside the bus, pacing up and down. He looks as if he's been cursing Mrs. Bertorelli and me for a good thirty minutes or more. He helps me stow my trusty tartan friend in the luggage hold and slams down the metal hatch. I climb up into the bus and a big cheer goes up. About ten different people want to know what took me so long.

Further back on the bus my best friend Lydia leaps up out of her seat and starts waving at me. "Here, Maddie! I saved you a place!"

"Hey, Madison. Did they strip search you?" The question comes from Brody, who sits with me in Compulsory English. He has gum in his mouth and his cap is on back to front. As usual, there is far too much interest in his round blue eyes.

His sidekick, Tanner, answers for me. "Like she'd tell *you,* even if they did!" Then he laughs like a hyena, and sticks his foot out to try and trip me up.

I roll my eyes and try to step over his leg. "No, they did not mistake me for a terrorist," I hiss, "but I'll let them know you're carrying explosives on the way back if you like."

Mrs. Bertorelli turns and yells in a voice that would halt a herd of buffalo. "Enough interrogation, Tanner Doyle! For your information, nobody got strip searched. I did offer, but they just said welcome to the United Kingdom and have a pleasant stay."

Everyone on the bus erupts in laughter, but she has their attention.

"Will you all sit down and shut up, so we can get this show on the road?"

The bus driver turns and glances warily at Mrs. B over his shoulder. I guess he hasn't met anyone quite like her before.

I head for where my friend is sitting, about two thirds of the way down, on the right hand side of the bus.

Lydia's great but she's always been the odd one out. She's a platinum blonde with braces on her teeth. Her style owes more than a little to Madonna's early look. Miniskirts and military boots, that kind of thing. She gets up and moves into the aisle and lets me take the window seat. She's generous like that, and she knows how much this trip to London means to me. I slump down and the bus starts to move.

Lydia gets out her (pink) cell phone and flips it open. "Your dad's been messaging me."

I shoot her an agonized look. "You're kidding."

"Nope. He's worried. Apparently you promised to call when you arrived."

"But I haven't arrived," I say, consternation brewing. "I'm barely out of the airport."

Dad is unbelievable sometimes. I reach inside my pocket for my phone, which I had obediently switched off when we got on the plane. Instead I encounter the crumbling edges of that piece of paper I picked up off the floor at the airport. Just the feel of it gives me a tiny thrill of anticipation.

Brody pipes up again. "Hey! Check out the Lamborghini!"

Everyone on the right hand side of the bus peers out of the window into the parking lot. Sure enough, there's a highly unusual car oozing down the street. A just-out-of-the-showroom kind of a car. Pale silver, not a mark on it, raindrops beading on all its gleaming bodywork. The windows are tinted and I can't see who's behind the wheel, but for some reason, I know who's inside it. I can feel it.

It's him. Mister Didn't-We-Meet-Someplace-Before.

"Oh man! That is one hell of a car," Tanner says. He's standing up in the seat in front of me, with his face pressed against the window of the bus, flattening his nose. He's practically licking the glass.

I'm guessing he looks like a ghoul from the outside.

Beside me, Lydia lets out a sigh. "That's two hundred thousand bucks worth of car. Right there."

I shoot her what I hope is a sympathetic look, but she frowns at me. I know that Lydia's family is dirt poor, and I know who paid for her to come along on this school trip too, and it wasn't them. I'm sworn to secrecy and I'm not even sure if Lydia knows the whole truth. Maybe she thinks it really was the school hardship fund that paid for it all. But I know it wasn't.

It was my dad. He didn't want me to make this trip on my own, so he forked out for my best friend's fare too. I'm glad he did – real glad – but it's created this tension between me and Lydia that I didn't expect. Maybe I'll get a chance to say something to her tomorrow. To clear the air. To apologize for having a generous dad – an overprotective, sentimental old fool of a dad who sometimes has more heart than he has sense.

It was a difficult call and he did what he thought was best. For me and for Lydia. I know he went over to her house and talked her parents into letting her go. Told them to forget their pride and take the money, for Lydia's sake. I'm glad they said yes. I hope she'll be glad too when she gets used to the idea.

Finally we are on our way, and in spite of being so tired, I look out into the dark night and try to catch my first glimpse of England, but all I can see is a big curving slip road leading to the freeway – or whatever they call it over here. The road up ahead gleams black and shiny in the rain, and traffic from the airport streams past. Red tail lights reflected on the wet road– that's about all there is to see. Not much to write home about yet.

Lydia has settled back in her seat to read her book. It's a dog-eared paperback with a creased spine, and I'll bet she's read it before. I smile.

I lean over and whisper to her. "What is this time? Vampires, werewolves, or shifters?"

"Vampires. They always win. Hands down."

I sit back and try to relax, but my mind is still buzzing from the encounter at the airport. I decide to allow myself a surreptitious look at the little piece of contraband in my pocket. I pull it out and unfold it gently, for although the paper is heavy, the edges are so fragile that they crumble away in my fingers. I smooth it out. I catch my breath and pray I won't be disappointed.

It's like the start of an old, old letter. Written in black ink. There's no name at the top and no signature at the bottom, either. Just a few words scrawled in black ink – and they could mean anything.

> *'Forgive me. In time you will forgive me. I'll be waiting for you at Heathrow, last Wednesday in August, in the year of our—'*

It doesn't say which year. There's a harsh black line trailing away from the last word, as if the person who wrote the letter had gotten interrupted before they finished it.

I gasp out loud, but it's not the words that shock me. I almost knew the contents would be cryptic. He was that kind of guy –

the enigmatic stranger at the airport. It's not the words that disturb me. It's the way those words are written.

The handwriting.

Fear grips my throat, like a cold hand around my neck. I take a few short sharp gasps for air, and Lydia looks up in surprise.

"What's wrong, Maddie?"

"Nothing!" I fold the letter up. I can't let her see.

"What have you got there?"

She reaches for my precious letter, but I snatch it out of her grasp. My heart is pounding in fear. "Nothing! It's just… a list… of stuff I had to pack," I say desperately, struggling to concoct something she won't question. "I think I forgot my cell phone charger. Can you believe that?"

"No," she says. "Your dad will have got you three spares."

I stare fixedly out of the window to hide my lies. I'm scared.

Lydia murmurs something about borrowing her charger when we get to the hostel. Then she leaves me alone and goes back to reading her book.

When my heartbeat has slowed down again, I take one more surreptitious glance at the letter, just to make sure I'm not seeing things.

But I'm not. Every detail is etched into my mind, correctly. The 'H' in the word Heathrow. The 'g' in forgive me – and the way the writer dots every single 'i' with a tiny little circle. Every detail is familiar.

I know the handwriting. The way the letters all lean backwards. The person who wrote this letter was left handed, just like me.

The person who wrote this letter *was* me.

# Chapter Two

The room at the hostel is tiny. Two beds on either side of a narrow strip of carpet, and a little nightstand in between. The nightstand is metal, like a filing cabinet, only short and squat. It has a small bedside lamp on it for us to share.

Lydia looks through the doorway in dismay. "We got assigned the room furthest from the bathrooms."

"Yes. But it's also the room furthest away from Mrs. Bertorelli. Did you pick that?"

A smile appears on Lydia's face and we high five. We stumble into the room, which seems extremely crowded once we get all our bags in through the door. There is hardly enough space to put the bags down flat so we can unzip them and get our clothes out. We have to take turns.

I want to tell Lydia about the letter. I've always told her everything. But I'm tired. In the dim glow of the low wattage, energy-saving light bulb overhead, I unpack just what I need for tonight and slip along to the bathrooms – dodging Brody on the way.

"Hey baby, I wouldn't mind being your bar of soap!" he calls out from the doorway of his room. He is dressed in only his boxer shorts.

"Cut it out, Brody! What ever happened to separate hostels for men and women, huh? That wasn't such a bad system."

"That's for monks and nuns, Maddie, not red-blooded guys like me."

Mrs Bertorelli emerges from her room, wearing an extraordinary purple housecoat that matches her hair. She gives him a withering stare. "Need help brushing your teeth, do you, Brody?"

"No, thanks, Mrs. B.," He bares his teeth for her to see. "All done. Shiny and white."

Brody has excellent teeth. In fact he's quite the all-American guy. Six feet tall, blond hair, broad across the shoulders, narrow in the hip. Shame he has the personality of a deranged cockroach.

I scoot into the bathrooms and freshen up.

When I get back to the room, Lydia says she's found my cell phone charger, so what the hell was I freaking out about on the bus?

I shrug. "Nerves. What's on the schedule for tomorrow?"

"Tower of London," she says, in the same bored tone she would use on a regular day at school.

"Cool," I say, wishing she wasn't making this so hard.

She sighs. "Amazing opportunity, yes. I'm very lucky."

I frown. Now's the chance to say I'm sorry about Dad muscling in and opening his checkbook, but I'm afraid I'll make things worse. Why does she have to have such a chip on her shoulder about it anyway?

Lydia sighs and starts putting those awful bendy curlers into her platinum blonde hair so she can look like Marilyn again tomorrow. Right now she is starting to look like Medusa with all the snakes.

I sit down on the narrow bed and get out my phone. I send a quick message to my parents to tell them I've survived the journey. I'm not sure what the time is back home, but they told me not to worry about that. My guess is they are sitting at the kitchen table with their cell phones out, waiting for news. They reply instantly, with panicky instructions about getting enough sleep, taking my vitamins, having a great time and not talking to strange men.

I tell them goodnight, and then I slip under the covers and try to settle down to sleep.

There is a long awkward silence.

I think about the discarded letter I found at Heathrow. It's tucked into the inside pocket of my jacket. In my mind's eye I see the young man who let it slip from his fingers, and something doesn't add up. The yellowed fragment of paper doesn't seem like the kind of thing that guy would carry.

Everything he wore and everything he had with him was brand new. Expensive and ultra modern. The suit, the bags, the Lamborghini.

It doesn't make any sense.

My feelings don't make much sense either. I shiver when I think of him. He was beautiful – he was breathtaking – and I can't forget his face. It is etched into my mind as if drawn in sharply by Leonardo Da Vinci himself. Only Leonardo could have captured that face – revealed some part of its true beauty.

I reflect on the bizarre conversation we had. He spoke to me. He touched my arm. Left me confused and bewildered.

"Lydia. You awake?"

"No."

In the morning, I wake to the unfamiliar sound of London traffic. There is another noise too, a weird knocking sound that I can only assume is an airlock in the ancient system of pipes and radiators that heats this room. Looks like it was installed in the Victorian Era.

I get out of bed and go look out of the window. It's an old sash window, and it's quaint and quirky like everything else around here. I see a green leafy square of grass below, and people walking from place to place. This hostel is owned by one of the London universities. Come October, this building will be home to real students. For now Lydia and I get to pretend to be college kids like we hope to be next year. It feels very grown up. We get dressed, in jeans and sweatshirts, and prepare to take on the day. I glance at the slogan on the front of Lydia's new shirt – the only thing she bought new for this trip.

My Boyfriend is a Vampire, it reads.

I roll my eyes.

At breakfast we all sit at long tables like some old-fashioned boarding school, and the grown-up feeling evaporates. We have eggs and bacon and hot coffee. Brody wants to know if either of us are afraid of the sight of blood, because the Tower of London has seen a hell of a lot of executions.

"Are you on their list for this morning?" Lydia asks him, feigning a note of hopeful optimism and a sweet smile.

They warned us that England would be cold, but today is warm and sunny. The last day in August. We wait on the grass for the bus. Some of the girls make daisy chains. Some of the boys make fools of themselves. Especially Brody.

We get on the bus and Mrs. B. does another one of her headcounts. Then she introduces us to a weedy looking guy with a moustache. He's called Nigel Puckett and he's going to be our guide while we're in London. Mrs. B. gives him a big build up like he was topping the bill on some Broadway show, and he stands there going rather pink while we give him a round of applause. He is wearing a Fair Isle vest and what appears to be a *knitted* bow tie. He has pleat-front pants, well-polished brown shoes and an old tweed jacket – complete with leather elbow patches.

"This is an unexpected pleasure," he begins. "My colleague Hugh Littlehampton was supposed to be guiding you through our fair city this morning, but he has been struck down with an attack of tonsillitis, which was very unexpected, since he gargles almost every day with salt water. So last night at quarter to nine, I received a telephone call from my other colleague, Dr. Basil Craig, Dean of History here at the college, inviting me to take poor old Hugh's place and… "

"Wake me up when it's over," Lydia says, and snuggles down in her blue plush seat, determined to ignore it all.

We take in a few of the sights en route to the Tower – and it's slow going because the traffic is heavy. Nigel does his best to fill us in about this and that, but even he runs out of steam after a while.

The driver lurches the coach into the parking lot in Lower Thames Street and we all get out. We troop along in a straggly line towards the Tower, and then we all have to wait while Mrs. B. sorts out our admission.

Then, I have an idea. I abandon my place in the queue and go find Mr. Pleatfront Trousers.

"Mr. Puckett," I say, and put on my best schoolgirl smile. "You're an expert on history, aren't you?. May I ask you something?"

"Er… yes. Ask away!" He's got that slightly startled look of someone who has set himself up as a bit of a know-it-all, but inside he's desperately hoping I'm not going to ask him anything he can't answer. His moustache is quivering.

I reach into the pocket of my jacket and get out the letter. "I found this. I wondered it you could take a look at it for me."

Puckett takes it, and has a closer look. It intrigues him, I can see that.

"Where did you find this, my dear?"

"A friend gave it to me."

I stand there wondering why I said that. Didn't want to admit to picking up random pieces of litter, I suppose. Besides, it's become sort of special to me now.

Puckett turns the piece of paper around in his freckly fingers, and looks up at me. "Where did your friend get it?"

"I don't know. I don't know anything about it. I was hoping you could tell me something. The paper looks old, doesn't it?"

"It's not paper," he says. "It's vellum."

"Vellum?"

"Vellum parchment. Made out of calfskin."

I try not to think about the calf involved.

"Vellum lasts much longer than paper," he says. "The writing is very odd, though. Anachronistic."

"What do you mean, *anachronistic*?"

"I mean odd. At the time when vellum like this was being made, nobody had handwriting like that. It's been written with a quill pen, I'd say. A feather. But the writing is modern."

"I noticed that." I'm suddenly in awe of Mr. Puckett. He knows a hell of a lot about vellum. I'm hanging on his every word now.

"Did you notice the faint trace of gold along this edge?" He says.

I hadn't, but now that he has pointed it out, I can see it clearly, glinting in the sun.

"It's a page torn from a valuable book. Such a pity. I think the writing must have been added later. Yes. I would have to conclude that this is a very old piece of vellum that your friend has been using to practice his writing on. Does that sound plausible?"

"Very." I smile weakly. "Thank you so much, Mr. Puckett. I'm so glad that other guy dropped out and we got you instead."

"You're very kind." He's thrilled to have been useful. I can see it. His pale gray eyes are bright behind his spectacles.

I'm no nearer to the truth. My 'friend' couldn't have written it. Not unless he happens to have identical handwriting to mine, which I doubt.

Suddenly, the abrasive sound of Mrs. Bertorelli's voice brings our little discussion to an end.

"We're in, everybody! We're in!"

She's waving her clipboard high above her head, since she is only about five feet tall, but she stands her ground like General Eisenhower. "This is the plan, so listen up! We hear Mr. Puckett's words of wisdom first of all, and then you'll have a chance to look around the Tower on your own. Do not get lost. This bus leaves at three-thirty sharp and I want you back in your seats at three twenty-five. Do I make myself clear?"

Mr. Puckett hands me back my letter, and I tuck it back into my jacket pocket.

"We'd better do as the good lady tells us," he says, and his moustache does another little quiver. He seems a little scared of Mrs. B.

"Yep. Don't mess with a woman with purple hair."

We go through the gates of the Tower and I'm moved by the thought of all the prisoners who have lived and died within these cold gray walls. Our footsteps echo on the polished stone floor, as we make our way to the main galleries. It's eerie in here, with its high vaulted ceilings and its museum smell. After the pale August sunshine outside, it seems cold too. For nine hundred years, people have been held captive here against their will. I can sense their desperation.

Yes, it feels like a place of death.

Mrs. Bertorelli ruins the moment by giving every student a questionnaire to fill in – as if we couldn't have soaked up a bit of history without that.

"A silly paper chase in the name of education," Lydia whispers to me, under her breath. "My favorite!"

"Yeah."

I hunt for a pen while an argument breaks out between Mrs. Bertorelli, Nigel Puckett and a large Beefeater – resplendent in a scarlet coat. They are all talking in hushed, we're-in-a-museum voices, but there is definitely some kind of power struggle going on. I tune in and see if I can work out why.

Apparently, it isn't quite the done thing to bring our own tour guide into the Tower. We're supposed to have a proper Beefeater assigned to us – and the Beefeater in question seems to be getting very hot under the collar. Mrs. Bertorelli is scowling at him and shaking her head, but in the end poor old Nigel backs down and Beefy gets his way.

We get frog-marched out to Tower Green for the full treatment. We gather in a circle around the site of the scaffold, and our Beefeater – a stocky guy with a boozer's nose – gives us a lurid account of how it was used.

"This is how Anne Boleyn finally lost her head," he informs us, amiably. "She was put to death with a sword, as befits a noble lady, and it is said that with one single blow, the executioner cut right through her delicate little neck."

This guy obviously enjoys his work.

"Of course, if the executioner was in a bad mood, it could take as many as five strokes of the axe to sever the head of the unfortunate victim… and that's exactly what happened in the case of Lord… "

I take a sidelong glance at Lydia, and bite my lip. She's hating this. She looks extremely pale. I know she's probably still tired from the long flight yesterday, and none of us got our full eight hours sleep last night. But she doesn't look right, to me. She is paler even than a platinum blonde should be.

"Now, if any of *you* was up for the chop this morning, the first thing you would do is pay your executioner – coz he ain't going to do it for free." Beefy gives another wheezy laugh. "And you'd want him to do a good job, wouldn't you?"

Brody nudges me. "You have to pay the guy to chop off your own head," he says in a low voice, right beside my ear. "But I guess you don't have to tip him afterwards, huh?"

I push him away.

Lydia is concentrating hard on her map, turning it round in her hands. I'm guessing it's an excuse not to look at the block. I can see her fingers are trembling.

Beefy's voice rises above the crowd. "Now let's talk about how to hang, draw and quarter someone, shall we?"

Lydia sways slightly. It's only a tiny movement, but I see it. I put my hand on her arm and try to whisper "Are you okay?"

It's no use. I see her mouth go slack, and her eyes glassy. Then her head goes back, and she just crumples into a heap on the floor. Like someone pulled the plug and all the air went out of her. Reacting as one, our group utters a rather melodramatic "Oooooh!" sound.

We all stare down at Lydia, taking in the deathly pallor of her skin, which tones so well with the silver and gray eye shadow duo that she applied this morning. Her legs are kind of splayed out in an undignified way, and her mouth is open.

"Lost one, 'ave we?" our Beefeater asks, with a leery, self-satisfied grin.

"Let me see what's going on, will you?" Mrs. Bertorelli prises her way through the crowd like she was opening up a giant clam.

Our Beefeater orders people out of the way on her behalf. "Let the dog see the rabbit!'

Mrs. Bertorelli peers down at Lydia in dismay. I feel rather useless and wish I knew what to do, but Mrs. B is on her knees in a flash. She starts patting Lydia's face to see if she can bring her round, tugging at the neckline of the Vampire sweatshirt so it isn't cutting into the poor girl's airway.

"Come on, honey!"

# Chapter Three

"Oh God... what's happening?" Lydia murmurs and her eyes flutter open again. She seems to get a bit of a fright when she sees that she has turned into the main attraction, lying on the grass on Tower Green. "Oh shoot."

Mrs. Bertorelli tries to haul Lydia up into a sitting position. "You passed out on us, honey. Did you skip breakfast?"

Suddenly, my brain clicks back into action and I kneel down beside my teacher. "Lydia's diabetic. Did she tell you that?"

"I guess it's on a list somewhere. Lydia, sweetie, have you got your meds with you, or are they back at the hostel?"

Lydia is sitting up now, examining a grass stain on her elbow. "I think they're in my backpack. On the bus."

"Shall I run and get them for her, Mrs. B.?" I start wondering if I can remember how to get back to the parking lot in Lower Thames Street.

"Yes, that would be helpful, dear, but let's get her inside first. Brody! Tanner! One of you on either side, please! We can't leave her lying on the grass all day."

"NO!" Lydia begs. "Not them. Please Mrs. B. – I'll never live it down."

Beefy the Beefeater suddenly gets all helpful and enthusiastic. "Lean on me, love. We'll get you inside before you can say London Bridge is falling down."

He ducks under Lydia's arm and gets her upright. She's still a bit limp, but he walks her back into the main building. The rest of the group straggle along behind. Brody's looking sheepish and Tanner is laughing behind his hand. Selena – part of a trio of girls who all wear the same brand of sunglasses – wants to know if we still have to finish filling out the questionnaire.

Mrs. B. says everyone has to wait in the foyer while she deals with Lydia, but I'm part of the exclusive little group that gets to go into a back room behind the desk. We get Lydia sitting down in there, and have a tense discussion about the medication.

Lydia apologizes for all the fuss, and says she thinks she got confused when we switched time zones.

"It could be worse, honey," Mrs. B. says. "On the skiing trip two years back we had a broken elbow, and in Crete one of the girls needed the morning after pill. I've seen it all."

Mrs. B gets on her cell phone to try to get hold of the bus driver. Lydia leans her head back against the wall and says she's got a splitting headache. She asks me to get her a drink of water, so I run and try to find a water cooler.

This proves rather more difficult than I thought. Water coolers seem to be less common here than they are back home in America. I hurry along a long corridor that I thought led to the refreshment area, but it turns out to be the way through to the weapons collection. I head back across the foyer and try the other side. Over there I get caught in a huge crowd of people who are on their way to see the Crown Jewels. I do my best to be pushy, but I get buffeted along in the wrong direction. Finally, I ask another staff member to help me, and he tells me to go up a flight of steps and I'll see a water fountain on the landing. I ask about cups and he finds some for me. The whole thing takes a lot longer than I planned.

When I get back with the little plastic cup of water, and find the room where Lydia was sitting, it's empty.

I wait for a few moments, holding the silly little cup. Then, I go back into the corridor and put my head around the door of the office next door. I wait for the admin lady to get off the phone so I can ask her if she knows what's happened. She's seems very preoccupied, but pauses mid-conversation and says she thinks they've gone to wait outside in the main entrance.

I go look out there, but I can't find my group. I go back to the enquiry desk, but it is unattended.

Okay, this is odd. No need to let this faze me. Not just yet. They wouldn't leave without me. They are here in this building somewhere. Or in the White Tower. Or something.

I start heading back into the main gallery, walking fast, looking to the left and to the right as I go.

I suppose they could have gotten worried about Lydia and decided to head back for the hostel. But even if they did, I reason, it seems unlikely that the ever efficient Mrs. B forgot to count up when she got everyone back on the bus – and even if she did Lydia would have spoken up.

I know she would.

I chase like a shadow around the various buildings that form the Tower complex. I'm a little angry with them all for putting me in this situation when I was only trying to help. I get out my phone and fire off a brief message to ask Lydia why they all took off in such a hurry, but there is no reply. I start worrying about Lydia and wondering if she went unconscious again. But even if they had to deal with that, surely *someone* will notice that I'm missing soon?

I sigh and tell myself that although I don't know where they are, they know where I am. I'll just stay here at the Tower until they put out an announcement and then I'll go down to the front desk and make another round of apologies. I slow down, and start loitering in front of some of the exhibits.

I hesitate in front of a display about the Princes of the Tower. Two boys, heirs to the throne, who lost their father. The oldest one is twelve – same age as my kid brother – but this boy is the young King of England, waiting to receive his crown.

Only his uncle wants it all for himself.

An unfamiliar voice speaks, just behind me.

"Hello."

I turn to see who it is, and catch my breath.

My heart does a double somersault in surprise. "It's you!"

"Yes, it's me."

The guy from the airport. He stands there, unsmiling. Hands shoved into the pockets of a tailored jacket. Eyes dark and soulful.

I gulp. I feel like a wild animal caught in a trap. He wants something. He expects something from me.

When I find the courage to speak, I whisper. "Do I know you?" I wish my voice sounded more confident, more assertive. Less wispy and afraid.

There is a long, long pause. He looks straight at me, studying me.

"Apparently not."

My breathing is too rapid, and I make a conscious effort to slow it down. "Should I know you?"

He doesn't answer me, but I notice that one of his dark sardonic eyebrows rises just a little.

It's unnerving.

I swallow and let my eyes run over the display board in front of me. Anything to dispel some of the intense awkwardness that

I feel when I'm with him. It's a sad story, about the Princes. They didn't stand a chance. They couldn't escape.

"What brings you *here*, of all places?" he asks.

"I'm on a cultural exchange trip, a high school thing." Only after the words are out of my mouth, does it cross my mind that I do not have to justify my movements to a complete stranger.

"You have come for no other *more specific* purpose?" he asks.

"No."

He frowns, and again, his gaze searches my face. This is so weird.

Suddenly I figure that if he gets to ask *me* weird questions, I can do the same. So I give it a try. "May I ask what brings *you* here?"

He shrugs. "I'm always here. I'm a Patron of the Tower."

*A Patron of the Tower*. That brings to mind images of dusty sponsorship committees and wealthy old couples who want their name on a brick.

He seems to sense my disbelief. "The Tower of London is a place of great importance to me. It's nice to be able to give something back."

"It's an amazing place," I murmur, politely.

He stares straight ahead – his eyes scanning the words and pictures on the display board. His face is sad, but perhaps he is moved by the story of the Princes. It captured *my* attention. In my mind's eye, I can see the two boys. I don't know why, but I imagine them with dark blond hair and blue eyes – my own coloring. Their fate intrigues me.

"Do you think they were murdered?" I say.

He gives me a sidelong glance. "Do you?"

"Well… no one really knows for sure, do they?"

A flicker of emotion crosses his beautiful face. He looks down and a lock of dark wavy hair falls over his brow. "It was a long time ago."

A wave of yearning floods over me. I am not a girl who gets 'crushes' on guys. I am not silly and giggly and I have never written anyone's name in a heart on a tree. But this guy – this raven-haired stranger with the glint in his eye – he gets to me.

Abruptly, he looks past me, and scans the room. "If you *are* with a school party… why do you appear to be alone?"

"I'm worried they might have gone without me."

"Gone without you?" There is skepticism in his voice, so I rattle through the story about Lydia passing out and the diabetes and the backpack.

He gives a short sigh, and another disconcerting dark-eyed glance. "You'd better come with me."

I hesitate. "I don't think I can do that."

"Don't be ridiculous. Let me take you down to the office and make some telephone calls."

I can't really object to that. It's probably what I should have done in the first place.

So, we walk. Not exactly side by side. He walks fast, with a slightly irritated expression on his handsome face, and I hurry along beside him, feeling like an idiot. We pass through various rooms with artifacts on display, all gleaming under the subdued museum lighting. A woman with a name badge on her shirt passes by in the opposite direction. "Morning, Johnny!" she calls out cheerily.

He smiles back, and acknowledges her too. A brief smile, professional and disinterested, but even that fills me with heartache. *Johnny*. His name. The first time I've heard it. I risk a curious sidelong glance at him, and he catches me at it.

"Johnny De Vere," he says, filling in the blanks.

He seems to resent that he has to.

"It's kind of you to help me out," I stammer.

"No choice," he says.

*Gee thanks. Sorry I breathed.* But I don't say it. I keep walking and say nothing.

Downstairs in the office, I hear him say his name again several times, in that warm, I-need-a-favor tone of voice that good-looking guys sometimes use on the phone.

"Johnny De Vere here. Tower of London. Yes. I'm trying to contact the organizers of the Ashwell High tour party. That's right. We have a young lady here. Got separated from the rest of her group. Madeleine, no, *Madison* Lambourne."

I look up when I hear him make that slip again.

He notices my reaction, and turns away from me, glancing casually at the artwork on the walls while the man on the other end of the line puts him on hold. I'm sitting on the chair where Lydia sat just a little while ago. Waiting to find out what I'm supposed to do.

I gaze down awkwardly at my sneakers and wish I didn't feel about twelve. At least I know that Johnny De Vere really is who he says he is. A Patron of the Tower. Everyone seems to know him around here. For a young guy he commands an awful lot of respect, too. Must be loaded. I hate that idea, though I'm not sure why. It's not like I have a chance with him anyway.

Then he cups his hand over the receiver, and speaks to me.

"Are you happy for me to run you back to the hostel at the college?" he says, innocently.

*Happy?* I stare back at him, while the idea sinks in. To drive through the streets of London with Johnny – presumably in a Lamborghini – fills me with a sort of nervous dread. On the one hand, I'd take any chance to prolong my encounter with this guy. I'd even get into his car – though this is exactly the kind of scenario that my parents warned me about and he does appear to be stalking me. All because I bear some resemblance to this Madeleine person he is so hung up about.

On the other hand, I need a ride back, and he has gone to every effort to convince me that he means me no harm. He's practically on the staff here and I ought to trust him. But the thought of being with him, alone in his car, trying to think up polite stuff to say? Terrifying.

I can't stand here all day, while he waits for my reply.

I nod, and stare back at him. "Okay."

When we get to the main entrance, I glance outside. I can see sunshine coming in through the door, but Johnny turns the other way.

"My car isn't parked on the street."

No, I suppose it wouldn't be. You couldn't leave a car like that just anywhere, could you? Not in London.

We stop in front of a pair of double doors and Johnny feels in his pocket for some kind of electronic key. He swipes it and leads me into the part of the Tower that the public never get to see. He leads me away through a maze of dark corridors and down a flight of stairs. I start to feel a little nervous.

We follow the signs that say 'underground car park' and end up in a small subterranean area full of expensive cars. It's cold down here, and either the drop in temperature or my nervousness starts to make me shiver.

"You like American cars?" he says, conversationally.

I guess he's trying to make small talk, but he's picked the one topic I know nothing about. Some people can talk for hours about torque, performance, and engine power. But not me. So I deflect the question.

"Do you?"

"Yes, I do. I have a Corvette. A red one. A Stingray."

"Really? Not a Lamborghini, then?"

He frowns. Perhaps he doesn't know I spotted him at the airport. Neither of us have mentioned that hideously awkward meeting yet, and perhaps it's best if we don't. He reaches for his keys, presses a button, and the Lamborghini lights up. We walk over to the car, and I can see that my mild remark has irritated him.

"Get in."

I obey him, obviously, once I get over the shock of the car door opening out and up, unlike any other car I've ridden in. The seats are real leather, I'm sure they are. They feel like leather and they even smell like it. I snap my seatbelt into the shiny metal clasp, and glance over at him. He's reaching out for the steering wheel, revealing the white cuffs of his immaculately dry-cleaned shirt. He's wearing gold cuff links. Now that he's so close, I catch a faint hint of his cologne, too, mingling with the new car smell. He turns his head to reverse the car out of the space and I try not to stare.

He's so... sophisticated. I feel so young, so awkward, with him.

He eases the car out past a gray concrete pillar, does a perfect three-point turn, and then drives out of the building and up the slope into the street.

We nudge through the traffic and it's all pretty slow until we get further away from the Tower. The car turns a few heads at the lights – and a few more as we speed along the street.

Soon we are heading down a busy main road, and I'm seeing all the things I thought I'd see. London buses, big black taxi cabs, streets teeming with people, terraces of smart townhouses with railings out front. Grimy brickwork. Shabby chic.

"Have you been a Patron of the Tower for long?"

A hint of a smile appears on his face. "Ages."

I fall silent, and so does he. So much for my first attempt at conversation.

"Have you always lived in London?" I say.

"No."

Another one syllable answer. Doing great so far.

Finally, he takes pity on me, and does some of the work. "I'm based in France," he says. "I inherited an estate in the Champagne region."

"Really?" I have visions of a beautiful old French villa and a riot of autumn color in the vineyard beyond. I smile. I've got a thing about champagne. I've never tasted it – my Dad won't let me – not until I'm of age. I have a secret ambition to find a way to try it, while I'm on this trip. The legal age for purchasing alcohol is lower in England – and at least one of the girls on the trip has already turned eighteen. But I'm not telling Johnny any of that. I try to think of something very grown up to ask him instead.

"Is your family in the wine trade?" I say, hoping I've struck the right note.

"I have no family. But yes, the estate produces champagne."

Oh my gosh, he just gets better and better. I stretch out my legs shyly, and I see that his glance travels there for a moment. I'm in jeans, but they're skintight, and I know I have nice legs. I'm guessing he can see that, too.

"This car is amazing," I say.

"Better on the open road," he says. "Same with the Corvette. I could show you what I mean, if you like?"

Thinking he means he wants to show me what the Lamborghini can do, I smile. "That would be nice."

"Yes?" he says, turning to glance at me for just an instant. There is a dangerous glint in his eye and it mesmerizes me. I catch my breath, and he turns away, focusing on the traffic.

For a moment, I'm unable to think about anything except how extraordinary he looks in profile. His smooth forehead, his dark brows, the aristocratic lines of his nose. The curve of his lips. His hair is softer today – more wavy – than it was last night at the airport. More casual. It curves around to touch his cheekbone, like the wing of a bird.

"Yes," I murmur, finally remembering that he's waiting for me to reply. I'm not quite sure what I've said yes to, but moments later we are speeding along a highway and I'm beginning to see what people love about these ridiculous Italian cars.

I experience a rush of sheer exhilaration, as the car pulls effortlessly away from the rest of the traffic and leaves them all for dead. So this is what two hundred thousand dollars buys you, is it?

But then, we pass a road sign that says 'Blackwall Tunnel' and a bolt of fear goes through my chest. I try to remember how to breathe. This isn't the way back to the hostel. But he's not taking me back to the hostel, is he?

# Chapter Four

Okay, now I'm in panic mode. I'm in a fast car with a strange man and I have no idea where he is taking me. I glance across at him, but he stares straight ahead as the motorway signs flash by. We are leaving the city of London far behind us. I am shaking inside, and I'm trying to hide it.

"Where are we going?" I say, with a quaver in my voice.

"You said you'd like to see the Corvette," he says, with a slight frown. "It's no distance."

Obviously his concept of no distance and mine are not the same. I swallow, trying to calm down. He's showing me his Corvette. That's the pretext, anyway. And technically, I agreed to this.

I am suddenly overwhelmed with a strong feeling that Mrs. Bertorelli would not approve of my decision to get into his car. My mother wouldn't like it either and my dad would be on red alert.

"Maddie. Is there anyone you'd like to call – to tell them that you are going to be a little late?"

I nod and fumble for my phone. I drop it in my anxiety and have to lean down into the foot well to retrieve it.

"Let me guess," he says. "Your screen saver is bright blue, and you have a picture of you and your best friend in there?"

This guy is unbelievable. It's like he's been spying on me my whole life.

I pretend this isn't as weird as it feels. "Predictable, huh?"

Then there is a long, long pause.

"I keep my cars at The Grange," he says – as if I ought to know it.

"Where's that?"

"In Kent."

I nod.

"I have an apartment in London, of course."

*Of course.* The guy has everything – except a sense of humor and the ability to put seventeen-year-old girls at their ease.

"The Grange is bigger, and it has land around it. More space for the cars."

I am so out of my depth. Come back Tony from my photography class – the first guy I ever kissed. He lived above a convenience store.

"Maddie, are you okay?"

I notice he's calling me Maddie now, like he wants to be one of my friends, though I never invited him to. I give him a worried glance. "I didn't realize it was going to be so far."

"Sorry. It was a little presumptuous of me to bring you out here."

"It's okay."

"And it was trusting of you to come along," he says, with a slight smile. "I might be a cold-hearted killer."

I pretend to laugh. Cold-hearted killer. OMG – he's got a nerve!

He asks me a couple of questions about what I'm studying and what I want to be. I give him the bare minimum. No need to tell the guy my life story.

We drive on through the English countryside. He takes an exit off the motorway that leads to a small town with the picturesque name of Swanley.

We drive on past, eventually coming to a leafy little village clustered around a beautiful old stone church. Johnny takes a turning marked 'The Grange'. He noses the car down a long driveway.

A beautiful house comes into view. Half-timbered and so old that the roof seems to sag under the weight of time. Johnny wheels the car round and comes to a stop. He parks in a patch of deep shadow beside the barn. He releases his seatbelt and gets out, and this time he goes around and opens the door for me.

I step out onto the gravel and look around. He seems to be waiting for my reaction, so I tell him I love the house.

"And the barn?" he says, meaningfully.

We both stare for a moment at the barn, covered in dark-green ivy. Huge curved beams hold up the walls of the ancient building. Beams that are dark and weathered with age.

"The barn's cool."

"You've seen it before?"

"Of course not," I say, and look up at him, in all innocence.

He studies my face for several seconds longer than is really polite, and then he leads the way over to his converted barn.

"The barn is even older than the house," he says. "Medieval, in fact."

"The age of chivalry isn't dead," I say, risking a teasing smile as he opens the heavy barn door for me.

He has several cars in there – not just the Corvette, with its sinewy curves and gorgeous, cherry-red paintwork.

I ask him what they all are and he tells me. There's a classic Jaguar, an E-type, and a World War Two jeep. An old Aston Martin – a beautiful shiny Lagonda – dating from the nineteen twenties. The guy even has a Model T Ford – black and shiny, like the day it left the factory. One hell of a restoration job.

"You like collecting old cars?"

He laughs. "No. I buy them when they're new, and I never sell them on."

His laughter isn't warm and friendly – it's hollow and bitter. The sound echoes up around the barn ceiling, with all its exposed v-shape beams. Echoing around in the darkness.

He's crazy. I'm in a barn with a crazy guy.

"You really *don't* understand, do you, Maddie? You don't know who I am, or *what* I am?"

"No. Please tell me what's going on, Mr. De Vere."

"Johnny. You knew my name before."

"I only met you today, Johnny." He's scaring me now, and I get flustered. "I mean yesterday! I met you for the first time yesterday."

"Yesterday and today. It's all the same," he murmurs. "Oh… Madeleine—"

"I am NOT Madeleine. Look, I want to go back to the hostel now. My friends will be worried."

"You don't like it here?"

"No. I have no idea why you brought me to this place, other than to impress me or scare me, or both. Why *did* you bring me here?"

"It was an experiment," he says icily. "And it didn't work."

"An experiment? Great." I march towards the barn door. "Well. Johnny. Would you please *stop* experimenting on me and take me back to London? Right now!"

# Chapter Five

We drive back to London in silence. He says he's sorry, more than once, but I say nothing.

I don't know what to say. It's the middle of the afternoon now, and the shadows are stretching out. Who knows what kind of trouble I'll be in, when I get back. I haven't had any lunch and it doesn't seem to occur to Johnny that I must be starving. He grips the steering wheel, with a grim expression on his handsome face. The traffic thickens as we get back into the city, and he has to concentrate.

Back at the hostel, he insists on talking to Mrs. Bertorelli. We stand in the entranceway of the hall of residence having an awkward exchange.

Her, and me, and Johnny Weirdo De Vere.

To my surprise, she's extremely polite to Johnny and thanks him again and again for taking care of me and driving me back from the Tower. She's been busy all afternoon dealing with Lydia – who passed out a second time just after I left and had to be hurried away to get medical attention.

"She's going to be fine," Mrs. B. says, apologetically. She smiles at Johnny, and pats a strand of her purple hair back into place. "But they're keeping her in the hospital overnight, for observation. It's a pain in the ass – I mean neck – if you ask me, Mr. De Vere. But I guess they want to be sure she's okay before they let her out. It put the kibosh on our little visit to the Tower of London, though."

"Yes," Johnny says, thoughtfully. "I'd like to offer some recompense to your party, if you would allow? To make up for some of the disappointment."

Mrs. Bertorelli touches his arm. "That's so sweet, Mr. De Vere. But it wasn't your fault the day turned out the way it did."

"No matter," he says. "I can offer free admission to the Tower for your whole party. It would be a shame to go back to America without having a chance to see it properly."

"Well, that's very generous of you, Mr. De Vere."

"Johnny," he says, and flashes her the most charismatic smile I have ever seen. I fold my arms in disapproval, and pretend to read a notice on the wall about dealing with harassment. But Mrs. B is lapping it up.

"Why, thank you, Johnny, for taking such an interest in us. Several of my students were very upset that they didn't get to see the Torture Chamber."

*Yeah, that would be Brody and some of his happy little friends, I suppose.*

"The chamber is… not to be missed," Johnny agrees, giving Mrs. Bertorelli another captivating smile. She's nodding and smiling at him too, like he'd just offered to give her a back massage and a foot rub.

Then his face takes on a sort of 'concerned' look. "There is one little favor I would ask you to do for me, if I may?"

"Oh, ask away," she says, "if there's anything in my power… "

"On our way over here in the car, I was telling Madison about our re-enactment nights at the Tower," he says.

I turn and stare at him in surprise. This is the first I've heard of it.

"Oh, you do historical re-enactments? How wonderful!" Mrs. B. is impressed.

"Yes. Enormously popular they are too. Trouble is, we're one short for tomorrow night's performance and since Madison is studying Drama, or so she tells me, I wondered if you would consider *loaning* her to us for a few hours? As a special favor? I'll take great care of her.'

*Say no. She has to say no.*

"Of course! Why, Madison, you lucky girl – to get an opportunity like that!"

"I don't know, Mrs. B. I ought to ask my parents first, don't you think?"

"Would you like me to speak with them?" Johnny says, smooth as silk.

"No! I mean, no thank you." I stare wildly at Mrs. Bertorelli, trying to use telepathy to tell her I would rather die than go to a re-enactment night at the Tower of London. With Johnny.

"The only reason I ask is that Madison would fit the costume nicely, if I am not mistaken."

He gives me one of those up and down glances that appraises my entire body, and I stiffen, feeling like I could die of embarrassment.

"Madison honey, I'll call them. Mr. De Vere has been so kind, and I know you just love dressing up. Your mom and dad will be okay with it, I bet they will."

He turns to me. "That's settled then. Tomorrow night. I'll pick you up at eight o'clock."

Oh. My. Gosh. I try to take stock of the situation. I think he just asked me out. I think that's what just happened. And my teacher said yes on my behalf!

I stare at him in stunned horror, but he ignores me.

He thanks Mrs. Bertorelli, very warmly, and then he goes. He pushes open the heavy glass fire door and disappears.

"Well. Wasn't he a darling? Such a nice, well-mannered young man."

I stare out through the glass doors into the street. I can just see the red taillights of the Lamborghini lighting up as he maneuvers the car out of the quad and drives away.

Mrs. B. turns to me and frowns. "He was a lot like that guy at the airport, wasn't he?"

I feign surprise. "Him? No. Don't think so. Just another guy in a suit."

She smiles at me as if I'm simple. "Maddie, honey. That wasn't just *any* suit."

In the morning, I go see Lydia in the hospital. It's an old Victorian building unlike any hospital I've ever seen before. You need to be over six feet tall to look out of the windows, for a start. But Lydia seems happy, and she looks better too. She's sitting up in bed reading an old copy of Vogue magazine. She's pleased to see me.

"Maddie!"

"Hey! You okay?"

"Yeah, yeah. I'm fine. But what happened to you? Mrs. B. was going crazy yesterday. She said if she had to tell your dad you were missing, the whole of our town would hear about it within hours, and if you didn't turn up again she'd lose her job and be the outcast of Ashwell Springs for the rest of her life."

I laugh, but she has a point. My dad is a local celebrity, you see. He works for the local radio station – he's got this show called 'Wake Up With Jake' and it's very popular. It gives him a rather unique position of influence in our tiny community.

I smile and give Lydia a hug. "Are they letting you out today?"

"Tomorrow."

"You're missing the trip."

"I'm not. I'm experiencing the ambiance. I'm eating British cuisine," she jokes, and indicates her abandoned tray of hospital food. We laugh, and it seems easier again between us.

"I'm sorry. About my Dad asking you to come on this trip with me," I say.

I can see from the look on her face that she knows *exactly* what I'm talking about. "He had some crazy idea that I'd be safer if I had my best friend with me. You know how he is."

"He's over-compensating," she says, picking at the sticking plaster that attaches a scary-looking tube to the back of her hand.

We both know why. Because Jake isn't my real dad. He's my stepfather and he takes his role very, very, seriously. And he's worried about me. About this trip. For reasons we definitely didn't discuss that night he made sure I packed my cell phone charger and he gave me his out-of-date Lonely Planet guide.

My real dad is here, somewhere in London.

Can't talk about that now either. I glance around the ward – no private rooms here – but nobody is taking any notice of us. They've got their own visitors.

"I wish you weren't stuck in here, Lydia. You're missing everything."

"Did Brody ask you out yet?"

I laugh. "No. But I have a date… if you can call it that. Mrs. Bertorelli jacked it up for me."

Lydia looks at me like I've lost my mind. "Seriously? Come on! That woman has been guarding our moral integrity like it was the Crown Jewels ever since we left home!"

I smile and move my hospital chair a little closer to the bed. "She practically begged me to go."

Lydia's eyes are bright with interest. "Oh my gosh! You have to tell me everything. All the deets – and don't go censoring all the best bits, Maddie!"

There's no way I can tell her *everything*. But Lydia's the best friend I've got, and I sure could do with some advice about tomorrow's fiasco. She knows a bit more about guys than me, and she might have some tips for surviving the night. So I start my story and do some heavy editing along the way.

"Well. I met a guy, yesterday, at the Tower of London… "

# Chapter Six

He'll be here in ten minutes.

I can do this. I can do this. I'm not nervous. I refuse to be nervous. No. I'm bloody terrified. I'd rather face torture on the rack than this.

We've spent the whole day trooping around the Tate Modern and the Natural History Museum and my feet hurt. It's been highly educational but I couldn't concentrate at all. Johnny De Vere. Johnny De Vere. Those words appear to me everywhere, in my fevered imagination. On little cards beside fossils at the museum. Underneath famous paintings. On billboards in the street. Earlier today, I even got out at Euston underground station and thought it said 'Johnny De Vere' on the sign.

My little room at the hall of residence seems lonely without Lydia. I have been ready for an hour. I brush my hair again and check my reflection. I look pale and scared and young. Round blue eyes. Long hair – but not in a glamour girl kind of way. Clean, shiny, schoolgirl hair.

I add a hint of Lydia's pink lipstick. I decide to try out her blusher as well and drop the compact on the floor when I hear the knock on the door. The little cake of pink makeup cracks and sheds powder across the carpet.

I have to let him in.

I open the door and I gasp. He is wearing his costume already. Instead of pants, he's wearing tightly-fitting hose, in an eye-catching bright red. I try not to look. On his upper half he's wearing a doublet – richly embroidered, burgundy in color – and over that a short cloak. Rather too short, in my opinion, given the tight-fitting red hose clinging to every contour on his legs. I try really hard not to look.

I drag my gaze back to his face, and find that his expression is stern and serious. A small red hat is perched on his glossy black hair.

"Good grief." I say.

"I'm glad you like it. Thank you. This one's for you."

He hands me a plastic carrier bag containing my costume. I peek inside the top of the bag and see something voluminous and black.

"Do you want me to change right away?"

"Please."

I make him go stand in the hallway, where I imagine he'll cause quite a stir – or at least get a lot of funny looks.

I pull out the dress, which is made of several acres of black velvet and is very heavy. I take off my normal clothes and struggle to get this thing over my head. It gapes across my chest, revealing my bra.

I realize there's an under dress in the bag – so I have to start all over again. Once I've got both bits on and fastened up the sash, I take a peek in the mirror and I'm rather pleased with the effect.

The dress is medieval in style. It has a wide V-shaped neckline trimmed with soft white fur. At the front, a triangle of fabric shows for modesty's sake. But the dress isn't unflattering – it's gorgeous. It clings tightly to my breasts, and it almost slips off at my shoulders, revealing my pale skin. The waistline is high and nipped in by a sash in gold brocade. The folds of the black velvet skirt are rich and luxurious.

In this dress I look like a woman. A lady of noble birth. I love this dress.

I smooth back my hair and add the last piece of the costume. I think it's called a snood. It's a type of golden hairnet to keep my long hair tidy. This one is amazing – it's decorated with tiny seed pearls.

Feeling a little more confident, I go open the door and let him back in. He does a rather gratifying double take, and nods his head in approval.

"I knew it would be perfect on you," he says, softly.

"Thank you."

We get a few wolf whistles, going down the corridor, and I'm guessing they were mainly for Johnny's legs. On the stairs I have to learn the art of picking up my skirts so I don't fall to my death. He takes my arm to help me, and I let him.

"I'm sorry… about yesterday," he says. "I hope you'll enjoy tonight."

Johnny's car is parked, illegally, right outside the building, so I don't have too far to go. We speed through the night to the Tower of London, and park in the underground lot.

On the way up through the complex, we pass by a doorway, partly hidden with a thick velvet curtain, and guarded by a burly Beefeater.

"What's behind there?" I ask, but Johnny doesn't answer.

He speaks sharply to the guard. "Where's the other guard? There must always be two. We have people wandering all over the Tower tonight and one of them might slip through."

"Sorry, sir. He was here ten minutes ago. I'll go and have a look, shall I?"

"Certainly not! You must never abandon your post!"

The guard pales visibly and promises that he won't.

Johnny and I go through to the main building and join all the other folk in their amazing clothes.

Everyone seems to know Johnny, and they all admire my beautiful dress.

"And why has nobody introduced me to this *attractive* young lady" says a cool voice behind me. I turn and see a tall thin man with an unhealthy pallid complexion.

"My sincere apologies, Randolph," Johnny says. "May I present Madison Lambourne, who is visiting us from America. She's agreed to step in and play a role in the proceedings tonight."

"Charming," the man says, lecherously. "So fresh, and so young. So divinely innocent, too. Johnny, you have done well!"

The tall man shakes my hand and his fingers are ice cold. I recoil from his touch, but I struggle to be polite because he seems to be the head honcho around here.

"Pleased to meet you, Randolph, thanks for letting me come along."

Then Johnny exchanges a few words with the guy, but I notice that he takes the very first opportunity to bow out of the conversation and hustle me away.

"He's dangerous," Johnny warns, speaking low to me, "you must avoid him, as far as you can."

"Why?"

"Later," he says.

He shows me through to the courtyard, where they have set up a little stage complete with proper lighting gear and high-tech sound equipment. The guests, who have all come along in medieval costume, are getting settled into their seats to watch the show.

We are re-enacting a scene from the time of the War of the Roses. Johnny is playing an aristocrat from the House of York. I'm playing the love interest.

Johnny takes me to wait in the wings and explains everything I have to do. Fortunately I only have two lines. I get to say "Sire, I will do as you bid me," and "Adieu."

It's not the most challenging role I ever played, but the audience is great and I begin to relax and enjoy the whole thing. I particularly enjoy the moment where Johnny bows down and kisses my hand.

"Sweet lady, let me bid thee farewell," he says. It reminds me of what he said at the airport and I don't feel so scared of him now.

"Adieu!" I say, with gusto.

We get thunderous applause and Johnny takes an extravagant bow, sweeping off his hat as he does so. I make a passable attempt at a curtsey. The whole thing seems to have been a huge success and I am flushed with enjoyment and pleasure.

We stay for the wine and cheese afterwards, but every time a waiter comes near us, Johnny shakes his head.

The waiter tries me instead. "May I tempt you with a glass of white wine, Miss?"

He holds out his silver tray in front of me. I feel a little guilty as I reach out and take one, wondering if I'm doing the right thing. Johnny sees my face and raises a quizzical eyebrow, as I take a cautious sip.

I blush. "My dad wouldn't approve of this," I explain.

"What the eye does not see, the heart does not grieve after."

I smile and take another tiny sip.

People keep coming up to Johnny and congratulating him on his performance, and they are very gracious about mine too. I begin to think Mrs. B. was right. I'm a very lucky girl. I realize that I don't want the evening to end, and judging by the look on Johnny's face, neither does he.

"You are not used to wine. Your face has gone very pink," he says, teasing me a little. He touches me lightly on the arm and nods in the direction of the open door. "Let me take you outside, where it's cooler."

I nod. I rather like the idea of strolling around the grounds with him. It is quiet and cool out there – very different from during the day when the tourists are clustered around their tour guides and you can't move an inch without getting in the way of someone taking a photo.

"We'll go through and look at the Thames, shall we?" he says.

"Oh yes! I'd like that."

Our footsteps echo on the cool stones, as we walk across the courtyard. It's quiet and eerie out there in the darkness, now.

Johnny seems to know where he wants to go. He heads across towards Traitors' Gate, and I go with him without a word. As we pass under the gate, he places his hand on the small of my back to guide me through the darkness. All I can think about, is that he is touching me, guiding me, taking me where he wants me to go. I notice the exact moment when that light touch disappears, and I miss it. I yearn for it.

He leads me through to look out over the river. At night the Thames is dark and melancholy, glimmering in the moonlight. We turn to face one another.

"I've waited a long, long time," he says softly, "for another chance like this."

I shiver. He is beautiful in this light; his features are proud and strong. His brow is inclined towards me, and his dark eyes are glittering.

"No more waiting," he says. He puts his hand on my waist to pull me close to him, and my body moves at his command. He seems very tall, standing there in the dark. Powerfully attractive, but terrifying at the same time. He is so close to me that I can feel his breath on my face – cool and steady. I'm eye level with that smooth hollow at the base of his throat. I'm afraid to look up at him, unsure what I'm meant to do next.

He leans in, closer. He brushes away a lock of hair that has escaped from my snood. He brushes it back over my shoulder, and he lets his lips graze my neck. I could die in an agony of pleasure.

He is trembling, as he kisses my neck. *He is trembling.*

He lifts his head up again, to look at me. There is a sort of aching sadness in his eyes that I am at a loss to understand.

"Kiss me properly, Johnny. Please. Just once!"

I will always remember this: his hands cupping my face, his mouth on mine, the taste of happiness and the tug of real desire inside me. My response is urgent, desperate. I lose myself in his kiss, pressing my body against his. Right at this moment, I'm in his power, and I know I would do anything he asked. I want this kiss to last forever.

He ends it first, turning his head aside to moan in pleasure and dismay.

I don't want him to stop, but I will not beg him for more. I feel mildly ashamed of my behavior with him. Everywhere he touched me burns with sensation. His kiss was intoxicating in a very adult kind of way.

"I'll walk you home," he says. His tone of voice is terse. Grim.

I hesitate, wondering what he means. We arrived by car.

On our way back through the grounds, he surprises me by taking my hand, though his face is stern and emotionless in the moonlight. Passing by the stage, we get stopped by a man in a giant black coat. His face is red and he seems to be in an angry mood.

"Randolph wants to speak with you – immediately."

Johnny frowns, glancing at me. He lowers his voice. "Is it about our plans for tonight?"

"Yes! the other man hisses. "There are some… security problems, one of the guards has had to go home. The girl can wait, can't she, De Vere?"

Johnny lets go of my hand, reluctantly. He leaves me by the door of the chapel, where there are plenty of seats for me to sit and wait.

"I'm sorry," he says. "But if it's a matter of security, I just have to go. Stay here. Wait for me."

He leaves me there, and I watch all the other actors and volunteers dismantling the set and packing up all the props that we used. They work fast, and before long there's no trace of our little dramatic production. Gradually, one by one, they say goodnight to one another and go home.

After what seems like an eternity it all goes quiet, and one of the Beefeaters says that I will have to go home. I don't want to sit out here all alone in the dark, so I get up and go look for Johnny.

I glide through the empty museum in my long black gown – feeling like I could easily play the ghost of some traitorous medieval lady. I pass by the place that we saw earlier, the old stone wall with the black curtain hanging down in front of it. But now, the curtain is pulled back, revealing a battered old timber door with iron clasps. Despite Johnny's stern warnings, there isn't anybody guarding the door at all. The two guards are gone. They have abandoned their weapons; two gleaming halberds with sharp curved blades are left leaning against the wall. The guards are nowhere to be seen.

There is an inscription, carved into the stone arch up above the door, and I go closer to read what it says. It isn't in Latin, thank goodness. It's in English, rough hewn into the stone, rather inexpertly. The graffiti of the past.

'Time and Tide Wait for No One' it says.

I smile. I know that old saying well. I put my hand on the door knob and turn it. I know that I shouldn't, but I'd love to see where it leads and what lies beyond.

I glance back along the corridor as I step through the doorway to see if anyone is coming, and the last thing I see is Johnny's face, as he runs around the corner.

"No!" He's shouting at me like a madman, his face contorted with fear – but it's like I can't really hear him anymore, or I don't really care. He's running towards me – full tilt – but I go through the doorway as if in a trance or a dream.

Johnny bellows a desperate cry of warning.

"DON'T!"

# Chapter Seven

I experience a feeling like falling – like I'm in a lift and it's plummeting down inside the shaft and no one can stop it. I hear a scream and I realize it's me. A wave of nausea and fear overtakes me and I brace myself for an impact. There is a blinding white flash as I hit the ground, and everything goes black for a moment.

I open my eyes. There is grass under the palms of my hands and pressed against my cheek. To my intense embarrassment, I have fallen flat on my face. I try to sit up before anyone sees me, and a wave of pain hits me. I've landed awkwardly. The palms of my hands are dirty and grazed, and my beautiful dress has mud across the front. I look around and try to work out where I am. Still in the Tower complex, but outside on the green? The configuration of buildings seems different. Unfamiliar. I seem to have fallen out of one of the lesser towers. After all – there are a lot of them: White Tower, Bell Tower, Bloody Tower…

I'm on the damp grass and it's raining, or rather drizzling slightly. I look up at the stone wall beside me and see that the doorway is a long way up. I must have tumbled over the edge of the parapet or something. I could have fallen to my death.

Then I glance to my right and see Johnny running towards me. Running through the rain. His face is almost as white and fearful as it was just a moment ago.

He reaches me and kneels down in the mud to see if I'm hurt. "Maddie! For heaven's sake! What did you do that for?"

"I'm fine. I'm sorry. That was so dumb."

He embraces me, holding me very tight, almost crushing the breath out of my body. "I was so scared for you! Let me see – are you hurt?"

"I'm fine. No bones broken – which is a miracle given that the door is way up there!" I glance ruefully at the door high up in the turret wall. What a dumb place to put a door. It was an accident waiting to happen. "Help me up, will you, Johnny? I think I must be sitting in a puddle of water. Feels like it, anyhow. My dress has gotten so wet!"

Wary and apprehensive, he disentangles himself from me, gets up, and then he extends his hand and hauls me to my feet. I inspect the damage to my dress, as far as that's possible in the dark shadow cast by the Tower.

"I think I've torn the front of it. I'm guessing the owner won't be too happy about me handing it back in this condition. I could pay for it to be repaired, maybe?"

Johnny gives a short, impatient sigh. "I had it made for you, Maddie."

I turn and stare at him. "You did?"

"I did."

"That's impossible. You only asked me to come along yesterday."

"Yes,' he says through clenched teeth, "and then I drove to the dressmaker and bribed her to stay up all night making that dress."

I'm stunned and I stare at him. His hair is damp with the rain. Damp dark locks hanging over his brow. "Why would you do that?" I ask.

He ignores the question. "Come on. We can't stay here."

My ankle feels suspiciously weak – as if I've sprained it, but I try to ignore the pain. I take hold of my train and lift it up over my left arm so it doesn't trail on the wet ground. Johnny takes hold of my other arm and pulls me along beside him.

We hurry across the wet grass and back onto a path. He steers me through the maze of buildings and to my surprise, we start heading towards the gate. He nods respectfully to the guards and makes me keep walking – fast. We go over a stone bridge that crosses the moat. It is eerie and dark, but I can see the water glimmering underneath.

"Why are we going this way?"

"Come on!" he says, urging me to walk faster. He pulls me along a dark street and we turn a corner into an alleyway.

"But, Johnny? Surely we have to go back in through the Tower?"

"It will be locked by now."

"No it won't. There were people still in there. What about your car?"

"I'll pick it up in the morning."

I see several men pass by who must have been at the re-enactment. Their clothes are like Johnny's, only not so nice. Their doublets are not embroidered, and everything they're wearing looks dirty and in need of repair. One of them stops and stares at me, and then he takes off his hat and gives me a respectful nod.

Johnny is guiding me along all the time, glancing left and right. I sense the tension in his body. He makes me walk on, and I struggle to keep up with him. My ankle is hurting like hell now. He guides me through a street where the houses are all half-timbered and lean close together.

I'm glad to have seen this part of London, though. It's very quaint. It has a real nostalgic feel to it. What's the term – *olde worlde* – that's right.

"What area is this, Johnny? What's it called?"

"Not so loud. People will hear you."

"So what if they do? I was just asking?"

"We're heading towards Billingsgate, down by the river."

"Why?"

"Because there's an inn I know down there. The only safe place I can think of to take you."

I start to feel nervous and uncertain again. "You want to take me to a bar? It's getting rather late for that, Johnny. Maybe you should just take me home – I'm not at all sure I want to go into a public place dressed like this."

"Trust me, it would be much worse if you weren't."

Gee, he's hard to fathom. I look up at him in my confusion, but his face is shadowy and inscrutable. "Weren't what?"

"If you weren't dressed like that."

I sigh in exasperation. He's not making any sense. I try to take stock of my surroundings – to decide what I must do. The streets are not busy, but those few people out and about are not like the ones we met at the re-enactment. They are poor and shabby and some of them are in rags. Some of them even look diseased. This is a horrible place and it scares me. Why does he always do this to me?

He's leading me down a street that smells of rotten fish and human waste. How dare he do this to me? We had a wonderful evening and shared that incredible kiss beside the river. Why does he have to go and ruin it all?

A wave of anger flashes inside me. "Johnny, I want to go back to the Tower! Now!"

He grips my arm tightly and shakes his head. "Not possible. It's your own fault. You went through the door."

His fingers are clenched so hard around my arm that it makes me grimace in pain. "Where are you taking me?"

"I told you. The Rose and Crown – we'll ask for shelter there. We can leave tomorrow."

"In the morning?" I protest. "Now look here, Johnny, if you think I'm spending the night with you then you've got a nasty shock coming! I am here to tell you that I am not that type of girl!"

"For the love of heaven, woman, hold your tongue! Are you determined to bring disaster upon us?"

"You go to the bar on your own, Johnny De Vere. I am going back to the Tower, and then I'm finding a tube station and making my own way back home."

I don't mean home, of course, I mean the hostel – the hall of residence – but the wrong word came out by mistake.

"You can't! You'll be dead before the morning if you try."

"Don't tell me what I can and can't do! Enough already, Johnny. Tonight was a big mistake!"

People turn and stare at me, amused by my display of temper, I suppose. An old man standing in his doorway, calls to his wife to come and see, and a dirty-looking beggar sitting one-legged on the ground, looks up and laughs at me.

I feel sickened by it all.

In desperation I pretend to stumble and in his surprise he releases his grip just enough for me to duck away from him and start running.

I break away from him and pick up my skirts. I hurry back the way we came – going just as fast as I can with a turned ankle. I'm in serious danger of wrecking the other one – the surface of the street is so uneven.

I run, with my heart thundering and a rushing sound in my ears. I'm hampered by my gown, which is bundled up over one arm. My bare legs are visible for all to see but I no longer care.

I try to head back the way we came, but the maze of narrow streets confuses me and it is so gloomy and dark. There don't seem to be any streetlights around here so I head for a dim light at the end of one of the alleyways, hoping to find my way back onto a main street.

About halfway down the alley I am whirled around, shoved roughly into a wall. I feel the texture of crumbling plaster – or is it dried mud – under my fingertips, and a lattice work of sticks underneath. I scrabble against it, but I can't get free.

Something thick and warm and hairy – a man's arm, I guess – is around my neck, suffocating me. I scream, but he silences my scream with a huge hand over my mouth. Something glints in the darkness, and I feel a pinprick of pain on my neck.

A knife. He has a knife.

I tremble. The blade of the knife is against my neck. The point touches my flesh and if I make the slightest movement he will cut my throat. I'm weak with terror, and my knees threaten to give way and shorten my journey to my inevitable, violent death.

"Unhand her, ruffian, or you'll swing for this!"

Johnny's voice in the darkness. I dare not call out to him though. The pressure of the blade is still there at my throat. It does not waver. In fact, my attacker, who I cannot see but I can smell, is laughing.

"Find your own sweetmeat, lad!"

Johnny inches nearer to me. Even in the darkness I can feel it. "Leave her be, or your life ends tonight!"

The older man snorts in disgust. "You're no match for me."

This time it is Johnny who laughs. "Indeed I am not. I will vanquish you and tomorrow your body will be on that stinking midden with the horse dung, where it belongs."

I sense a frisson of fear go through the hefty body of the evil man who holds me. His beard is touching my face and his foul breath nauseates me. Still he refuses to release me.

I see a flash of steel and a dagger is drawn. "I warned you." Johnny's voice is low and menacing. A whispered curse in the darkness.

In an instant the men engage in one swift lunge. The knife falls from my neck and clangs onto the cobblestones at my feet. I sense Johnny's body close to mine, but I can't see him. I can't see what's going on at all. The sound of metal rasping against metal chills me, and then there is a cry of pain.

"Please! Have mercy!"

Johnny's voice answers him – stern and cold. "Would you have had mercy on the girl, you foul dog?"

The man who attacked me falls to his knees with a heavy thud. I stand quaking with terror in the dark alleyway, unable to move or speak. Then, an even more chilling sound – my attacker, on his knees, begging for his miserable life.

"Please, sir, please. I didn't mean her no harm!"

I tremble and try to touch Johnny's arm. "Let him go!"

A tense moment passes. A black silence. I almost wonder if my plea for mercy came too late. Perhaps the deed is already done and the evil man lies dying at my feet.

But then, Johnny speaks. "Begone! The lady's heart is warmer than my own. She spares thee."

In the darkness the man struggles to his feet, panting with fear. He doesn't stop to look for his knife. He starts running – running away from us down the dark alleyway. As fast as he can go.

I listen, hardly daring to breathe, until I can't hear his footsteps anymore.

Johnny takes my hand, and though I want to recoil from his touch – I don't. He has saved me. He has saved my life.

"Come on!" he says, angrily. "I find the stench of that ruffian's blood detestable, and we *must* find a safer place than this. London is full of cut-throats, Maddie."

Johnny pulls me along by the hand and we head towards the light again. My dress is trailing in the filth, but I no longer care. We come out onto a wider road – but there are still no street lamps. I'm shaking, but it is all becoming clear.

I look up at the face of the man who has just saved my life.

"The moat," I whisper, my voice shaking with fear. "At the Tower of London. There was water in the moat."

"I know." His voice is terse. Cold.

"But the moat was filled in," I say. "Ages ago."

"I'm sorry. You were never meant to see… "

I'm shaking uncontrollably now. "Where the hell are we, Johnny?"

"We're in London," he says, quietly. "and the year is 1483."

# Chapter Eight

"Make way!" Johnny shouts as he carries me into the inn. There is laughter and merriment here, people clanging tankards together and telling jokes – an irony, that they should all be so happy and relaxed, when I am shaking with fear. Johnny pushes his way through the small crowd of late-night revelers who are enjoying ale and wine in a room no bigger than my bedroom at home. There is a lull in the noise and the men turn and stare at us. The smell of unwashed bodies is overpowering. I am nauseous with fear. I press my face against Johnny's velvet doublet and try not to look.

I must have passed out or something, when Johnny finally broke the news about where, or rather *when*, we have ended up. I remember screaming at him that it couldn't be possible, I remember beating my fists against his chest and begging him to take me back where I belong – back to the hostel, back to the familiar world of Lydia and Brody and Mrs. Bertorelli. I remember him holding my wrists tight and telling me he would help me, but I had to agree to do exactly as he said. I remember struggling until my wrists hurt and the tears ran down my face. Then I remember collapsing against him in fear and distress and after that... a blank.

I hear Johnny calling out for Annie Atkins, whoever she may be.

I hear an unfamiliar female voice, above the jangling noise all around me. "Good sir – what have we here?"

"A lady, gently bred, taken sick. I must ask for your best chamber, madam."

There is a pause, and I risk peering out to catch a glimpse of a buxom woman in a brown linen dress. She's looking at me like I'm some kind of leper.

"Taken sick, is she? Does she carry some vile contagion, sir?"

She isn't keen to have us here, I can tell.

Johnny sounds impatient when he answers her. "No, by my troth, she does not. Tis but the frailty of her sex."

I suppose I should be grateful that he can speak the lingo so fluently, since we find ourselves stranded in a nightmare world and we need help. Instead I hate him. I hate him and I blame him for luring me in to this dreadful, dangerous place. I hate him for not taking me back where I belong. The fact that he's talking like a sexist pig doesn't seem to help at all.

He takes on a more persuasive tone of voice. "Please Annie, you'll be handsomely paid if you can provide us with food and lodging for the night. I've heard you are often kind to *travelers*."

The buxom woman lowers her voice. "I know you. You're from the Tower."

I look round sharply. Something about the meaningful way she lingered on the word 'Tower' alarms me.

Johnny hesitates too – and I'm guessing he wants to be real careful about what he says.

"We come to London to pay our respects to the new King," he says tersely.

"Aye," she says, with a funny look. A look that does not convey much respect for the King – whoever he is. She sniffs. "This is not a place normally frequented by courtiers, sir."

"No. But we have been set upon by vagabonds. Fortunately we have eluded them – we have money and can pay our way."

He sets me down on my feet for a moment, so that he can feel in his pockets for his money. He tosses some coins down on the counter, and waits for a response.

The woman gathers them up greedily, and tucks them away.

"Best chamber in the house, good sir. At your pleasure and disposal."

She reaches for a bunch of old-fashioned keys, and indicates that we should follow her. She leads us through to the back of the pub, and out into a square courtyard beyond. A rickety wooden staircase no wider than a fire escape leads up to another level. There are rooms up there, accessed by a balcony that looks down on the courtyard below.

The woman stops in front of one of the doors, fumbles for the key, and opens up the room. We follow her inside and take a look. She lights a couple of candles from her own, and stands back so we can admire the place.

It's not a large room, and it feels a little chilly, but there is a comfortable looking bed made up with coarse linen sheets and woolen blankets. I sit down on it, grateful to be away from all the prying eyes and laughing faces of the men drinking downstairs. I sink into a mattress that I'm guessing is filled with hay or something. Smells like hay in here, and lavender. Quite a pleasant smell. My legs are still trembling from the shock and it feels good to be able to sit down. I look at my feet and see how filthy my shoes are.

"I'll send up hot water, shall I?"

"And hot stones," Johnny says in a tone that conveys authority, "to warm the bed. The lady feels the cold."

Mistress Atkins gives him a polite nod, and then she goes. I'm thankful she made no enquiries about Johnny and me. I mean... he only asked for one room.

I'm left alone with this strange man who has befriended me, lied to me, kissed me, and faced death in the dark for me. I have a thousand questions for him and I don't know where to begin. I give him a long hard look, and his dark eyes glance away from mine.

He's uncomfortable alone with me, I can see it. Guilty, too. He walks over to the window – which has no glass in it – and opens up the wooden shutters as if he needs some air.

I find my voice and try to speak. "You've got some explaining to do, Johnny De Vere."

He nods, and runs a hand over his face. He clears his throat, but he doesn't say anything.

I get impatient. "Well? Start talking. Start explaining what's going on!"

He swings round to face me. "You went through the door, Maddie! Why did you have to go through the door?"

"I don't know. I was just curious. There wasn't anybody around to ask, so I just opened the door to take a look."

"You were never meant to see any of this."

"No. I can see why you were so worried about security, that's for sure."

"I'll kill them," he says bitterly, "those useless guards! I'll kill them when I get back."

"I can believe it! You drew a knife on that guy in the street like you'd done it plenty of times before!"

"It was either that or watch him slit your throat. For me, there was no choice."

Instinctively, I put my hand up to my neck where that beast of a man tried to hurt me. I can feel the place where the point of the knife poked into my skin, and I rub it ruefully. There must be a droplet of dried blood right there on my neck, because when I dislodge it accidentally, fresh blood stains my fingers.

Johnny stiffens. He sort of grips the window frame and gasps, as if he's short of air.

"It's nothing," I say. "Do you have a handkerchief or something I could borrow?"

He takes a few gasping breaths of air and covers his mouth with his hand.

Feeling more than a little impatient, I get up and look around the room to see if I can find something to press against my neck and stop the bleeding. Not much chance of a complimentary box of tissues in this place, that's for sure. He acts like he's ready to jump out of the window when I go near.

"What is *wrong* with you, Johnny?"

"I… find the sight of blood… disturbing," he says.

I frown at him. Disturbed by the sight of blood, huh? This sits a little uneasily with his James Bond act in the alleyway.

"Just cover it up, woman, please. Here, use this."

He reaches into his doublet, and tosses me a lace edged kerchief made out of fine, old linen. For some reason this reminds me of that letter of his – the one he tossed on the floor at Heathrow. A lot of things are falling into place now.

I press the handkerchief to my neck and stare at Johnny. "You do this a lot, don't you? Go back into the past?"

A dark figure walks right past the open window and there is a knock on the door. I feel a moment of panic wondering if he overheard what I just said. But I suppose it could have meant anything.

Johnny opens the door and lets in a boy about nine years old. He's holding a wooden tray.

"Some broth, for the lady," he says, nervously. "And some mulled wine for you, sir."

Johnny speaks to him, irritated by the interruption. "Set it down there, on the table."

The little boy does what he's told and then he takes a sneaky glance at me. I figure I must look a real mess. I've lost my snood and my hair is all over the place. The hem of my dress is filthy and my shoes are caked in mud, or more likely horse dung. Actually, I had been wondering where the smell of horses was coming from, and now the mystery is solved.

"Someone's coming up with them stones you wanted," the boy says, wiping his nose on his sleeve.

"Thank you," I murmur, staring at the boy's clothing. He has a little brown tunic on, with a hood, pushed back, and he's wearing green stockings of some kind. He looks like a miniature member of Robin Hood's merry men. Happy holidays, everyone, trick or treat!

I'm going mad. I'm definitely going mad.

When the boy has gone. I turn back to Johnny and he glances warily at me.

"Close the shutters, so we can talk."

To my surprise, he obeys me. He pulls the wooden shutters closed and fastens them with an iron clasp. There isn't a single chair in the room – just the table where the candles burn and my bowl of broth is steaming gently beside the jug of aromatic mulled wine. I invite him to sit on the bed.

He sits, looking stiff and uncomfortable, some distance away from me.

I ask the most important question first. "Why can't we go back to the Tower? Isn't that the way home?"

"It is, but we can't go back straight away. You see – the gateway is like the river itself – it is governed by the tides. We have to wait for when the tide turns, that's how it works."

I pause, thinking about this. He could be lying, or he could be telling the truth. There was that saying about time and tide written up above the door.

"When the tide turns – you'll take me back, right?"

"Of course. You shouldn't be here. "

"What about you? You've been here before, haven't you? You talk to everybody like you were born here."

He looks at me, and his dark eyes are full of sadness. "I am… a traveler… a rather weary traveler. I am part of a group of…

people… who look after the gateway to the past. We guard it. We defend it. Fiercely."

"But you get to go through the gateway, don't you?"

"Yes. Sometimes I'm assigned duties. Things that have to be done, to protect the River of Time."

"The River of Time?"

He nods. He looks deadly serious. The candlelight flickers on his face.

This is surreal. "So it's always 1483 when you go through the door, is it?"

"No. Far from it. Each month with the waning of the moon the time beyond the door changes – entirely at random, or so it seems."

'Okay, let me get this straight. The moon changes, and you open the door and it's a different time and place, is that right?"

"Oh, the place is always the same. London. It's always London. It's the time that changes. Every new moon it's a different phase of time. When I heard it was 1483 this time, I flew back from Paris straightaway. I have unfinished business here."

"What unfinished business?"

He pauses, then he shakes his head. "Regretfully, I cannot say."

"But it was important enough to fly back from Paris at short notice, and that's why you were at the airport that night."

"Where we met," he says softly.

"Where you mistook me for somebody else," I remind him, and a look of pain crosses his face.

"You must try to understand, Maddie. With my... lifestyle... I meet a lot of people, in some very strange situations. You are the very image of ... that girl."

The way he says 'that girl' has me a little worried. "She hurt you?'

Suddenly his face flickers with anger. "She lied to me. Betrayed me. Left me for dead."

Gee, this guy has a bit of emotional baggage, to say the least.

"Forgive me," he murmurs, seeing the way I'm looking at him. "It was a long time ago."

"It's okay," I say.

There is a pause. We are both at a loss to know what to say or do next. There is no clock in the room, but if there was, I'd be listening to it ticking, unable to express any of the complex feelings that well up inside of me.

He reaches out, and takes my hand.

I do not push him away. His touch is welcome, and I accept it gratefully. I curl my fingers around his, and squeeze his hand. A silent acceptance of some kind of bond between us.

"I will protect you, as best I can," he promises. "I'll take you back to the Tower tomorrow, and when the tide turns I'll show you how to reach the door. You can forget all about all this."

If I want to forget. Right at this moment, I want him to comfort me. I've been attacked in the street and dragged through hell. I've been told things that would traumatize most people, and I've had to nod politely and say "Okay, so that's how it works".

I don't want any more talk. Not now. I want his arms around me. I shoot him an agonized look and he seems to understand. He moves to sit beside me at last.

"Johnny, hold me. Please."

His arms are around me, cradling me, and I can feel his kisses in my hair.

There is a loud noise right outside the door. "Hot stones, sir!" says a deep male voice from outside.

Reluctantly, Johnny gets up and lets the man in. A wiry-looking guy comes into the room carrying heavy stones wrapped up in some sort of cloth. Is this Mr. Atkins, I wonder? He is accompanied by a young girl about my age, carrying a jug of hot water and a bowl.

We seem to be getting every member of the staff one by one – I suppose so they can satisfy their curiosity and get a good look at us. The girl arranges the bowl and the jug on the table, and then comes over to the bed and asks me if she can turn back the covers. I get up so she can do this, and then she takes the stones from the man I'm guessing is her dad, and she pops them into the bed to warm it up for us.

That's when it hits me. I'm sleeping in this room with Johnny. We hardly know each other, and things have moved way too fast already.

When they leave us, I glance at him and he glances at me. Surely he's thinking the same thing. He's a man who knows how to get what he wants. He's already shown that to me. If we curl up together in that bed, I fear he will expect more than I'm ready to give. A lot more.

"You should drink your soup," he says stiffly. "Before it goes cold."

"I'm not hungry."

But he passes the bowl to me, and I obediently sample the aromatic broth.

"It's good," I say, sounding slightly surprised.

Johnny scowls at me and paces over to the window again. He makes sure the shutter is fastened tight.

I drink my soup but he doesn't even touch his wine.

I try to calm down. I use some of the water to wash my face, and dry it on the piece of old linen that the girl laid beside the bowl. I dither about taking off my shoes and generally find every excuse to delay getting into that bed with him.

I take a few sips of the wine, and find that it tastes absolutely excellent – it is warm and spicy and reminds me of Christmas. I decide I'd better not have any more because I need to keep my wits about me.

Johnny says he'll protect me, yes. From anyone who comes to this room. But who's going to protect me from *him*?

I glance nervously up at him. He's undoing his doublet, rapidly, making quick work of a dozen or more little buttons down the front. He shucks it off in one easy movement and leaves it on the end of the bed. Underneath, he's wearing a linen shirt, and he loosens the fastening at the neck. He places his belt and his dagger on the table.

He's a dangerous man, and I'm alone with him for the night. And yet, I am not afraid. His tenderness to me is revealed more and more, with every hour that I know him. He is unlike any man I have ever met, or will ever meet in my lifetime again.

He hesitates, fingers hovering on the strings that tie up his pants – I mean his hose. He looks up at me. A blistering look that burns me, deep inside. I am standing over by the table, wondering if now is the moment to snuff out the candles, though the last thing I want to do is extinguish the light. Not when it lights up such a beautiful, beautiful sight as Johnny in that open-neck shirt.

"Sorry," he says. "I am getting ahead of myself. Should I wait outside while you take off your gown?"

"I… have nothing to change into."

"Sleep in your shift. Many women do."

*And you'd know about that would you?* I'm tempted to ask, but I don't.

"I suppose I could," I say reluctantly.

Suddenly he seems to see the real reason for my hesitation.

"Look, Maddie. It's just for one night. Stop looking at me like I'm a monster. I'm not going to seduce you, if that's what you're worried about."

"You're not?"

"I am a gentleman, Maddie. You can rest assured of that."

My face is scarlet, like his hose. I know that. "Okay."

I haul my dress up over my head, and he offers to take it downstairs so the servants can brush the mud off the hem. I agree to this and while he's gone I rake my fingers through my hair, since I don't have a comb.

Then I hop into the bed. The stones have made the bed warm and cozy. The linen sheets are a little coarse compared with the poly-cotton sheets I'm used to but they are not uncomfortable. The scent of fresh hay and lavender is really rather nice. I snuggle down and rest my head on the pillow.

In a moment or two he returns and snuffs out the candle, carefully. In the darkness he removes his hose. I turn over in bed so it doesn't seem like I'm watching him.

He slips into bed beside me.

His body spoons with mine, and I feel his breath on my neck. He strokes back my hair and tells me that he'll watch over me while I sleep. *While I sleep!* How can I possibly fall asleep, with him and his long muscular limbs brushing against me? His touch leaves me tingling like he's conducting electricity into my whole body. So I just lie still and try to keep my breathing slow and steady while he whispers soothing words and strokes my hair.

This is the sweetest, scariest experience I have ever had with a guy. I'm a virgin. I've never had a real boyfriend before.

Is this strange, secretive man really my boyfriend?

I don't know. Only time will tell.

# Chapter Nine

I wake to the jarring sounds of human activity. Strangers passing by our shuttered window, talking in loud voices. People shouting hello to their neighbors and emptying their slops out in the street. I remember where I am, and why.

Medieval London starts early. Too early.

I brace myself for a most unusual day.

I shift position gently, trying not to wake Johnny. He looks like a sleeping angel, fallen from some Italian fresco, lying beside me in the bed. His eyes are closed. His long dark lashes rest softly on his cheek. Yet something about the careful regularity of his breathing makes me suspect that he's not really asleep.

I have never woken up with a guy before. Surreptitiously I turn my head away from him and rub the sleep out of my eyes. I hate to think what kind of a tangle my hair has gotten into overnight. I comb through it again with my fingers and hope for the best. When I look back at Johnny, he's watching me.

"You are very beautiful," he says, as if he knows my thoughts.

"I knew you weren't asleep."

"Did you, indeed?" He puts a hand to my face and smoothes back a strand of my hair. I flush in embarrassment. This intimacy seems too much in the cold light of day.

"I can't believe we just spent the night together," I say, before I can stop myself. Then I regret blurting it out.

He gives me a strange look – and there is sadness in his eyes. "You really don't remember, do you?"

"Remember what? Yesterday you told me I only reminded you of Madeleine – are you saying something different today?"

He sighs and turns his head away. "I'll get up and go downstairs. See if I can get us some breakfast."

"My dress. Remember to fetch my dress for me, Johnny. I don't feel decent in this." I tug at the linen shift I'm wearing. It's creased and it's falling off one shoulder.

"Very dissolute, darling. I agree."

He smiles and leans across the bed and kisses my bare shoulder, making me blush even more. It never ceases to amaze me how easily he has slipped into all this – when for me it is still very new.

He gets up and gets dressed and I try not to look as he fastens his hose up. Then he goes downstairs. While he is gone I wash my face in cold water left over in the jug. I glance down at the dagger on the table and wonder if he'll use it today.

He returns with my dress over his shoulder. He carries another tray.

"We need to call room service to take the other one away," I say to him, in a teasing tone. Seems like the only way to deal with all this is to use a little banter now and then.

"Phone through to reception, if you like," he replies, putting the tray on the bed in front of me. "Ask them about internet access, while you've got them on the line."

I stare in dismay at the tray. "Good grief, what's all that?"

"Pease porridge," he says. "And ale."

"Is that what they eat?"

"Yes. Why do you keep talking about 'them' all the time? They're not aliens, you know, the people who live here. They are flesh and blood. Like you."

"Sorry."

"Try to eat something," he says. "You'll feel less jittery, if you do."

"You want me to drink ale? At five-thirty in the morning? Johnny, I can't!"

"Try some of the pease porridge then. They warmed it up specially for you."

I turn my attention to the contents of the little wooden bowl. It looks a bit like hummus, only it's green. I put my finger in, and take a tiny taste.

It's not bad, but it's kind of… sludgy.

"Thanks, but no thanks. I could kill for a hot cup of coffee though. But I suppose I'm all out of luck."

Johnny shoves the tray aside and stands up. "Ungrateful wench."

He goes and gets his belt and fastens it on, sheathing his dagger as if he does this every day. He turns and looks at me and frowns. "I'll have to take you with me to the Court."

"The court? Is someone you know on trial or something?"

He rolls his eyes, like I'm a stupid child. "The Royal Court."

"Oh. Okay."

"You'll have to stay out of the way. And out of trouble. Maddie, if you make trouble you have no idea what the consequences might be."

No. I don't. And he doesn't seem to want to fill me in on much, does he? I nod, trying to look helpful and obliging. "Okay."

A girl arrives with a bag containing brushes and combs. She curtseys respectfully at Johnny and then at me. She offers to help me with my hair. Johnny seems to think this is a great idea and he makes himself scarce again.

I sit on the bed and let the girl comb the tangles out of my long hair. She tries very hard not to pull it, but it's gotten into such a mess overnight that some pain is inevitable.

"Such lovely hair," she murmurs. "The color of rich honey."

I smile weakly, and let her pull it away from my face, combing it back from my brow with a little water to make it smooth and compliant.

She dresses my hair very nicely, and I begin to feel normal again. But then to my dismay, she reaches in her bag for some strips of white linen that look a bit like bandages. She starts arranging pieces of linen over my head, and before long my hair is completely hidden.

"Do I need all this," I say, as she winds another bit of linen under my chin – making me look like I've broken my jaw.

"You can't go bareheaded my lady, 'tis not proper."

I sigh and resign myself to my fate, hoping the end result isn't too awful. She adds a padded circlet of linen which fits around my head like a rubber ring – and more bandages. She stands back and holds up a small, dull looking-glass so I can admire her efforts. Swathed in all that white linen I look and feel just like a nun.

Certainly, the effect is very… medieval.

"Purity itself," says Johnny, standing in the doorway with a bit of a smirk on his face. I poke out my tongue at him, and the servant girl gasps and stifles a giggle.

Downstairs, in the public part of the inn, Johnny talks to Mr. Atkins about procuring a horse. The mistress is still in her bed, but several other women are bustling around. The smell of fresh bread baking in the oven comes from somewhere nearby.

I vaguely wonder if the Royal Court will be back at the Tower. I keep wanting to go back to the Tower, even though it's not time just yet. Perhaps I imagine I'd be safer there.

"The landlord has secured us some horses," Johnny says. "It's a good thing you know how to ride."

That makes me look up sharply. I love horses, I always have. I love to feel their warm, nuzzling breath in my hand, I love to groom their satiny flanks and most of all I love to ride. I learned when I was ten. There are lots of great places to go horse-riding in the Midwest. But how does Johnny know about all that?

"I never told you I could ride."

"Let's just say I have an… insight… into these things. Make haste, Maddie, and come with me to the stable yard. It is two and a half miles to Westminster and I have business with the King and his ministers."

"The King?" I say, in a questioning tone. "And here's me thinking you came through the door to help me out."

"I did. Your welfare has become very important to me. But I have other business here too."

I open my mouth to ask what kind of 'other business' he means, but he shakes his head.

"You must not ask questions. Not now."

The servant girl who helped me with my hair appears and hands Johnny a large black riding cape. "Is this the kind of thing you had in mind, sir?"

"Yes, it looks excellent. Thank you, Gwen, you did well to find me this."

He presses some coins into her hand and she seems very pleased. Johnny swathes himself in the heavy cloak, and puts the hood up over his head.

This puzzles me. It's cloudy and gray outside – classic English weather – but it isn't really cold.

We go and meet our horses and I'm surprised and delighted with mine. She's a lovely mare named Poesie, dappled gray and white.

She allows me to pet her, and I stroke her warm neck. "Johnny, she's gorgeous!"

He smiles as if this pleases him and offers to help me up. I only have one tiny problem, and that's my velvet dress.

Johnny lowers his voice. "It is customary for a lady to sit sideways, Maddie."

"But there's no side saddle."

"No. The lady has no actual… control… of the animal, you see. She just sits on the horse and someone else leads it along."

I don't like the sound of that. "You won't let me ride?"

He looks apologetic. "You are supposed to be highborn, Maddie. A gentlewoman does not ride astride. You will draw less attention to yourself if you sit sideways and let me lead you, if you please."

I want to tell him to go to hell. I want to tell him that I'm a damn fine horsewoman and if he will slit the seam of my dress with that horrible dagger of his, I will get up there and prove it. Instead I scowl and let him set me on the horse like I was four years old. Then he leaps up into his saddle, takes up the reins, and pulls me along like a toy.

For most of the first mile I am fuming with rage.

In this fashion, we ride through the cobbled streets of the City of London, which turns out to be quite tiny in comparison to the urban sprawl I saw from the bus yesterday. Yesterday – what a strange concept. A yesterday five hundred years into the future from today.

We head towards Ludgate Hill and Johnny points out St Paul's Cathedral. I look up expecting to see the great dome rising up against the skyline, but of course it isn't there. Instead there is an imposing Norman building with a tall, thin spire. From inside the depths of his dark hood, Johnny gives me a wry kind of grin.

We ride along the Strand – a broad main street that takes us out of London and into open fields. Growing produce to feed a hungry city, I suppose.

"Covent Garden," Johnny informs me, gesturing with his gloved hand to the green fields on our right. *Gloves, in early September*, I'm thinking. Is that what you have to wear when you visit the King? If so, how come I haven't got any?

But there are other, more important questions I need to ask him. Since we are riding through open country and there is no one around – save a few laborers in the fields – I decide to ask him a few, right now.

"Johnny? You said you are here on a mission."

"Yes?"

"I know it's top secret and everything, but since I find myself… involved… is there anything I ought to know?"

"I don't know the full story myself," he says. "Patrons are rarely given all the information – just a set of instructions, that's all. But I was told that one of the Patrons turned maverick and went off on his own – tried to change things for his own personal gain. This is strictly against our Code."

"And you have to track this guy down?"

"Yes."

"And then what?"

"I have not yet had my briefing, but I would guess that my mission could be to assassinate him."

This shocks me. "You might have to kill one of your own group?"

"I would, if I had to. My first duty is to the River of Time."

"Do you have any idea who the maverick is?"

"No, though I have my suspicions. I expect to receive my instructions soon."

"Johnny, tell me who you think it is – I won't breathe a word, I swear."

There is a long pause, while he considers this. "It's hard to imagine any one of us being foolish enough to break the Code."

"What about the creepy guy who spoke to us at the re-enactment? Randolph?"

"Maddie," he says, with a wry smile. "Randolph is the Chief Guardian of Time."

"What about that other guy – the one with all the fur on his coat?"

"You mean Arthur – he's been with us since the Dark Ages. He's one of our oldest serving Patrons and I don't believe it's him. No. Perhaps it's Simon," he says airily. "He joined us recently – during the Second World War – and I've always had my doubts about him. He could easily be the turncoat."

We keep going until the Palace of Westminster can be seen, tall and imposing up ahead. With the palace looming closer, Johnny asks me how I want to be introduced when I'm received at the court.

"I don't know. I'll leave it up to you."

"Well, obviously we have to have a story. You are not my wife. The King knows I have no sisters. None living, anyway."

"Are you supposed to be a friend of the King?"

"Everyone must appear to be the friend of a tyrant, unless they want to end up with their head on the block. But no. I loathe the man."

"Does he suspect that?"

"Yes," he says. "Which is why I must pay my respects to him today. So prepare to meet Richard the Third."

I gulp. "Richard the Third? The Duke of Gloucester?"

"Yes. The very same. People call him by other names too – less flattering ones. Crouchback, for example. Richard the Turd. The Wicked Duke."

"Not a popular guy, then?"

"No. But he likes to think he is. If he comes anywhere near you, Maddie, curtsey low. You can do that, can't you? And don't turn your back on him either, or sit down in his presence unless he asks you to."

"Okay."

"And don't say 'okay'. Please don't say 'okay'."

"What do I say instead?"

"As little as possible," he says tersely. "I'll introduce you as my betrothed. But it is really most irregular that we are traveling together with no servants and no chaperone for you."

"We're going to raise a few eyebrows at Court then, aren't we?"

"We certainly are." He seems distracted for a moment, as if he's thinking hard. "They'll want to know your name and where you hail from."

"I'm from Ashwell Springs, Illinois."

"Those words must NOT pass your lips, Maddie. It is 1483, for heaven's sake."

"Where then? Where do I come from?"

"I was thinking, perhaps from France? I'm supposed to be a courtier with French ancestry. It would make sense if you came from Champagne, like me. Champany they call it here."

"Okay. I mean, yes. Champany."

"Good. You're catching on. How's your French?"

"Non-existent, Johnny. Are you sure I shouldn't have stayed at the inn?"

"Too risky, I'm afraid. I have to keep you where I can see you, at all times. For your own protection."

It's nice that he cares so much about me, but at the same time I'm noticing that this 'protection' he's talking about is starting to seem more like twenty-four hour surveillance. His decision to take me to Court seems unbelievably risky. They won't believe my flimsy cover story, and I seriously doubt my ability to keep up the act. It would be much better if I stayed out of sight.

* * *

At court we are received into a large room where a group of ladies and gentlemen are laughing and talking. Everyone is wearing costly clothing, similar to my own. I'm very, very grateful to whoever it was sat up late last night brushing all the dirt off my dress. I notice that there is a small tear on one of the sleeves, and it has been mended neatly. There are tiny stitches closing the gap where the fabric gave way.

Johnny goes off and gets involved in a rather secretive conversation with a courtier in a peacock blue doublet. I stare goggle-eyed at some of the clothing. Several men here wear 'parti-colored' hose – one red leg and the other in green!

A group of important-looking men enters the room, and my heart flutters in fear. I have no idea what King Richard looks like, so I plan to take my cue from the other women and curtsey when they do.

Trust Johnny to abandon me, just when I need him most!

All the ladies seem to be bobbing down in front of a small man with one shoulder slightly higher than the other. He has brown hair – which he wears rather long – and pale, piercing blue eyes. His clothing is magnificent – his doublet is in deep blue silk and crimson satin, and the front is studded with jewels. His hat is black velvet – worn in extravagant folds, held back with a giant gold brooch.

This must be the King. He makes his way along a row of people, and I wait in anticipation for my turn. What if he asks me about France or something? I've never even been close to France. Unless you count Quebec in Canada, where my family spent our vacation last fall.

I could so easily screw this up, and if I do, I'll blow Johnny's cover as well as my own. By the time the King turns to me I am practically a nervous wreck. I'm shaking like a leaf and my knees don't have any trouble at all giving way for the curtsey. No trouble at all. I bow my head and stare at the King's extraordinary shoes.

He turns to the courtier at his side. "And who do we have here?"

"Your name, good lady?" the lesser man demands, and after a moment I realize he's talking to me.

I'm still practically on my knees, and I dare not look up. "Maddie Lambourne, of Champany," I say. It comes out a cross between a whisper and a squeak.

When the King speaks, he sounds slightly amused. "Arise, Madeleine of Champany."

*Madeleine – that name again.* He thinks I said Madeleine, and he's the King so I'm not going to correct him. I rise to my feet, knowing that I'm pale as a ghost. The king extends his hand, and I take it. His touch is very cold. He presses his lips to my hand lightly, and then looks at me with a condescending smile.

Johnny appears through the crowd – looking a little flustered that all of this has taken place without him being around.

"John De Vere," he says, apologetically. "You will remember my father, sire. We claim our lineage from the Counts of Champagne."

"Ah, yes." the King says, with a blistering look. "He was loyal to my brother, was he not?"

"He is loyal to his country and his King," Johnny says, and makes another exaggerated bow. This time his fingers sweep the ground, I notice. It looks a little stagy and fake, in my opinion, but it seems to pass muster.

Johnny waves his hand in my direction. "Gracious Majesty, may I introduce my intended bride?"

The King smiles. "I have met the enchanting Madeleine."

I shoot Johnny an apologetic look. He stares straight back at me, and his face goes stark with horror. How unfortunate that it had to be *that* name, the name that seems to mean so much to him.

Johnny struggles to recover his composure. "Indeed?"

"Yes," says the King, "but she's as mute as a nun!"

Everyone laughs hard. Especially Johnny and me. After a moment or two, the King moves on, and Johnny turns and stares at me – his eyes questioning mine.

"Well?"

"He misheard," I say, knowing he's upset. "He thought I said Madeleine. I wasn't going to argue with him."

Johnny frowns anxiously, and for a moment, he seems lost in thought. But then he runs a hand over his face and gives a defeated shrug. "Madeleine it is, for now."

It is hot and stuffy in the room and I feel as if I just might faint. My velvet dress is far too hot for early September, and it's turning out to be a warm, muggy day. My palms are sweating, and surreptitiously I wipe the perspiration on the folds of my dress. The whole room is smelly – though fresh rushes have been strewn on the floor. But there are far too many people in here – and dogs – spaniels, I think.

The king is laughing with a knot of people at a little distance away. I am anxious because Johnny seems so worried. I lean in and whisper in his ear.

"I'm sorry – if I handled it wrong."

He turns to me and touches my face – the part of it you can still see with all that linen wrapped around me.

"You did everything that was expected of you, and more."

I look at him gratefully and ask him if his work is done for today.

"Not quite," he says, "but we can slip away if you like. Let me take you outside, into the garden."

We walk down a long walkway completely shaded by hawthorn hedges. We hardly say a word. We reach an enclosure where there are lots of flowers and lots of dense greenery including sweet juniper. The scent of rosemary wafts towards us from somewhere close by. Just to our left, there's an arbor, a bower where birds sing. They flutter away as we approach, and we sit down together. I look up and marvel that you could have such a garden in London – the wooden arch above us is covered in delicate vines with heart-shaped leaves and pink and white flowers like little bells. We sit down and enjoy the cool shade.

"Bellbine – such a sight to see," he says a little sadly. "It is treated as a weed in our world."

He sits close to me and takes my hand, and before long we are lost in a little place of our own – a golden moment where all that matters is his beautiful face, and his lips so close to mine. His breath is like a soft breeze against my flushed cheek, his midnight hair brushes against my forehead, and his lips – his lips are on mine. For me there is no choice but to surrender all my senses to him. He tastes of sunshine and champagne, and I cannot get enough of him. I respond, eagerly, though I know I can never match the pleasure he is giving me. Sweet, tantalizing kisses that make me so happy. Loving, giving kisses that arouse my body, my heart and my soul.

We are so busy sharing surreptitious kisses that it is several moments before we realize that there is a very private conversation going on, just the other side of the arbor.

"They must die," the first man says.

I stiffen and so does Johnny. We draw apart and try to remain still and silent.

Through the leaves I catch glimpses of the man's clothing – a black doublet and a cloak trimmed with fur. But I can't see his face. I hope, desperately, that he cannot see mine. A more moderate voice replies, in a pleading tone.

"But my lord duke, they are the sons of our late king—"

"Bastard sons."

I look at Johnny, aghast, and he looks back at me. I want to ask him who they are talking about, but he places a warning finger on my lips.

The second man speaks again. "They are children, and the world abhors the killing of a child."

I hate to be an eavesdropper, but there is no way we can give ourselves away now. I am almost too afraid to breathe.

This is a deadly plot and we must not make a sound, or the two men will know what we have heard. I hold my breath and listen as the conversation unfolds.

"Why must they die? Their uncle Richard is already crowned. What need has he for fear?"

"If either one of those boys survives – they'll always be a threat to old Crouchback."

"Our gracious sovereign would not think kindly of you if he heard you use that name. And yes, I suppose they must die," The man pauses for a melancholy moment. "Who will be assigned to put an end to the boys?"

"Someone from among our midst will step up for the task – or at least to hire the fellow who has the mettle to do the deed – there will be great riches in store for the one who solves this… vexing problem, for the King."

"What man would risk his mortal soul to do such a thing."

The other man laughs. "One who values riches in this world more highly than riches in the next, I should think. I've heard it whispered that if no courtier can be found, then Richard will hand the matter over to those creatures in the Tower. They have no mortal souls, and thus it makes no difference to them. If *they* commit this crime they will not burn for it in hell's eternal fire."

The sound of mild laughter. The men move away.

"Was he talking about the princes? The ones who were held prisoner in the Tower?"

"Yes. Edward – our rightful King, and his nine year old brother, Richard, who was taken there to join him. Oh Maddie, his poor mother tried to lie and said he was sick with a terrible fever – she would have said anything to keep him out of the clutches of those who seek to destroy him. But it didn't work. They took the boy from her, and she mourns for him as if he was already dead."

"But they're both alive – and those men – they plan to kill them tomorrow night."

"Yes, they do."

"Those boys are still alive," I say, as the possibilities dawn in my mind. "Is there no way we can warn them?"

Johnny's face stiffens. "Maddie, they have to die. They are pawns in a game, that's all. A complicated political game. None of our concern."

"They're children, Johnny. Just kids. They didn't ask to be born heirs to the throne. They shouldn't have to die for it, either."

"Maddie. I am a Patron of the Tower and my job is to protect the River of Time. It is strictly forbidden for anyone to interfere with the past."

"But you're interfering with it all the time – just by being here."

"I am under strict orders not to alter the seminal events of our nation's history. I would pay a very high price if any of the other Patrons found out I had broken our Code."

"But… what about the things you DO change – don't they have an effect? What about that man you nearly killed last night? And the money you gave Gwen this morning? And introducing me to the King? You still say that you can't alter anything?"

"Keep your voice down, Maddie, for both our sakes."

"Seems to me you do what suits you, and not what you *ought* to do. There are two children locked up in that horrible place, and bad guys all around. How can you stand by and let this happen?"

"I have no choice, Maddie. Things must happen as they were meant to happen. Come on. We have to be getting back to the Tower. We need to be back there before two-fifteen or we'll be stuck here for the rest of the day."

On horseback we make our way slowly through the streets in the direction of the Tower. I keep quiet and say nothing, but only because we're heading for the Tower again – and if what I read that day at the museum is true – those two boys are there right now. They are still alive – living, breathing human beings with thoughts and feelings and hopes and fears. Mostly fears, I should think, if they have any idea what fate lies in store for them.

I decide to bide my time. Maybe, when we get back inside the Tower there'll be a chance to give Johnny the slip, then I can go see if I can find those kids.

Somebody ought to step in and help them, and I guess if Johnny won't do it, then it's going to have to be me.

# Chapter Ten

At the gatehouse of the Tower of London, Johnny has some trouble getting us back in. He argues with the guards while I stand there wishing I was invisible, hoping they don't want to ask *me* any questions.

There are four guards on duty. The most senior of them is an officious-looking man with a large beer belly, who says he has heard nothing about a visit from anyone called John De Vere.

Johnny gives an exasperated sigh. "If you don't believe me – send for your Constable. He will verify what I say, but I assure you that I am here at the request of Dr. John Argentine, physician to Prince Edward, to treat the boy's toothache."

The man laughs and exchanges glances with his friends. "We don't go talking about Prince Edward anymore, do we boys? Not since he was declared a *bastard*."

Johnny colors, as if he's just made a foolish mistake. "I am well aware that the boys have been declared illegitimate, but old habits die hard."

I'm standing here thinking that if he keeps making slips we could soon find ourselves in some serious trouble. I bite my lip in my anxiety. It wasn't like this last night – but I suppose they *would* be more careful about who they let in, rather than who goes out, wouldn't they? That's logical.

"Yes, well, we're loyal to the new King, aren't we boys?"

"And so am I," Johnny declares hotly. "Only this morning I have had an audience with him at Westminster."

"Yes, but you ain't got no papers, have you? Nothing with a proper seal on it. These days we can't be too careful, and you need something official, to get in here."

Johnny passes a gloved hand over his pale face, inside the hood of his heavy cloak. He's getting impatient now. I shift from one foot to the other and send him a supportive look.

"I demand that you fetch the Constable of the Tower – Robert Brackenbury. He's a personal friend of mine!"

Johnny's eyes glint dangerously, but the man just scowls back.

I'm really not liking the way these two keep upping the attitude. Surely we could do without blood on the doorstep today?

"The Constable don't like to be disturbed for *all and sundry*," says the man, with unpleasant emphasis.

That's nice. All and sundry. Mercifully, Johnny doesn't rise to the bait. He just stands there and he won't go away until they go get this Brackenbury guy.

When Brackenbury appears he's wiping his mouth with a napkin, as if he's been enjoying his lunch.

"De Vere?" he says, in astonishment. "I wasn't expecting you until tomorrow."

Johnny nods at me and shoots him a dark, secretive look. "Our plans got changed."

"I see. Well, you must come with me."

"Finally," Johnny murmurs, as the guards fall back to let us through.

Brackenbury takes us to his private apartments inside the Tower complex. He lives in great comfort. The place is furnished beautifully and he has servants waiting on him all the time. He's obviously well-rewarded for being in charge of the palace – and the prison that it has become.

But soon it's clear to me that Brackenbury's a worried man. Our arrival on his doorstep has flustered him, yes, but he's nervous and edgy anyway. Brackenbury dismisses his servants, in order to speak to us alone.

"The King's men have asked me to surrender the keys to the chamber, De Vere. I don't know how much longer I can hold them off."

Johnny gives him a dark look. "You must try. Just a little longer."

I interrupt. Unwisely, maybe. "Are you talking about Richard and Edward? The Princes in the Tower?"

Johnny turns on me. His dark eyes warn me to be careful.

Brackenbury sighs. "I've been praying for their deliverance all morning. They are too young to die. But my first loyalties lie with the King."

"Courage, man," says Johnny. "The decision will soon be taken out of your hands."

Brackenbury's face is white with fear. "That's what I'm afraid of, don't you see? It's awful having them here. I want no part in the destruction of those two young lives. No part, you understand?"

Johnny touches the man's voluminous sleeve. "Take heart. I have a message for you, from the ones who guard the door at the Tower."

I frown. Okay, so this guy, the Constable – he knows all about the door and the time travel, does he? I suppose if he's in charge of the place, he'd *have* to know. Plus, he hates the idea of killing the Princes, and I respect him for that. But he's a coward.

He won't kill them and he won't save them either. That much I've worked out.

Apart from that, I have no idea what is going on.

Brackenbury studies Johnny's face anxiously. "What is the message, young man?"

"It is this: Randolph's time has come. Do you understand?"

"Yes. Randolph's time has come."

I want to insist that Johnny tells me what this all about, but he says we must hurry or we'll miss the tide.

Brackenbury takes us through a paneled door behind a wall-hanging in his living room. He leads us up some narrow spiral stairs, up and up and out through a small door that takes us onto a small stone terrace overlooking the gardens of the Tower.

It's breezy up here and Johnny holds on to the edge of his hood to prevent it blowing back. I glance dubiously down over the edge of the parapet and realize how easily I could have been killed.

"This is dangerous." I shiver and pull the fur-trimmed collar of my dress a little closer around my shoulders.

"My way of life is dangerous," says Johnny.

I turn and look for the door – the door back to our world.

It's just an old timber door, recessed deep into the stone.

"When they built this door," I ask, "did they *know* what they were building?"

"No time for hard questions now."

Another worrying thought crosses my mind. "Johnny?"

"Not now. We need to go through before we are seen."

"But, Johnny, it's important, and it's something I need to know!"

"What?"

"When we get back – to our own world – will time have passed there too? Is that how it works? Or does it stand still while we're away?"

"Time never stands still, Maddie. Time is a river, remember, it flows on both sides of the door. Hurry up!"

"But that means I've been missing for hours Johnny! I've been gone all night."

"Yes, I'm afraid so."

"I am going to be in so much trouble when I get back!"

Brackenbury looks over the ramparts at the eddying currents of the Thames. "The tide is turning, De Vere. Now is the moment."

With confusion and fear in my soul, I head towards the door.

"Wait, Maddie. We must go together. When you get to the other side... there will be consequences."

I look at him, in horror. "You mean... if someone goes through who isn't supposed to go through—"

"In theory, you could be executed, yes. It would depend on what we thought you had seen."

"That's terrible! You can't kill people for their curiosity."

"You must travel with me. Take my hand."

But somehow in the whirling, swirling sensation that follows, I lose my grip on Johnny's cold, smooth fingers. I fall endlessly, and I'm sure I must be screaming but I can't seem to hear any sound. Bright flashes of color blind me, followed by a whiteout like I'm caught in a blizzard.

Then nothing. Silence.

This time, I find that I've fallen onto a hard, polished floor. The surface is cold and shiny against my cheek. I hope I haven't cracked my skull.

I look up to see two burly men staring down at me. Beefeaters, pointing the sharp bits of their shiny metal halberds at me.

"Please! Don't shoot – I mean – stab." I raise my hands, like I'm trying to surrender.

They hesitate, and glance at each other, wondering what the hell they are meant to do next. I guess this situation doesn't come up all that often.

The next thing I know, Johnny lands on top of me. I feel the weight of his body on my back and his breath against my ear. We spend a long embarrassing moment spread-eagled on the floor, before we disentangle ourselves and sit up – bruised and cursing.

"It's perfectly alright," Johnny announces, with far more dignity than I would have managed. "Don't worry about the girl. She's with me."

The sharp gleaming points of the weapons are retracted, and the men stand at their ease again. These guys seem to trust Johnny.

I only wish I could feel the same way.

Johnny helps me stand up. Then he spends a few moments explaining to the men that this assignment needed a 'third party' – meaning me, I suppose – and it has all been cleared with Randolph and they need not fear any questions from him.

He flashes them a confident smile, and removes his gloves and his cloak. "Everything is going according to plan," he says. "*Exactly* according to the plan."

I stand there feeling awkward in my long dress, with one foot bare and one still in its shoe while Johnny tells his story.

Why do I get the feeling that not all of it is true?

"Come on, Maddie, we'd better get you back where you belong," he says, in a lordly tone of voice. He hands his discarded cloak and gloves to one of the men, who looks a bit bemused but doesn't complain.

We head off down the hallway in the direction of the lift. I assume we are heading for the underground parking lot until we make a turn down another corridor that I've never seen before and end up outside a door that says 'J. De Vere' on the front.

"I'll just get changed if you don't mind, come in and sit down if you like."

I go inside the room without a murmur. I've gotten rather accustomed to doing what he wants in the last forty-eight hours. It's a plushy, modern office with a leather chair behind a big oak desk. Not new, but all of the very best quality. It has some nice artwork and a view out over the grounds. Johnny may have seen me from here, that day when I came to the Tower with my class.

I sit down in his big leather chair while he finds his regular clothes and gets changed as if I'm not there. I pretend to look out of the window like I'm used to all this, but inside I'm anything but happy. Mrs. Bertorelli will be having kittens by now. Someone will have told her I didn't come back last night. After all, Lydia wasn't there to cover for me.

We were supposed to be going to Hyde Park to visit Speakers Corner. Then some free time to spend shopping in Oxford Street on our own. But by now anything could have happened. The police may be involved. If my parents have been told, then my dad may have decided to hop on a plane and come look for me, or something crazy like that.

I am in trouble right up to my neck. And it's all because of Johnny. Dangerous, sexy Johnny, who right this minute is hauling off his old-fashioned linen shirt and reaching out his long, muscular arm to get a modern shirt down from the hanger on the back of the door. His back is rippled with muscle – even though he's very slim. My gaze flutters over the shapely contours of his shoulders, the curve of his neck, and those dark locks of hair that nestle just there, where his shirt collar sits. He pulls on the shirt and I tear my gaze away as he turns around and starts doing up the buttons.

In a valiant attempt to pay him no more attention, I glance down at some of the papers on his desk. It's all perfectly ordinary stuff. Letters about Patron's meetings. Requests for donations. Memos about this and that. There is just one thing of interest to me, though. Lying on the desk, is one of those cards with a barcode on it. The type of card you swipe to get through all the 'no entry' doors at the Tower.

"Cufflinks," Johnny says, frowning slightly. "Are my cufflinks over there?"

"Nope, don't think so," I say, moving a few things around on the desk, pretending to have a good look. My fingers rest for a moment on the swipe card, and the thrill of possibility runs through me. What if I….?

"Must be in here, then," he says. He picks up a plastic bag standing over on the floor by his filing cabinet. He opens the bag and searches through the contents, looking for his missing cufflinks. While I commit my crime.

Surreptitiously, I slide the card towards me. I reach the edge of the desk and let it drop to the floor. Then I put my foot over it and wait for the chance to pick it up.

He locates his cufflinks and asks me to help him put them on. I smile and say that I will. I fumble with them a bit, mainly because I'm nervous, but I get them fastened in the end.

"I can do them myself," he admits, "but it's rather nice to let a pretty girl help me out once in a while."

I wonder – with a twinge of jealousy – how often that happens, but there's no way in hell I'm going to ask. When he turns and reaches for his jacket I seize my chance. I reach down and get the swipe card. My dress doesn't have any pockets, so I slip it into my shoe.

He puts on his dark blue suit jacket, which makes him look a little older than twenty-one. He adjusts it and then says that he's ready to go.

I leave the Tower feeling like I've stolen the Star of Africa, instead of borrowing some old swipe card that probably doesn't even work. We head downstairs to find the Lamborghini, and at last he drives me back to the University to face my fate, whatever that may be.


We don't even kiss when he drops me off. Johnny says goodbye, and we do not even kiss. The warm, sensual kisses of this afternoon are just a golden memory, and the mood is different now. He drives away in his silver-gray car, and I turn and go inside. I go in through the double doors at the hall of residence, and the place is deserted.

Everyone's in Oxford Street, I presume.

Or else they're all out looking for me. That's an awful possibility.

I hurry upstairs to my room to get out of these ridiculous clothes. I step out of the black velvet dress and the golden kirtle. I fold it all up and put it back in the plastic bag. I pull on my jeans and a comfortable stretchy top, and I tidy up the makeup I spilt when I was in panic mode.

*I've seen the past.* The faces of the people I met are engraved on my mind as clearly as those of my classmates. They all whirl around in my brain. The woman at the inn, and the boy who was dressed like Robin Hood. The servant girl who made me look like a nun. The courtiers in the garden, plotting death while the bell vine danced in the summer breeze.

There has to be some purpose – some reason why I saw and heard what I did. One thing's for sure, I'm not leaving things alone now, knowing that there *is* a way back. Johnny may be bound by a sacred code, but I've made no such promise.

I put my contraband card in the pocket of my jeans, and then I hear a loud knock on my door. Time to face the music.

I open the door, but it's not the quite the face I'm expecting. It's an unshaven, male face, with a huge grin.

"Brody?"

"You are in so much trouble!"

"I know. What are you doing here?"

"I slept in. Missed breakfast. Mrs. B. hammered on my door at eight o'clock but I yelled at her to go away. Said I didn't want to go shopping. She told me I'd have to catch up with the others in Hyde Park, so I didn't miss the educational part of the tour. You can tag along with me if you like."

I'm suddenly thrown by this new piece of information. "I thought it was Hyde Park this morning and shopping this afternoon."

Brody smiles. "Don't you ever read your itinerary?"

I swallow, trying to take all this in. "No, I can't say that I have."

"Looks like you got your own itinerary going on anyhow. What's the deal with Mr. Pantyhose?"

I scowl at Brody, not liking his attitude to Johnny at all. "None of your business. How do we get to Hyde Park?"

A tiny, tiny hope kindles inside me. Maybe my absence hasn't been reported at all. Not yet, anyway.

Brody slips an unwelcome arm around my shoulders and gestures down the hallway with the other hand. "Just follow the yellow brick road."

I roll my eyes and look at his arm as if it was a dead rattlesnake on my shoulder.

Brody grins.

"Come on, Maddie. I'm your passport out of trouble, aren't I?"

"I suppose," I admit grudgingly. I lock up my room then we leave the building together and take the tube to Hyde Park.

At Hyde Park, crusty old Nigel Puckett is standing to attention, giving a sort of mini-lecture to a group of bored students. The teenagers are all sitting in a semi-circle on the grass, squinting up at him in the weak afternoon sun.

Mrs. Bertorelli is pacing up and down a small distance away, making urgent calls on her cell phone. The minute she sees us she stabs a jeweled finger at her phone to end the call. Abruptly, I should imagine, if you were the person on the other end of the line. She marches up to me and Brody to give us a piece of her mind.

"Madison Lambourne! If I could, I'd put you back on a plane to Chicago right now! Why oh why have you decided to be the thorn in my side? You, of all people, Maddie! Normally such a nice, polite girl!"

I've let her down and she has every right to yell at me. I know that.

Suddenly nobody is listening to Nigel anymore. All twenty-six students have their full attention fixed on me and Mrs. Bertorelli. Actually, even Nigel is staring at us now.

Mrs. B. folds her arms. "Well. Young *lady*. Where have you been?"

I don't like the emphasis she gives to the word 'lady' given the circumstances.

"I slept in," I say, borrowing Brody's story.

"Not in *your* bed you didn't. I checked. Last night. Several times. And then again this morning, just before I left to get Lydia out of the hospital. Your room was empty every single time."

"She was with me," Brody says, with a sly, sheepish kind of grin.

I turn sharply and stare at him in horror.

Brody shrugs. "Yep, well. I guess everyone's going to know we're… an item… sooner or later."

I know that my face must be draining rapidly of all its color. The sheer awfulness of my *entire class* thinking I spent the night with Brody is too horrible to contemplate.

Mrs. Bertorelli turns to me and puts on that mortally shocked teacher-face she's really, really good at. "Madison Lambourne. This isn't the kind of behavior that will make your parents proud, is it?"

"No," I whisper. It's the kind of behavior that would make my father reach for his rifle and hunt Brody down like a skunk, is what it is. And after he was done I'd be tempted to ask for a turn to put a hole or two into him myself.

But for now, I'm caught. If I tell her the truth… there's no way I can tell her the truth. I have to go along with this. I have to let everyone think I… oh my gosh… with *Brody*. My face floods with shame.

"She's seventeen, Mrs. B."

Mrs. Bertorelli looks up at him, sharply. "I'm aware of that, Brody. I know where we all stand, under the law. But that certainly doesn't make it right."

"I'm not saying we went the whole way."

"Brody!" I say. What color comes after scarlet, I wonder? What's next in that range of shades that goes along with deep personal shame?

He nudges my arm. "I mean all we really did was—"

"Save it." Mrs. Bertorelli's voice is crisp and impatient. I sense that twenty-seven people sitting behind me would have liked to have heard a little more. But she puts up her hand as if she was stopping traffic and tells Brody to go and sit down.

He lollops over to the rest of the group and there is a lot of suppressed laughter and punching Brody on the arm. Slapping him on the back. Like he'd scored a home run.

My angry teacher turns to me. "Madison. I'm disappointed in you."

I nod.

"I'm thinking maybe you're a little disappointed in yourself," she says glancing over at Brody, who is demonstrating his ability to cross his eyes while turning his mouth inside out with his thumbs.

I sort of blink and then I nod. "Please don't mention this to my dad. He really doesn't need to know."

"No, he doesn't," says Mrs. Bertorelli, and her tone is surprisingly sympathetic. Her gaze stays with the rowdy teenagers, who are all lolling around on the grass taking pictures of each other and sending texts to their friends back home. "But you know, honey, Ashwell Springs is a place where nothing stays secret for very long. So you better have your story straight by the time you get back."

I nod gratefully, and she pats my arm and tells me to go join my friends.

I go and sit down on the grass next to Lydia. She looks a little pale and wan after her bonus trip to the hospital, but otherwise a lot like Lydia.

"Hey, Maddie, what's going on?"

I am reluctant to start on the story, especially with Brody around.

"Talk later," I murmur apologetically.

Soon, we all board the bus again, and it takes us back to the Thames for our River Trip – one of the much-advertised highlights of our tour.

The weather is clouding over and it has turned a little colder now. It doesn't feel like summer any more, and it certainly doesn't seem all that great a day for sitting in an open-top boat listening to a muffled commentary about Festival Hall and what they are doing about pollution. Whatever they're doing, it isn't working. The water looks like mud.

I gaze across the brown, murky waters of the Thames and look out for the Tower, looming up ahead. For a wild moment I wonder if I could ask the driver if he would let me off there so I could go back inside. I keep thinking of those two kids locked up in there, and in my head there's a voice that says the same thing, over and over again. "They're still alive, Maddie, they're still alive."

"What the hell is wrong with you?" says Lydia, putting her hand on the sleeve of my jacket. "You look like you've seen a ghost."

"Oh, nothing."

"You thinking about your dad?"

"What?"

"Your real dad."

"A guy who disappears when I'm two years old, skips off to London and never sends me a birthday card cannot be called a 'real dad'"

"No. I guess he doesn't qualify, does he?"

"No way."

"You reckon he's still here? In London?"

"I have no idea."

"You gonna try and find out?"

I look up at her. Her pale platinum blond hair is straight today – I guess they didn't let her wear her curlers in the hospital. It is fine and straight and it blows this way and that in the wind as the boat makes its painfully slow progress up the Thames.

"Do you think I should?"

"Yeah. Why not? Look him up. Go ask him why he ran out, and listen to his tale of woe. Or just check him out and see if he looks like you."

I smile. She makes it sound easy.

"I tell you what. Tonight, we could spend some time on the Internet and see what we can find out."

"Look, Lydia – it's a nice idea, but… "

The old guy up front is asking us if we have any questions, and suddenly it hits me that I do. I start waving my hand in the air.

"Excuse me! May I ask what time the tide turns today?"

The boatman smiles at me. "Well, well, a person interested in all things nautical," he says, "and a young lady too, no less!"

I color up a little, because everyone is looking at me again, and I've already had plenty of that. "Just interested."

"About half past eleven tonight, young lady. Why do you ask?"

"I wanted to know if there are any superstitions about high tide on the River Thames, that's all."

"Superstitions? No, love. Londoners don't hold with all that. We're *realists*, miss, and *pragmatists*, that's what we are!"

Lydia rolls her eyes, and whispers to me. "What about all that stuff they were telling us the other day about how if the ravens ever leave, the Tower of London will fall down?"

"I guess it's just pragmatic to go on feeding them so we don't have to test that one out."

She laughs and suddenly I have the overwhelming urge to confide in her. "Lydia – last night, while you were in the hospital – I wasn't with Brody. I… I spent the night with Johnny from the Tower."

"Oh my gosh! No! You didn't do it with him, did you?"

"No!" I say, feeling like my cheeks are blazing. "I only just met the guy!"

"I'll say. Maddie – I never thought it would be you going wild on this trip. I'd understand if it was me. No wonder you've been acting weird."

I glance at her nervously, wondering if I did the right thing.

She pats me on the arm. "He's a step up from Brody, at least."

I feel a pang inside, just thinking about him. Johnny, I mean. "I don't even know when I'll see him again."

"He didn't arrange another date?"

"Not exactly. He has my phone number though."

"Have you got his?"

"Yes. But I'm not calling him."

"Playing hard to get, huh?" Lydia says.

I bite my lip. *Not very.* "Lydia. He's no ordinary guy. He's… scary."

"Sexy scary or scary scary?"

"Both. He's involved in something – at the Tower – and I need to go back and help him."

"No!" Lydia obviously can't believe what she's hearing. Me – involved in something – with a sexy, scary guy? This is going to take a bit of explaining, and I haven't got either the time or the inclination to do that.

"I might need you to cover for me tonight. I could easily slip away for an hour or so, as long as they don't find out where I've gone."

"I want to know everything, Maddie. Tell me."

"I can't. Not right now. Just cover for me tonight and then maybe tomorrow there'll be something to tell."

Lydia stares at me and then she covers her mouth to hide her smile. She thinks all I want is another chance to be with Johnny. She has no idea what I really want. No idea at all.

We are heading slowly past the Old London Docks, and the guide picks up his squeaky microphone again and starts telling us something of their history.

But I'm not listening. I'm plotting my escape.

My plan goes something like this: as soon as the bus drops us off at the University, I'll turn around and go straight back out again. I'll go to the nearest tube station and catch an underground train and head for the Tower. If I manage to get there before they close, I'll pay a normal adult admission into the Tower. Then I'll hide somewhere – not sure where yet – but I'll think of somewhere, and wait until everything's quiet. When it's safe to come out, I'll try out my new swipe card and see if I can find my way back to the doorway and… but what about the guards? That could be a problem. I have to think of a way to divert the guards. And the door to the Princes' chamber is guarded too… but everyone has their price.

Think fast, Maddie Lambourne, think fast!

# Chapter Eleven

It was almost too easy, at first.

I got into the Tower at two minutes to five – the guy on the door said I was lucky to get there before he had to say no more admissions. I lurked around the galleries and the Torture chamber. I deliberately avoided going outside onto the Green, because Johnny's office looks out that way and I was determined not to be seen.

Right now, I'm waiting beside the water fountain on the second floor. I've spotted a little CCTV camera up in the corner, and I'm watching and waiting for it to pan away from me so I can make my next move.

I see my chance and I take it. The camera swings away and I walk silently across the polished floor and swipe my card beside a 'STAFF ONLY' door. I wait with bated breath for the beep, expecting disappointment, but to my delight the door unlocks for me to pass through. Now all I have to do is find a secure hiding place – somewhere I can sit out the long wait. Closing time is at five-thirty, but then I still have to wait until after the ceremony of the keys, and that's nearly four hours from now.

I find a janitor's cupboard, but I walk on by because the most likely time for that to be needed is just after the last visitor has gone home. The next place is much more hopeful – a little room with the shades drawn down, full of stationery supplies. I find a spot behind an old whiteboard and crouch down to begin the long wait.

I begin to regret missing dinner, and I'm uncomfortable as hell. But no one comes near me, and I see the color of the light coming through the shade changing and fading as the sun gradually sets.

Later, I wake with a jolt – and realize I must have been asleep. If I've missed the tide then everything I've done so far will be wasted. I check my phone to see the time. The bright blue light flashes on and I see that it's still only ten past ten. Still another hour or more to go.

Finally, after what seems like an eternity, I decide it's time to leave my little room and do what I came here to do.

I open the door and go into the hallway, moving as silently as I can. I find the nearest fire alarm, mounted on the wall. I take all my courage in my hands. I break the glass and set off the alarm. The whole place resounds with screaming sirens and I feel like a hooligan. My heart beats wildly while the shrill sound wails through the air, making my ears throb with pain.

I have to remind myself that I am doing this for the right reasons. Two boys are locked up in this place. Here, within these walls. And yesterday I heard two men plotting to end their lives. *Only yesterday – over five hundred years ago.*

I must hurry. I get my swipe card ready and run along the deserted corridors. I struggle to remember the route to the door – the portal – whatever you care to call it. I don't care as long as it's still there and it works. I hear footsteps coming towards me, and I duck into a darkened doorway, and wait there with my heart thundering while the guards run straight past.

I am frozen to the spot with fear. I tell myself that I chose this. I wanted it, and I can't stop now. Not when I stand just a few feet from the door – inches away from success.

I swallow hard and look up to see if I am watched by CCTV. They don't seem to have any up here. I must ask Johnny why. But then it occurs to me that from what he has already told me there are some things go on in this place that nobody ought to see.

I walk towards the door and check the time yet again. Go now, Maddie. It's time to go now. I hurry towards the door – almost expecting to see Johnny running round the corner like he did last night. But this time I go through, unobserved and brace myself for the fall.

I land better this time, rolling like I'm a paratrooper or something. I don't know why I did that, but it worked. I get up cautiously. Nothing sprained and no bones broken. It's going well, so far.

I'm out on that little parapet again. This time I know the proper way down. I steal through Brackenbury's secret door and out through his living room.

I make my way across the darkened courtyard and head for the place I believe the Princes are held: the Garden Tower – which only later acquired a more sinister name.

I slip inside. The floor is strewn with rushes and smells of urine and damp, moldy water, which seems to be dripping down the wall.

I get my phone out of my pocket to check the time. It says there's no cell phone coverage – obviously – but the display lights up and shows the date and time. Or rather, it shows *my* date and time.

"Who goes there?" comes a rough, male voice behind me.

I've been caught, before even getting near the chamber where the boys are held. I turn around slowly – fearing for a moment that the man holds a gun. A smile almost comes to my lips when I realize my mistake. No one here carries any kind of firearm. They haven't invented them yet, you silly girl.

He may, of course, have a dagger… and that could be a painful way to die. I hold my phone close against my chest, and curl my fingers around it tightly. "I've come to visit the captives."

"No one goes near my prisoners. What have you got there? I saw it show a light?"

"Nothing."

"What is it? A lantern?"

"… Yes, that's right. Nothing of consequence."

He steps closer, trying to see what I'm holding. "It cast a most eerie light upon your face – and yet it is so small it cannot have much of a wick inside it. Let me see."

"No!" I stuff it away into my pocket and back away from him.

He looks tempted to manhandle me for it, but then he notices something else. "You're a woman, dressed as a knave!"

Ah. My clothing – the tight blue jeans, and the hooded sweatshirt – he mistakes them for the garb of a young boy.

He wheezes with lusty laughter. "Are you a little harlot?"

"No. I am no such thing. I have come to see the boys. I am sent from their doctor, with a salve."

"A salve?"

"Yes. Some medicine, for the older boy, the one that has the toothache."

"Aye, well, he won't have to worry about that much longer." The man grins a wicked, leering grin. "Begone with you! I've heard naught about a visit from the doctor."

I get out a tiny pot of pink lip gloss with little sparkles in it, and I show it to the man, who takes it in his huge, dirty hands and examines it with childlike curiosity.

"Well, I've never seen the like! That's not goose grease, is it?"

"Nope. It's been specially prepared for the boy – Edward."

The man puts his giant nose close to the little pot of lip gloss and sniffs it suspiciously. "Strawberries?"

"Give it back, it took the apothecary hours to prepare."

"It's a fancy preparation indeed, though there isn't very much of it."

"It's marvelous stuff – and I must take it to the boy immediately."

The man smiles. "Only if you let me see that lantern of yours."

I hesitate. Could it have repercussions – showing him my cell phone? I hope not. I put the lid on my lip gloss and tuck it back into the front pocket of my hooded top. Then I reach for my phone. I get a strong feeling that Johnny would be appalled if he could see me now.

"Give me the key then, and you shall have the phone… I mean… the lantern."

The man pauses, studying me. The key hangs from a thin leather strap dangling from his belt. His fingers touch it, but he makes no move to untie it and give it to me.

I look up, with what I hope is a persuasive expression. "The boy will be less trouble to you once I have applied the salve."

The man raises a quizzical eyebrow, but he's weakening. He really, really wants to get his hands on my phone. He unties the key from its leather string, and we do the exchange, cautiously. I take the key. He takes the little black plastic phone.

"How do you make it show a light?"

I show him how to slide it open, and he marvels at it, and moves it this way and that so the blue light shines on the dank stone walls.

He grins. Intrigued by it. "It is most marvelous small," he says. "And the light it casts is a very clear blue. Is it done with woad?"

"I have no idea. Why don't you sit down with it and try out all the features, while I slip in and see the boys."

He grunts and leans against the wall, completely absorbed by the new toy I have given him. I leave him there, stabbing huge grubby fingers at the touch-screen, while I walk along the corridor to find the right chamber, with the all-important key pressed tightly into the palm of my hand.

I find the door. It's a heavy timber door. The kind you'd want if you were keeping valuable political prisoners inside. I glance left and right, but there's no one around except my new friend the jailor – and he is real busy right now.

I enter the room, and glance around. Two narrow beds, some abandoned objects on the floor – a spinning top, a book or two, some discarded clothing – but no kids.

The boys themselves are nowhere to be seen. I scan the whole chamber, but there is no sign of life or movement. The beds are rumpled, but empty. Perhaps I'm too late. Maybe someone has got here before me, and they are already gone.

But I was so sure they said…

I sit down heavily on the bed, and try to figure out where to from here.

After a while, I hear a sound. Coming from under the bed. Someone shifting position. Someone who has held his breath a long time, taking a gasp of air.

I kneel down and lift the blankets. I see a face squinting at me.

"Hello?" I say. "Are you Edward?"

"No," the boy whispers with fear in his eyes.

"Are you Richard, then?"

He inches away. I reach out to try to stop him but he slithers away from me.

There's a pause. Then the boy bolts out from the other side of the bed and hurls himself across the room. He ends up cowering beside an oak chest, looking guardedly at me. Another voice speaks. Behind me.

"Surely, they would not send a girl to kill us."

I swing round to see the older boy standing behind me. He is just about my height. I meet his wary blue eyes for the first time. Staring at me. I stare back at him for a moment – taking in the sight of this grubby twelve-year old boy.

His face is swollen and bruised, but his features are fine. He has a long, sad face. His hair is vaguely similar in color to my own – dark blonde – but his has a hint of auburn in it too. It falls down to his shoulders, and it needs washing. He's been crying – a lot, by the look it. Rivers of tears have run down his face, streaking it clean here and there. He stares back at me from under painful, swollen eyelids, waiting for me to make my next move.

This is the boy who was born to be the King of England.

I remember the way Johnny bowed low in the presence of the man who took this child's kingdom from him. I try to recreate that bow, letting my fingers touch the floor. When I lift up my head and look into the boy's eyes again I imagine there is less hatred. Perhaps.

"You dress like a boy, and you bow like a courtier, but I am not in the mood for pranks," he says. He has the intonation of a prince.

My confidence falters, but I try to find my voice. "Neither am I."

"Who are you?"

"I am… Madeleine of Champany." It seems best to stick to the same line for everyone, for the time being. "I… I wanted to warn you, sire. About a plot… against your life."

The boy stares at me. Unimpressed.

"Madeleine. I await the hour of my death as patiently and as fearlessly as I can."

His reaction throws me off for a minute. But then I remember what I'm here for. "I… I want to help you to escape it, Sire, if you'll let me."

He turns his head away, as if I had slapped him. He passes a hand over his grubby face – the gesture of a much older, careworn man.

"I used to believe there were men who would lay down their lives to help me and my brother. But we have waited for weeks and weeks, and no one has come near. We are forsaken. We are dead already. Why have they sent you? And how did you get in when everyone else has failed?" His voice is an urgent whisper in the dark.

"I am in a… unique position," I say, knowing I'm not doing that well at explaining this, but not daring to give too much away. I reach for the key and fish it out of the back pocket of my jeans. "Plus – the jailor let me borrow this."

The light is poor. Edward reaches out and takes the heavy metal key from me so he can get a proper look. His fingers are warm and they tremble a little – which fills me with compassion for his plight.

"The key to this chamber," he says, with a note of bitterness in his voice. "Would that you had come sooner, dear lady. Now I fear that all three of us will die."

"There is still time. I overheard a discussion about… you and your brother, and we have a few days in hand."

The younger boy takes in a sharp breath at this point, and I am struck by how awful it must be for a nine-year-old boy to be on death row.

Edward's face is ghostly in the moonlight that comes through the casement window. He hands me back my key. "I do not believe you can save us, but it is kind of you to come. We have very few visitors now. Will you stay and talk with us a while?"

I smile. "I kind of have to stay, bcause I can't get out the way I came for at least another six hours. So you're pretty much stuck with me for now. But when I do go back, I'm taking you guys with me, if you'll agree to that?"

Edward gives me a melancholy look. "Sometimes my brother and I while away the time by inventing stories, Madeleine. About how we could escape this dreadful place. We find it a comfort in the dark."

"This one's for real."

His face mellows, but I can see that he doesn't believe me. He's gotten used to waiting to die. He touches my arm lightly. "You can tell us your story, if you like."

The other boy creeps out of bed and kneels down so he can hear our whispered conversation a little better. He seems a lot younger than Edward somehow. He is smaller and slighter than his brother, though similar in so many other ways. His nightshirt is loose and I'm guessing he feels the cold, for he is shivering. He reaches out and gets a blanket from his bed and wraps it around himself for warmth. He could easily be my own little brother, wrapped up in his quilt on a cold frosty morning back home in Illinois.

I smile at him, but he just stares warily back.

"It's okay," I say, before remembering I'm not supposed to use that word. "I mean, it's going to be alright."

"I have never seen a girl wearing hose before," he whispers.

I look down at my legs – encased in blue jeans – and I can see what he means, I suppose. "Seen one of these though, huh?"

I pull my hood up over my head and make a funny face, Brody-style. I guess I look really grotesque because the boy almost cracks me a smile.

Almost, but not quite. I guess a few months spent locked up in here would destroy anyone's sense of fun. So, with six hours to kill and no surefire way to get them back out through the door in broad daylight, I start outlining my plan.

# Chapter Twelve

I've only been in the room a couple of hours when things start to go wrong.

Richard is sleeping in his blanket at my feet and Edward and I have been talking through the night – he's asking me all kinds of questions I can't answer, about my world.

He wants to know if all the girls dress as boys, and if so, what do the boys wear? He wants to know how many horses my father keeps and how many villeins are on his estate. I misunderstand at first and tell him that where I come from a 'villain' is a bad guy, and to the best of my knowledge my dad doesn't keep company with them. This makes Edward smile, for the first time in our short friendship.

"A wise father, indeed," he says, with a sigh. "For since I came to London, after my father died, I have *only* met evil men."

"Is there no one on the staff here who would help us? No one we could trust?"

"Not one. When we first arrived the servants were nicer, but they have all been sent away. These days we have but one man who comes in and delivers food from time to time. I'm sure he's loyal only to my uncle – he used to work in his house, you see —"

There is a noise. Footsteps, coming towards us, and angry voices too.

Edward's eyes flare and he grips my arm. "I'm sorry, Maddie, for anything you are about to see!"

I dive under the bed as the keys rattle in the door. Richard is awake in an instant and he takes up his place behind the oak chest in the corner again.

"Where is she?" demands an angry voice.

From under the bed I can see the man's shoes, and I know them; I've seen them before. This is Randolph – the cold, sickening man I met on that first night I came to the Tower. He's their leader, and he's looking for me.

"Where's the girl!"

Edward cowers in bed. "Sir… I know nothing… I swear… "

Two other men appear in the doorway, and then another one, carrying a lighted torch – flaming red and orange – sending sinister shadows dancing across the walls.

Between them, they start pulling the room apart.

"I'm here."

No need to prolong the hunt when the outcome is inevitable. It will only make things worse for the boys. I crawl out from under the bed, and Randolph's henchmen grab hold of me – one on each arm.

I see that all four men are dressed in the right clothes for this place. For this time, I should say. Their cloaks swirl about them as they move and their daggers glint in their hands. Randolph sheathes his knife, now that I've been caught.

"What wild folly is this then, my girl?"

My first thought is how hateful it is to have someone as revolting as Randolph calling me that name: 'my girl'. But this is crazy. The game is over now.

Nevertheless I lift my trembling chin and try to speak. "Randolph. How enchanting," I say.

Which was a mistake, because he brings his angry face close to mine. Close enough for me to see the yellow stains on his teeth and to smell his foul breath on my face.

Then he slaps me hard and my head swings to the right with the blow. I clench my teeth and ignore the stinging pain. I can see poor little Richard trembling and cowering down on the floor by the oak box in the corner. Hardly daring to look up.

The man in front of me slaps me again. Harder, this time. "You may pay for your disrespect with your lifeblood, girl! Have you no understanding of that?"

"If you have any power over this at all, Randolph, why haven't you used it to set these boys free?"

"Their fate and yours is sealed… my sweet."

He almost spits at me when he says this, and maybe that's why the hatred burning inside me gives me more strength than I ever knew I had.

"Life is full of surprises, Randolph. Nobody's fate is *sealed*."

He laughs. "You will learn. Tonight, you will learn. Take her downstairs – deliver her to the others. Tell them, she's a present, from me!"

The two men pull me away, and all I have time for is one glance over my shoulder at Edward's scared young face. I try to mouth one word, and one word only. A word that will give him some hope.

"Tomorrow."

I see him nod, almost imperceptibly, as the men lead me away.


I am taken into a chamber where about twelve men are gathered – all wearing long dark cloaks. More lighted torches burn brightly at the walls, sending plumes of black smoke curling up to the ceiling. The room smells of burning tar and some other more sinister aroma I can't quite recognize at first.

Blood. I think it could be blood.

My knees are weak and my mouth is dry.

Inside my head, I pray for strength. More men come in and pass right by me. They move slowly in a kind of procession, and the first one carries a cup – a chalice I think it's called. An old, old chalice made out of some kind of metal, chased in gold.

Their hoods are up over their heads, but I get glimpses of their faces now and then. The men start chanting – like monks or something, I don't know. I find myself drawn by a pair of glittering black eyes staring at me from across the room.

I know those eyes.

The man in the hooded cloak holds me in his gaze.

I shiver.

It's Johnny. I know it is.

At first I feel a rush of pure relief. He's here. My heart leaps.

He'll help me, of course he will.

But he makes no move. He shows no sign of recognition other than to keep me in his sights. Those dark eyes, burning bright in the torchlight, never leave my face. Gradually, the stark reality sinks in. He's here because he has to be here. He hasn't come to rescue me.

This is his life, all this. The fire and the chalice and the chanting. These men – one of whom has already told me I will pay with my life tonight – they are his *friends*. These predatory, angry men.

He's one of them.

Johnny is a predator and I am the prey.

Yes. Finally I understand what he is, and what he wants with me.

Tonight, I will indeed pay for my curiosity, and my foolishness, and my hopeless, misguided… love.

I will pay for it in blood.

# Chapter Thirteen

I am asked to kneel.

I'm guessing this is one of those moments when you have to do what's expected of you, like paying the executioner before you die. So I kneel.

Randolph takes a few paces forward and tosses my phone down in front of me. Its black plastic case comes apart as it skitters across the floor.

"You have disturbed the equilibrium of time," intones Randolph. I think that's his way of saying I've angered him beyond what he's prepared to put up with.

"Judgment must be immediate and final," he says, and he looks at me with a hideous leer. Then they all start talking about me as if I wasn't there. Muttering and murmuring about what they would like to do with me. Talking about tasting my blood.

But another man steps forward, and pushes back his hood. He is Arthur, the one that Johnny said was loyal.

"Randolph. May I be allowed to speak?" he says.

Randolph inclines his head, as if he was the Emperor of Rome.

Arthur clears his throat. "If this girl does, in fact, have a role to play, then we will be endangering the River if we… *extinguish* her at the wrong time."

I have never had to listen to anyone talking about 'extinguishing' me before. It isn't easy to remain silent and still. My inner fears are screaming, and my heart is telling me to run. I stare at Johnny and will him to speak.

"She has no role," says Randolph. "She's not one of us."

Then Johnny tears off his hood and rushes forward. "She does! She does have a role to play and you can't kill her or you'll all die."

"Johnny?" The word escapes from my lips like a whispered prayer, but he does not answer me. He doesn't even look at me.

He turns around wildly, challenging each and every one of the men with his stare. His jet black hair glints in the firelight, and his eyes are burning bright.

"I was there, remember! The first time around – in September, 1483. She must go back, it is her fate! If you change that, I cannot even imagine what will happen!"

Randolph begins to laugh. "You speak with great *passion*, John, and I think we all know why."

A ripple of amusement goes around the circle of men.

"You do have a rather *personal* interest in the subject, don't you, De Vere?" Randolph says, with a sickening smile.

"I do. But my first loyalty is to the River. I am sworn to serve the River, and serve it I will. She has to go back. I have seen her before. I remember her. She has done nothing wrong – she is only fulfilling her fate. Arthur? Will you believe me? Simon? Anyone else?"

Randolph wheels round angrily, cutting the air with the edge of his hand. "He lies! His cold heart yearns for the warmth it can never enjoy. He is at the mercy of his *feelings*, like the frail human being kneeling there! We have no reason to believe him."

Arthur steps forward again. "We have no reason to disbelieve him, either. He has served faithfully on this committee, Randolph. He has a right to speak. You cannot deny him a hearing."

Randolph snorts with annoyance. "I've heard him. I've heard all I need to hear."

"And now you would dismiss him, because you dislike him, and kill the girl for sport? What if John speaks true? We will all suffer the consequences of our actions if we are governed by our lust for blood tonight!"

Another man steps forward. "I say we put it to the vote."

There is a general murmur of agreement, and even Randolph shrugs and nods his head.

The vote? My whole body shivers with fear. They are going to put me to the vote. They might as well have said they were putting me to the sword. My life, my future, my hope of saving Edward and his brother, it is all in the hands of these men. Randolph is their leader. I've seen them all bowing and scraping to him. If this is an open ballot, then perhaps my fate *is* sealed.

"Take her into the next chamber to wait. You go with her, De Vere."

"He has a vote," Arthur points out. "He must be allowed to use it."

"I'm aware of that," hisses Randolph, "but we already know where his sympathies lie."

Johnny comes over to me, and reaches out to help me get to my feet. I want to push him away, but I am weak and wobbly and I need to lean on him. He takes me into a small dark chamber, lit by a single candle in an iron sconce on the wall. There is a seat by the casement window, and he leads me over there. It is still dark outside and it is cold sitting there. My hooded sweatshirt is much too thin to stop me from shivering. Johnny takes my hand, and his fingers are cold too. How could I have been so blind?

"Do you want my cloak?" he says and puts a hand up to undo the clasp.

"You are at least as cold as me," I say in a voice that sounds as if I've screamed myself hoarse.

"Yes, but I do not feel it," he says, in a voice that is hollow with pain.

We wait, and every minute seems like an eternity.

"Why didn't you warn me, Johnny? About those men?"

"I'm sorry. It was outside my control."

I'm not sure that I really believe that. I know I've let my curiosity lead me into danger, but he's been guiding things the whole time. Besides, he is not to be trusted. He is one of them.

"Why did you tell them you *remembered* me?"

"It was the only way I could think of to make them spare your life."

"Will it work?" I say, searching his face for the truth.

He glances out of the casement window, into the darkness beyond. "It has to work."

*He is as scared as I am.* I can sense it, though he hides his feelings well.

We keep on waiting. I watch the patterns cast on the wall by the flames that burn in the sconce. "Does the voting take long?"

Johnny shoots me an unsettling glance. "The longer the better. It means there is some dissent."

"So this… delay… it means the jury's still out?"

"Yes."

We wait in silence, for what seems like hours. Outside, I hear the birds begin to sing, and the night sky begins to give way to the dawn.

I turn on Johnny suddenly and anger flashes through me. "I'm supposed to wait here while they decide if I live or die, am I? I'm supposed to accept their decision as if it was fair?"

"Maddie," he says in a grim, warning tone. "You must try to remain calm."

"No!" I leap to my feet and try to make a run for the door. "I'd rather take my chance out there on those streets than wait around in here."

He is in front of the door – barring my way in an instant. He is slim but he is strong. He places his body weight against the door while I shake him and pull at him in a vain attempt to get past.

"Let me go! You should at least give me a chance to save my own life!"

"I can't. It is my duty to guard you."

"And what if they decide I've got to die. Will you do your duty then, and hand me over to them? Johnny! Tell me the truth!"

He stares down at me, bracing his shoulder against the heavy timber door. "I do not believe the outcome will be the one you fear."

"How can you say that? How can you stand there and talk like everything's going to be okay, when those… monsters… are in there, drawing lots for who gets the first taste?"

"Maddie. Think about what I said in there. Your fate is already written. If they change it, we are all lost."

"Stop talking in riddles the whole time! You are the most awful man I ever met, and I can't believe I ever wanted to be close to you! You don't care about me at all! You're *inhuman*, that's what you are!"

"Yes. I am," he says bitterly, "and you would do well to remember it."

"Let me go!"

"I'm trying to help you, Madeleine!"

"Don't call me Madeleine! That is NOT my name!"

After another futile bout of tugging at his arm and pulling at the iron catch that holds the door, I sink down onto my knees on the floor. I burst into hysterical desperate sobbing. I bend my head forward until it almost touches my jeans, and cry my eyes out.

I sense Johnny kneeling down beside me and I know that he's trying to work out if he should take hold of me to offer me some comfort. I can almost feel his awkwardness and guilt. But my heart hardens and I resolve that if he does lay a hand on me – I'll shove him away.

"I… I'm not ready to die, Johnny, there are so many things I want to do with my life."

Gently he tries to soothe me with trivial questions about my hopes and dreams.

Between my sobs I tell him all of it. The big things, like going to college and helping my step-dad Jake with his radio show, and the little things, like wanting a taste of champagne. I even admit that I wanted to meet my real dad, just once, to understand why he left.

"How can you let a beast like Randolph take it all away?"

"I could fight him, and one day I will," he says. "But it will not be me who vanquishes him, Maddie."

"How do you know?"

Johnny gives a sort of hollow laugh. "Travel broadens the mind."

I assume, from this deliberately puzzling statement, that Johnny means he has traveled to the future, at some other point in time. Jeez, this is getting complicated. It's messing with my head.

"How did he get to be so powerful?"

Johnny shrugs his shoulders. "Men like that have their methods – mainly ruthless ones – of gaining the support they need. King Richard was the same."

That's when we hear a loud knock on the door.

Johnny leaps to his feet, grasps the iron ring that serves as a door knob and pulls the heavy door open.

Two words. Two words that shape my future and seal my fate.

"She lives."

The man delivers his message curtly and disappears, and I am left alone again with Johnny. He does not say 'I told you so,' he's smart enough to know not to say that. Gently he encourages me to get to my feet and leads me back to the window seat. He fetches me a drink in a leather flask – some sort of alcohol, I think. He is wise enough too, not to make conversation. I have nothing left to say to him.

We have to keep waiting, even now. We have to wait for the tide to turn. But this is a different kind of waiting; much more like the dull, uncomfortable hours that pass when your flight has been delayed.

Finally they call us. They say the tide is right. We troop along the corridor in silence. Me, Johnny, and all those other men. Walking along feeling numb and tired. We go through the door to our own world. We pass the two guards with their shining halberds, standing to attention. They nod politely, as if we've just finished our shift. *Punch your time-card, Maddie. Grab your coat. It's time for you to go home.*

Johnny puts his long cloak around my shoulders and says he'll drive me.

The last remnant of defiance inside me makes a comeback, and I shake my head. "No. I'd rather take a cab."

"As you wish," he says, glancing away.

I give him back his cloak. I want nothing from him. Nothing that gives him an excuse to come find me again. He insists on waiting with me, standing in the street in his outlandish clothes, waiting for the taxi to arrive.

When the sleek black cab turns up, I lift my chin and get in to the vehicle without even saying goodbye. I tell the driver my destination, and I keep calm and composed just until we turn the first corner and then the tears start. I cry all the way back to the University.

I'm blinded by tears as I pay the driver and turn away. I have no idea if I gave him too much, and I don't care. Nothing like that seems to matter anymore.

I go upstairs to my room and Lydia lifts her sleepy head off her pillow as I open the door. She looks up at me through half-closed eyes. "Did you do it?" she asks.

I fling myself, in tears, onto the bed.

She wakes up in a hurry after that. "Hey, Maddie! What the hell happened to you?"

"I can't. Not now. Don't ask me."

She gets out of her bed and comes over and sits on the edge of my bed. She shakes my arm. "What did that guy do to you? Maddie! What did he do?"

"He's a... he's a... vampire, and I never want to see him again." I bury my face in my pillow, and give way to noisy sobs.

Lydia rubs my back sympathetically. "Okay, okay. He's a creep. You're better off without him, I guess."

I sit up. I stare at her. I blink. She doesn't get it, does she? I said the word, and she thought I was just… expressing my disgust. Like calling him a rattlesnake or a yellow-bellied skunk.

Lydia flashes me a rather odd look. "He did have an *awesome* car."

I frown at her in disbelief.

Lydia gives a wistful sigh. "Oh well, never mind, Maddie. Plenty more fish in the sea. If you don't mind settling for a guy who rides a skateboard instead."

I stare at her open-mouthed, with the tears still wet on my cheeks. She reaches for the little box of tissues that she keeps by her bed, and pulls one out for me. "Here you go."

"Thanks," I murmur, and dab at my face with it, mainly to be polite.

"So… if you don't mind my asking. Which base did you get to, before you realized he wasn't quite… The One?"

"What?"

"Come on. You set out expecting a hot date. You were all excited about the guy. You come home crying your heart out. At what point did it all start to go wrong?"

I let out a kind of bitter, broken laugh. What do I tell her? The part where they point their daggers at me, or the part where they vote about drinking my blood?

There's a long pause, punctuated by a couple more shuddering breaths on my part and another tissue and a moment spent wiping my eyes. "He's not the guy I thought he was, okay?"

"Okay," Lydia nods, and then she shrugs and goes back to her own bed. "I guess you'll tell me about it when you're ready."

I nod too, knowing that there's not a snowball's chance in hell that she'll *ever* hear the whole truth. Not from me.

"Try to get some sleep Maddie, if you can. Big day tomorrow."

I glance at the bedside clock. "It *is* tomorrow. It's nearly six a.m."

Lydia groans. "Then I guess we might as well forget about sleep. We have to be on that bus again by seven-thirty."

I frown. I am too broken-hearted to care which tourist attraction is scheduled for today, but the mention of the early start time has me worried and I can't remember why.

Lydia sighs. "Bath on Wednesday, remember."

"What are you talking about, Lydia? Nobody said anything to me about taking a bath."

She rolls her eyes and starts explaining it to me slowly and patiently, as if I was very, very dumb. "We are leaving London today. We are going to stay in the historic City of Bath, where we will be admiring the Roman remains."

"No!" I say, suddenly fraught with panic. "I can't go! I can't just *leave*!"

"Maddie. The tour leaves today. You are on the tour, whether you like it or not. You signed up to see Bath, remember, and since Johnny has turned out to be such an… arrogant clown… I'm surprised you're so unhappy about it."

"But… Lydia! I promised! I promised Richard and Edward I'd go back!"

"Richard and Edward? Who the hell are they?"

I stop dead in my tracks. I can't tell her about Richard and Edward. And I can't go back for them, either.

I've made them a promise I can't possibly keep.

Lydia looks at me with rising alarm. "You've been acting weird now for days. Really, really weird."

"I know, I'm sorry." I put my hand to my throat, "I… I think I'm going to throw up."

# Chapter Fourteen

I'm on the bus, and we are getting further away from London with every passing minute. I have failed. I stare disconsolately at the endless gray-green hedges flashing by and the constant stream of traffic going the other way. Motorway signs loom up ahead: Reading, Swindon, Hungerford…

Places I've never been to, places I don't want to go.

I did *think* about not getting on the bus. I even had a half-baked plan. I was going to let them put my tartan bag on the bus, same as everyone else, so as not to arouse suspicion. I was going to get on board, put my stuff on the seat, stow my coat in the rack up above. Act normal. Follow the drill. Then, I was going to ask Lydia to cover for me while I snuck off back inside the hostel.

I was hoping they'd just drive away without me, if I could get Lydia to lie for me. But when it came to it, I failed.

For a start, it would have meant telling Lydia why I wanted to take such a drastic course of action. She'd have been worried sick and she'd try and talk me out of it. Plus, Mrs. Bertorelli was super-vigilant with her head-counting this morning – checking us all off on that master list of hers – I could see there was no way it was going to work. She stood there, blocking the aisle, shoulders squared like a linebacker on the defense. No way was I getting past her when she was in a mood like that.

So here I am. On the bus. Heading for the historic City of Bath.

The gentle sound of the engine is kind of soothing in a way. Perhaps this is all for the best. Forget about Johnny. Forget about the past. Forget about all the things you can't change.

My cell phone buzzes. Yeah, I put it back together and it still works just fine. I lift myself up slightly so I can slide the phone out of the pocket of my jeans. I check to see if it's a message from Johnny. In my heart of hearts I'm hoping that it's him, but it's not, it's my dad. He's awake early, as usual. He's fixing himself some breakfast and wants to know if his little girl is having the time of her life.

You could say that, I suppose.

I text back. "Having a wonderful time. Miss you guys!"

Oh, the lies we tell our loved ones.

Lydia sees what I'm doing and shoots me a sympathetic glance. "Time for a bit of KPC?"

My mind has gone blank, due to lack of sleep. "What?"

"KPC – Keep Parents Clueless."

"Oh yeah, yeah. That's right."

If only I could talk to someone, right now. Really talk to someone. But I can't. I can't even open up to Lydia. Not about all this.

So I turn away and look out of the window. In the silence of my mind, I revisit the same questions, again, and again, and again. What if you could change the past? What if you knew something was going to happen, something really bad, and you thought you could find a way to stop it? Wouldn't it be your duty to do something? Wouldn't it be your duty to… at least… try?

Lydia touches me gently on the arm. "Maddie?"

"Yeah?" I say, not even bothering to turn around.

"I've got something to tell you. I meant to say it the minute you came in – but I was sleepy and you were so upset… "

I almost resent having to turn and face her, but I do it, because she's a good friend. "What is it?"

She hands me a small slip of paper.

I take it, and gaze down at an unfamiliar address written in pink fluorescent felt pen in a very round hand. "What is this?"

"I looked him up on the internet last night, and that's the address where he works. It's a magazine."

She has me totally confused now. "Who are you talking about?"

"Who do you think, Maddie? Santa Claus? We went over this yesterday, and you said it was a good idea."

I frown at her in total confusion. "What?"

Lydia rolls her eyes. "Bill Lambourne. The guy your mom was married to for five years. Your real dad."

"My dad?"

"Yeah. That's where he works. I thought you'd be majorly excited. Took me hours to find it. But don't bother thanking me or anything – that's okay."

"Sorry Lyd. This is… overwhelming. Thanks."

Okay. I have in my hand the address of the man who is my biological father. My own flesh and blood. And just like everything else that is of any importance to me – he's in London.

I give a deep sigh. "He's in Marble Arch. Not much I can do about him, now."

"There's a number. You could call him," Lydia suggests.

I tuck the piece of paper into my jeans pocket. "Yeah. Or he could call me."

Which is something he hasn't done in fifteen years.


What with meeting some heavy traffic near Maidenhead, and pulling over for a bathroom stop after Swindon, it takes us nearly three hours to reach the outskirts of Bath.

When the bus finally pulls into the city it's already mid-morning. The weather is kind of British. A light breeze, with pale gray clouds scudding across a paler gray sky. But to my way of thinking, the soft light really suits the beautiful old city. I gaze out of the window and I love the way the gracious old buildings all stand to attention for us as the bus glides by. I marvel at the perfect curve that forms the Royal Crescent and the pristine green lawns beyond.

It's all so refined, so proper, so lovely.

"First stop – the Bathhouse!" yells Mrs. Bertorelli, whose voice could definitely stop traffic if she tried.

"Door fart – everyone wait for the door fart! There she blows!"

*Brody. Who else?* The door of the bus opens with its usual pneumatic snort and Brody and the boys on the back row all whoop with delight.

We get off the bus, grateful for the opportunity to stretch our aching limbs. We troop along the street, round the corner, and up the stairs leading to the Roman Baths.

"Brace yourself for another dose of culture, folks!" says Lydia, accepting a sheet of paper from the woman on the desk. "Oh, no. Not *another* questionnaire?"

Inside the building, I try – real hard – to think about Romans instead of princes in distress and boyfriends who didn't pan out so well. I walk around the water's edge and I try to picture all the rich Roman guys coming here to take a bath. I see them lounging around on stone benches beside the pool, relaxing in the idle, steamy heat. I picture the slave boys, fetching and carrying for them, massaging and shaving them. I try *not* to think what other duties might have been involved.

We go downstairs to admire the source of the hot spring – the only one of its kind in Britain. We study the intricacies of the ancient plumbing and the under floor heating system – a technological marvel in its day. It's incredible when you think about it. I can't believe all this stuff is so… *old*.

I'm just checking out the bronze head of the Goddess Minerva when Brody sneaks up behind me. He places a large warm hand on my back.

"Beautiful, isn't she?"

I smile. "I was thinking she was kind of creepy."

"She reminds me of you."

I give an involuntary laugh. "What?" Coming so rapidly on the heels of my remark about being creepy, that did not sound good.

He struggles to clarify things for me. "I mean – she's like this strong woman, you know. A warrior girl."

"She's lost her helmet," I say, reading the plaque. "And most of her gold leaf seems to have peeled off."

"Yeah. I guess she exfoliated too much, huh?"

I give him a withering look.

"Anyway," he says, moving in a little closer. "She's a goddess, isn't she?"

"Yeah. Minerva. Goddess of wisdom, and war. And poetry too. Hey – that's a mixed bag, isn't it?"

"Yeah. Just like you."

"Oh, so I'm a mixed bag, now, am I?"

"Nope. I meant goddess. Definitely goddess. Like old bronze face here, in her shiny box." Brody leans forward and peers at the ancient statue, scratching the stubble on his chin. "Now you come to mention it, that up-lighting ain't doing her any favors, is it?"

I blink. "Jeez, Brody, you say the *sweetest* things."

"Yep. Lunch on my table today – okay, babe?"

I look at him in amazement. "Babe?"

He chortles, and pretends to get bashful. "Aw! She called me babe!" he says, loud enough for the others to hear.

"Did not," I murmur, but it's a feeble protest. I am too tired and unhappy to care. Last night changed everything for me.

Brody gives me a sheepish, male grin. "See you in the pump room, then?"

"Yeah. See you there," I answer in a dull heavy voice. Well I can't actually *avoid* seeing him, can I? The pump room is our next scheduled stop.

I go upstairs and stand lost in thought in the gift shop. I'm supposed to be buying souvenirs. Something for Mom and Dad, and something for my little brother. And I mustn't forget

Grandma. She has to have something too – to thank her for lending me the giant tartan bag – the one that led me to Johnny.

I don't know what to get. She doesn't need a little plastic Roman guy in a toga. Or a pen with a shrink-wrapped image on it that's meant to be Jane Austen, but looks a lot like a zombie to me.

Postcards. Postcards are safe – and you don't have to write all that much. Only, we all send emails now. Or picture texts. But I have to get them something. This is so hard. Then I see a little decorative plate with a picture of a cottage by the sea. I pick it up, and take it to the counter clerk.

She bustles about looking for some tissue paper to wrap it up for me. "That's a lovely one, isn't it? Hand painted locally, you know?"

I look down, and it is only then that I notice the inscription round the edge, written in soft curly writing that's a little hard to read.

"Time and Tide wait for no one."


Later, in the Pump Room, we all mill around near the little fountain thing, sampling the health-giving waters of the spa. The place is crowded and it looks like there's going to be a long wait before we get seated for lunch. Mrs. B. has gone off someplace to find a staff member and hurry things up, and we're all soaking up the Regency elegance and ignoring our rumbling stomachs as best we can. Some of the other students are talking about all the nice stuff they've got on the menu here – Georgian cuisine, whatever that it – but I don't even want to think about food.

I'm standing there holding my glass of water, and my thoughts are miles away. About a hundred and twenty miles, to be exact. I feel a wave of hopeless despair, now that I fully understand what Johnny is, which is so different from what I hoped he could be. Jeez, was I really so dumb that I thought I could have a relationship with a man like that?

Brody interrupts my reverie. "He dumped you, huh?"

"Go away."

He doesn't. Instead, he puts his big thick football-player arm around me. His meaty hand rests heavily on the waistband of my jeans. He even tucks his thumb inside and sort of strokes it against my skin.

"That tickles, Brody. Cut it out."

He doesn't. He grins at me instead.

I roll my eyes. For half a second I seriously consider using my glass of mineral water to cool his ardor, but that wouldn't be at all nice, so I don't.

"Just trying to cheer you up," he says and pulls a clown-face. "I don't like it when you're sad."

"I… I'm not.."

"You can't lie to me, Madison. I've been watching you this whole trip, and I know what's going on."

I sigh. "I would doubt that very much."

"I know it started with the Lamborghini guy. But it doesn't have to end that way." Brody scans the room to see where Mrs. B. is, but it's okay, she's nowhere to be seen. "You've got… options."

"I know you're trying to help, Brody… it's just… it's going to take me a while to get over this. He was… different… special… unique."

He lets out an impatient sigh. "Women. You're so shallow. It's all about the car, isn't it?"

"What? I didn't give a damn about the car!"

"Well, okay. No problem. I believe you. But just imagine him driving round town in one of them little mini cars – you know the ones that look like a biscuit box with a union jack painted on the top? Or picture the guy on a moped with one of those little put-put engines under the seat. He's driving round London on one of those."

To illustrate his point, Brody does an impression of Johnny squealing round a corner on a scooter, complete with sound effects. I laugh, I just can't help myself.

"Is he still so different… special… unique?" Brody puts on a high-pitched, lovesick voice when he says that last part.

"You're funny."

For half a second, I almost feel like I need some comfort from this blundering oaf-boy standing right here, beside me. His body is warm and comforting against mine. Solid and fleshy. He puts his warm, damp hand back on my waist, letting it slip under the edge of my shirt.

"Got ya!" he whispers in my ear.

The blond stubble on his chin grazes the side of my face, as he nuzzles closer. I catch a whiff of his breath, which smells strongly of mint-flavor gum.

But then my heart aches for Johnny.

Beautiful, sophisticated Johnny.

Bloodsucking, scary Johnny.

Brody's hand is no longer on my waist. It has traveled down south. He nuzzles close and says. "Great opportunity being so far from home, isn't it? How about you sneak along to my room tonight, babe? Everyone thinks we've done it, anyhow."

His touch is so totally unlike Johnny's that I can hardly bear it.

"Brody. Stop," I say, and swing round to face him, mainly so he has to take his sweaty hand off my derrière. "Stop this right now. Look. I'm really sorry, but I don't feel… that way… about you."

"What's wrong? You only date guys who wear red stockings or something? Shall I go get myself a pair?"

"No."

He sighs deeply, but he isn't really abashed. "I can wait. One of these fine days you'll wake up to the fact that you want me. You'll realize what you've been missing and you'll be *desperate* to make up for lost time."

Lost time. I gaze into the distance and reflect on those two words.

Brody shrugs and mooches away. He's the sort of guy who will always keep trying to get what he wants – even when the odds are stacked against him.

I bite my lip.

Even a guy as shallow as Brody doesn't give up as easily as me.

After lunch we are free to go explore the city, and Lydia and me and some of the other girls head off towards the shops. In the town square we find that all the tourists are queuing up to get a ride in a big old sedan chair – and Lydia's keen to join them.

For a small fee you can get yourself paraded around the shopping precinct in a red velvet box just big enough for one person to sit inside. It's a funny little contraption – it has little drapes at the windows and it's all trimmed with red bobbles that dance merrily in the afternoon breeze. I suppose it's a bit like a rickshaw only it doesn't have any wheels. It has two long struts mounted on either side, and it gets carried along by two hefty looking guys dressed up like eighteenth century footmen.

Lydia's turn comes around, and I take a picture of her sitting inside the chair waving like the Queen out of the window. The footmen take their places and pretend that the chair is too heavy for them to lift with just one slender teenager inside.

Everyone laughs and I take more photos of the guys kidding around.

"Don't wait up!" Lydia yells out as the men bear her away.

I loiter around in the town square, waiting for her to come back, photographing anything that looks vaguely old. I guess it's time I started doing what I'm supposed to be doing on this trip – absorbing the culture and having a good time.

In less than five minutes, the little procession is back.

Lydia bounces out onto the pavement, laughing and flushed with excitement. "It's awesome Maddie! I wish we had one of these back home."

Pleased that she's happier today, I try to join in with the banter. "Yeah, it would be cool if we had one at school, wouldn't it? We could use it to get to class and back."

Now it's my turn. I pay my money and open the little door and step inside. Might as well try it, everyone else seems to think it's a lot of fun.

Not that I should even be thinking of having fun at a time like this.

"Where to, love?" one of the footmen says – and I know it's only a joke, because they always go the same way, round the block and back again.

"London," I say, wistfully.

"Need to catch the two o'clock express for that, love."

He snaps the little door shut and I settle back and try to enjoy the little jaunt, with his words playing havoc in my mind.

*The two o'clock express. London. I saw a signpost to the station when we were on the bus, not long before we got dropped off to go to the Roman Baths. It's only one-thirty right, now. What if I...*

We turn a corner by a quaint little shop that sells candy, and my classmates all disappear from view.

*Even if I have to walk, I could still make it in time. What if I leave now? What if I hightail it out of here, right now? I could be in London in time to catch the tide...*

I check my wallet to see if I have enough cash. Train fares are expensive here, but yes, maybe, I do.

*This is crazy, Maddie, you can't just up and leave...*

We turn another corner and I see a row of taxi cabs, waiting on the other side of the street. On impulse, I lean out of the little window and yell at the guy at the front.

"Hey mister, don't turn back. I want to you to drop me right here."

# Chapter Fifteen

I get the train back to London, and I text Johnny's number on the way.

"I need to see you. No questions, okay?"

I wait with bated breath. Fearing he will not reply.

Why should he? I've been nothing but trouble since the first moment he saw me, and yesterday I screamed at him, swore I never wanted to see him again.

I meant it too. But… I do want to see him again. Even now that I know what he is. My phone buzzes and a stab of anxiety spears through my heart. I check the phone, with shaking fingers.

Thank heavens.

The message is from him. The address he gives me is for a place named Riverside Apartments, and the postcode is SW1.

I tap in a message: "I'm on my way". But right before I press send, I add three meaningful little words: "Are you alone?"

I hold my slim black phone cupped in my hand, with the plastic getting warm as I wait for his reply. I gaze out of the window and worry about what tonight will bring.

"Very alone. I thought you said no questions."

I smile and text back. "I didn't mean me."

After that I get several more messages. All from Lydia. Most of them along the lines of *"WTF! You get in a sedan chair and then you just disappear?"*

I feel terrible, but I don't reply.

More messages come. More and more.

"Mrs. B is really mad! Get your butt back here!"

"She says she's gonna call up your parents, Maddie."

After a while, I switch off my phone.

In under an hour and thirty minutes the train pulls in to Paddington station. I go look at the underground map and try to figure out how to get to his apartment. Looks like I need to head to a place called Pimlico, on the Victoria Line. But that line doesn't run from here so I have to take the tube to Oxford Circus first. I'm staring at the underground map trying to work out the route when one of the other names leaps out at me. Marble Arch. The place where my 'father' works.

I check the time. Not quite three thirty.

He'll still be at work. My… dad. It seems so weird to think of that faceless stranger as my father. Yet without him, I wouldn't be here. I wouldn't exist.

I'm curious – it's always been my downfall. I want to know what he looks like, what he sounds like. I want him to know what *I* look like. I've changed quite a bit since I was two.

Johnny doesn't know what time my train was due to arrive. If I take an extra hour getting to his place – so what?

Johnny can wait.

I buy myself a ticket to Marble Arch, and go stand with all the other people waiting for the train, acting like I do this every day.

I find the building and take the elevator up to the sixth floor. The doors open and I walk nervously towards the reception desk. It's plushy. Busy too. Women in business suits, men with briefcases. Lots of plate glass windows so everyone can see how hard everyone else is working. Fancy-looking lighting on the walls. Exotic tropical plants looking impossibly shiny and green.

I'm a fish out of water in a place like this. I move silently across the squashy carpet towards the desk, and the receptionist senses that I'm here and looks up.

"Lost?" she says. She's has oversize shiny white teeth and pink lipstick. She wears a silk shirt and a permanently cheerful smile.

"I'm here to see Bill Lambourne," I say. Might as well say it like I mean it. It's the whole reason I'm in the country, after all.

She keeps smiling, and she nods, but I can see what she's thinking. *Like hell you are.*

"Do you have an appointment?"

"I'm his daughter."

That surprised her. I guess he goes around telling people he never had any kids. Or maybe he doesn't. Maybe he's got four ginger-haired sons or something. Keeps their photos in a row on his desk.

The toothy lady picks up the receiver of her fancy phone system and presses a button, leaning her head to one side, and tucking the phone in under her ear. She smiles at me again, and mouths "Just one moment" while I try to conquer the feeling that my knees are about to let me down.

She can't get Bill on the phone.

A tall guy with a camera bag slung over one shoulder passes the desk. Stops to speak to Toothy, like they are drinking buddies or something, and says he's off now.

I'm standing there wondering if this could be him, but I have a sort of mental checklist in my head, and I don't think this is the one. I'm sure the real guy will be taller than Mom, because she never dated anyone she didn't have to stand on her tiptoes to kiss. He'll be about forty-five, and he'll have blue eyes – coz I had to get them from somewhere, and Mom's are brown.

"Seen Bill?" Toothy asks, with a nervous glance at me.

"Boardroom," the guy gestures back down the hallway. "They shouldn't be too much longer. They were on the last item when I left."

"Great! I'll just go and wait outside." Acting with far more courage than I've really got, I march straight past her and go look for the boardroom.

"No, no," says Toothy, leaping out of her seat. "I think you'd better wait here!"

But I take no notice, I'm already halfway down the corridor. Boardroom, boardroom, where is the boardroom? I see a closed door about two thirds of the way down, with a shiny glass panel beside it. I go closer so I can look in through the panel.

I can see some men in there, behind the plate glass. All sitting round talking about stuff. It's not a stiff formal meeting – most of the people in there look kind of artsy. Some of them look bored, and most of them are acting kind of casual. One guy is leaning way back in his chair. Hands behind his head. Fingers interlaced.

I stand there, hovering between waiting and going straight in. After all, I've only got an hour. Some meetings take a heck of a long time and I can't hang around all day. I reach out and touch the brushed chrome door handle. I'm almost on the verge of opening the door when the toothy lady from the desk bustles past and makes the decision for me.

"I'll let him know you're here."

"Oh, please don't. I can wait!"

But she's already gone in. So I stare hard through the plate glass to see which guy she picks.

Coz that guy, the one she speaks to, he's my dad.

I can see her apologizing to everybody for bursting in. She goes around the back of the table, squeezing past people's chairs. Then she leans down beside a guy with a beard streaked with gray. She whispers a few words in his ear.

He looks up and his eyes lock with mine. Yes, his eyes are a little like mine, I suppose. Only his are cold. They do, however, betray his emotions, which seem to include shock – though it is well controlled – and something else.

Anger.

Okay. He's not all that pleased about this impromptu reunion. I suppose I should have expected that. After all, there hasn't been a phone call in twelve years. There isn't going to be a beaming smile and a bear hug, not from this guy. I keep on staring at him, through the glass, as he and the receptionist share a quick exchange of words.

He'll come out in a minute and I'll get to talk to him. For the first time in my life, I'm going to have a conversation with my father. In my mind, I start rehearsing a couple of openers I could try.

*Hi there, Dad.* Do I call him Dad? *How's the world of journalism treating you?* I suppose I could call him Dad. He is my father… but it seems kind of disloyal to my other dad sitting at home with mom, waiting for me to call.

I see the guy get up out of his seat, and my heart goes all jumpy inside me. He shouts out a jovial apology to the big guy in the orange shirt who seems to be in charge of the meeting. He shoots me another icy glance.

I'm jittery with anticipation, and I alter my speech in my head. *Hi there, Mr. Lambourne, I hope you don't mind...*

Then to my horror, I see that he's heading for another door at the far end of the room – one that I hadn't spotted before. He's going out the back way. The coward. He's not going to talk to me at all.

In an instant, he's gone. Hurrying down the stairs. The receptionist looks up at me through the glass and I can hardly bear the pity in her gaze.

I stare into the room. I feel kind of blank, as if all the emotion in me just packed up and left. Like him. That man with the beard who shuffled his papers together, shoved them away and scuttled out the back. My father.

The guy with the cold blue eyes that are not like mine at all.

The receptionist comes out again, and gives me a sympathetic smile. "Terribly sorry about that. He doesn't mean to be rude or anything."

"He doesn't?"

"No. Not at *all*." She puts a lot of feeling into that last word – making it sound sort of musical and meaningful – like she's determined to convince me that Bill Lambourne is being completely maligned and misunderstood. "It's just that… he's catching a train to Paris tonight. He's on a *very* important assignment at the moment, you see."

"I see."

"Would you like to leave him a message, perhaps? I'll make absolutely sure that it reaches him."

I stand there. Blank. Emotionless. Unable to think of anything I'd like to say to him right now.

"No message?"

What kind of message could I leave? A card saying 'I called but you were not at home'? A postcard of the Empire State Building? A message in Morse? A distress call?

"No."

"I'm really, really sorry." She sounds genuinely sympathetic, in a British sort of way.

"It's cool," I say, but my voice betrays me. My bottom lip trembles. I know I have to get out of here, and fast.

I look down at my feet. My sneakers are not so new now. I've been trekking round London in them for days. I just have to put one foot in front of the other until I get out of here. In my head I can hear my mom's voice. *"You can't change the past, Bill,"* she's saying, and he's saying *"You're goddamn right, and that's why I need to move on."*

Jeez, I'm going to break down and cry in a minute. I turn and make my way swiftly towards the main doors. I head across to the elevators and jab the button six times, like it's going to respond to the urgency of my call.

I feel the hot tears of humiliation welling in my eyes. I won't give in to them, I swear that I won't. The doors open for me, and I'm in luck – it's empty. Just goes to show that you can't lose them all. I step in and let it swallow me and take me down, down, down, away from the scene of my crime.

I leave the building and emerge onto the busy street, and I gulp the air gratefully, inhaling the familiar scent of passing traffic as if it was pure and sweet.

After a moment or two, I look left and then right, trying to get my bearings. Yes. I must walk back the way I came – past the traffic lights and the tiny sweetshop selling chewing-gum and cigarettes and magazines about William and Kate.

I'm going to see Johnny. I need to see Johnny. Everything that just happened will fade away like a bad dream. I need never tell anyone I tried to see him. My father, I mean.

I follow the surge of people heading down into the mouth of the tube station, and hurry down the steps, pressed on by that strange sense of urgency that Londoners transmit to one another in the last little while before the rush hour begins.

I'm lucky here, too. There's a train just disgorging all its passengers onto the platform. I chase down the last few stairs and run to get on board before the doors close.

On the train, I sit in the least crowded place I can find, and as we speed through the dark tunnels I turn and look at the girl's face I can see reflected in the grimy window beside me. She's not smiling. At one point, a couple of tears run down her face, but she swipes them away and won't give in.

One more station to go, so I try and pull myself together. No more tears. I don't want Johnny to see me with my face all puffy.

I get off the tube at Pimlico station, and take a short walk through a pricey-looking neighborhood full of tall Victorian houses painted cream. The roads here are lined with trees too – which you don't see in other parts of the city. The houses are jammed with cars parked along both sides of the not-very-wide street. I'm guessing all those big old houses have been divided up into expensive, one-bedroom pads.

Johnny's apartment building is right alongside the river. I catch glimpses of grayish brown water through the gaps between the buildings.

I see the name on a satin chrome plate: Riverside. That's the one. A double-fronted place, stately and imposing and… smug. It has a sort of concrete chute leading down to an underground parking lot, but I pass it by and head for the front steps. Standing under a portico made of marble, I find the doorbell and buzz to be let in.

A porter answers the door. Not Johnny. Just a porter. He frowns when I tell him the number of the apartment that I want.

"He doesn't like visitors, that one. And you say you've been *invited* up there?"

"Yes. Call him up and check if you like."

He lifts up the phone and presses the button, while I wait. Amazing how in a few words someone can make you feel like you've got no right to be there.

"No reply, love," he says, with an unpleasant grin. "I told you, he keeps himself to himself."

I frown and wonder what I can say next that will convince him to let me in, but just then a voice behind me interjects on my behalf.

"It's alright Phil. She's with me."

I turn and see Johnny hurrying lightly down the stairs. Today, he's dressed in a white shirt – the kind of shirt that any young executive might own – and a pair of ordinary gray pants, belted low on his narrow hips. He wears no tie and his top button is undone, revealing a pale triangle of skin.

"Hey!" My voice cracks with emotion. I want to reach out and embrace him, but I'm too scared to do it just now. I stare at him, drinking in the sight of the man who has come to mean so much to me.

"Maddie." His tone is even. "Good to see you."

Although he came down the stairs, Johnny presses the bell for the elevator this time. Out of courtesy for me, I suppose. It arrives and the doors glide open and we go inside. It is mirrored on three sides, and I catch a glimpse of my own anxious, young face. But in the mirror there is no sign of Johnny standing beside me.

No reflection. He casts no reflection.

This freaks me out more than a little, but I try to control the trembling and the fear. He takes me up to his apartment on the fourth floor. He lets me in and I gaze around. It's ultra-modern. In fact it's over-modern and minimalist and bare. The carpet is pale gray. The walls are white. The plate glass window that showcases the Thames is spotlessly clean. Unlike the river beyond.

I stand in the doorway and stare at it all in dismay. It is such a stark contrast to the crowded, colorful places we've visited together in the past few days. It is as if the real Johnny doesn't live here anymore. He packed up and left and the cleaners came in and vacuumed all trace of him away.

"Come and sit down," he says stiffly.

He leads me through to the lounge, where there is a black leather couch opposite a large screen mounted directly onto the wall. The TV, I suppose. Do guys like him sit round watching the music channel, I wonder? Do they rent melancholy movies about paranormal love?

"There's a great view of the river," I say, as I perch myself nervously on the edge of his brand new couch.

"Can I get you a drink?" he asks.

"Yeah, yeah. Whatever you're having," I say. Then I cringe at my choice of words. Johnny smiles sadly, but he makes no reply. He goes away to fix me a drink.

*Love.* Is that what I feel for him? I shouldn't be here, and yet I am. What compels me to be with this… creature… who can never love me the way I want to be loved. What hopeless devotion is this, that lured me here to this sterile, lonely place to make absurd small talk about the view?

He returns with a flute-shaped glass. "Champagne?"

"I've always wanted to taste it." I say, but I don't take the glass.

"So have I," he says, with a haunted look in his eyes.

"You've never …"

"No. Of course not. It was invented long after I… turned."

I pause, trying to make sense of all this.

He turns the sparkling glass around, holding it up to the light. "There was a monk, named Dom Perignon, in the seventeenth century. His blend of the very best grapes, expertly pressed, gave the world its first taste of champagne. The sparkle was a lucky accident, perfected in the nineteenth century. They say that champagne is the taste of France. Warmth, sunlight, and all that is worth celebrating in life."

He hands me the glass, and his cool fingers graze mine as I take the fragile stem from him. I look into the glass miserably as it fizzes away without a care. An effervescent, golden drink – one that calls for happiness and good cheer. If I was clever with words I'd propose a toast, but… under the circumstances, it doesn't seem right.

"You can't share this with me?" I ask, my heart a little giddy with nerves.

"No," he says.

"Then I won't drink it either," I say, and I place it down on the floor at my feet.

"Why not?" he says, sitting beside me. "I thought you wanted to taste champagne."

"I did, but not if you can't… "

I notice that a slight smile has come to the corners of his lips and I'm glad I made the choice that I did.

"What pleasure can I take in it, Johnny, if you can't drink it too!"

"Maddie, come here!" He pulls me to him in an instant and his lips are on mine. Between urgent, eager kisses, he says. "You're as sweet as ever! Oh, Maddie, this is the taste I long for. Your lips. You. The scent of your hair. Your sweet, soft skin next to mine."

We tangle together wildly for a moment, hungry for each other's mouths. I launch myself at him, and I kick over the glass of champagne with my foot. I hear it fall and turn to see it lying on its side, with the liquid spilling out and fizzing onto the pale gray carpet.

"Oh my gosh. I'm sorry! Shall I get a paper towel? I—"

He pulls me away. "Leave it! Just kiss me. Kiss me again."

I laugh at him, but he means it. I hear the low – almost threatening – note of passion in his voice. I let him pull me close. I let him tilt my head back in his hands and take my mouth fiercely, as if he has been waiting for this for a very long time.

But then I pull away, and I tell him I came here to talk.

"Okay," he says, and we separate and sit with a little space between us. I notice he isn't flushed. Not like me. Well I suppose he wouldn't be.

He looks agitated though. His dark eyes are wild and glittering, and his midnight hair is beautifully tousled. His shirt has pulled free, and I see that I've left a trace of lipstick on his cheek.

He glances away from me – like he's expecting the Spanish Inquisition.

"Will you tell me everything?" I ask.

"Probably not," he says, with a rueful smile.

Dear heaven, I love that smile. It distracts me from my purpose but I fight the urge to tangle with him again.

I take a deep breath. "I don't know where to start, Johnny. There are so many questions I need to ask. What about this for openers? When and where were you born?"

"I was born in 1462. In Kent."

I keep my breathing slow and steady, trying not to let my voice shake as I go on. "Kent? That's nice."

"Yes. It's very nice in Kent."

"1462? Fourteen-freaking-sixty-two? Are you serious?"

"Of course I'm serious. I'm rarely anything but serious now."

This is true. He's a serious kind of guy. That kissing we just did was pretty serious too, and the memory of it still warms my whole body. I struggle to remain on course. "So you've been twenty-one for a hell of a long time."

"Yes."

"You've been… drinking blood… for a hell of a long time too."

"Yes."

He sees my revulsion – and it saddens him. I can tell.

"Maddie, I have to. I tried starving myself once. I have great strength of will and I lasted many days. I wanted to die. I tried to die. But the hunger overcame me."

That sounds awful. I swallow and I don't know what to say. "I… these questions… it's not working, Johnny… I shouldn't have come!"

I get up. I straighten my shirt and I act like I'm going to walk out of his apartment and out of life again.

But he lays his hand, gently on my arm. "You're not leaving this time, Maddie."

It's a statement. Not a request. No pleading or begging. He just knows I don't mean it. I sit down again, this time a little closer to him.

He puts an arm around me and nuzzles my ear. "Why not let me do the talking?"

"Okay. So talk." *And it had better be good.* Because I'm pretty sure that my mom and my dad and my grandmother and everyone who cares about me in Ashwell Springs, Illinois are not going to like this.

"I was born in Kent, where my father, who was French, was given an estate in return for his loyalty during the war."

"Which war was that?"

"The War of the Roses. Don't interrupt."

I smile weakly at him and shut up.

"I had an idyllic childhood growing up in the south of England – a garden of paradise it was, back then. I also spent time in Champagne, where my father had another estate. When I was about nineteen my father became ill, so I used to try to help him, to ease his workload a bit. I went to Champagne to look after things there. I was there about two years, and there I would have stayed. But then, all this trouble began. The English King died unexpectedly, leaving an heir only twelve years old. Well, to cut a long story short there was a power struggle, and Richard – the man you met at Westminster Palace – succeeded in snatching the throne. He wanted everything that belonged to his nephew and would stop at nothing to make his avaricious dreams come true.”

I shift uneasily on the leather couch. “The boys told me as much.”

“You’re lucky to be alive after that little escapade, Maddie.”

“You think I don’t know that?”

He flashes me a wry look. “Anyway, my father wrote to me, explaining the turmoil that the country was in. I set out to return at once, and arrived in England just after the coronation. I was on my way to London to pay my respects to the new King – much as I hated him – when I was… lured away. Lured into the path of danger and death – the death of my old self, anyway. It was my own stupid fault.”

“Why?”

“Because I was human. I was male. I saw a pretty girl and I thought I could help her. She took me on a merry dance, I can tell you.”

“Madeleine?”

He nodded. “She destroyed me and I wanted to kill her, for what she did!”

He scowls and his face darkens with anger. The strength of his emotion about this woman both scares me and makes me jealous. I wish there had never been a Madeleine. I wish he would think only of me.

"Johnny, you said yourself when we spoke of this before, that it was a long, long time ago. Can't you just forgive and forget?"

"I was wretched – when they changed me, Maddie, I was wracked with pain that lasted for weeks. And when my strength returned I was a… beast. A vile, angry, monster with a thirst for blood I could not control. My old self was gone."

I shiver.

"I'm sorry," he said. "This is an unpleasant topic of conversation. Let us talk of other things"

"No! I want to know! I want to know how you lived, Johnny, all through those years, and when you started going back, and why?"

"That would take all night, my sweet."

"Give me the elevator version – anything – I have to know a bit more."

He sighs. "I refused to return to my family – they must have given me up for dead. I haunted London for a while and then every other lonely city in Europe, drinking only when I had to. Hating myself for what I had become. I searched for Madeleine, endlessly. I had one letter from her, asking me to meet her. She told me where to meet, but she didn't tell me when. I went to the place, year after year. I saw it change from a deserted heath into a busy modern place. But it was no good and time moved on. The French revolution came and went. The Terror. For a time it made things easy. If I thirsted for fresh blood all I needed to do was stand by the guillotine and wait."

"Johnny that's revolting." I squirm and look nervously at the door as if I might need an escape route pretty soon. But I need to hear more.

"I lived on through the centuries, I saw wars fought and won. Leaders changed, politics changed. Gradually, I learned how to control my passions. I found ways to quench my thirst that did not require the death of a human being. Why is it always assumed that a... *person like me*... must bleed his victim white? Or that he must kill at all, for that matter? Your family eats meat, I dare say. But you do not slaughter your own beef for the table, do you?"

"No." This is enough to make me seriously think about becoming a vegetarian, I can tell you.

"Well, neither do I."

"So what do you do instead?"

"These days I belong to a scheme. I receive blood as if it was an essential medication. There's an organized network set up for... people like me. It is delivered to my door by a courier, and I drink only what I have to, to sustain my life."

"That seems… more civilized."

"My thoughts exactly. I can take my poison in a glass, and feel almost human again." He gives a rather angry, bitter laugh which reminds me of that first disastrous visit to the Grange, where he keeps his Corvette. "Of course," he says darkly, "there are… others… who prefer a fresh kill. Barbaric creatures. They hunger for the thrill of the hunt almost as much as they hunger for the blood itself."

"Are they here? In London?"

"Yes. Which is why you need to allow me to protect you."

I reflect on all this. He could be lying to me. I am willing to face that fact. All this could be an act to suck me in.

But he's had a dozen chances now, and I am still here. He hungers for me, yes, but he doesn't want to destroy me.

"What's the whole deal with the Tower?"

"Ah. The Tower," he says, and his expression changes. "The chance to revisit some of my old haunts. The chance to set things right, or so I imagined, at first. Who wouldn't give anything for a chance like that." He sighs, heavily. "I found my… *friends* at the Tower, in 1665, just after the fire."

Something about the way he says *friends* sets off warning bells in my head, but for now I let it go. "The fire?"

"The Great Fire of London."

"Johnny, were you in London when that happened?"

"Yes – and you may be aware that fire is one of the few things that a… man like me… must fear."

"Fire could kill you?"

"Yes?"

"And sunlight – I noticed you are wary about sunlight."

"I burn easily, yes."

"What about silver, does that work?"

"I've only seen it attempted once, and it didn't turn out so well. What is all this about, Maddie? Do you want to know how you can kill me, in case I misbehave?"

My face flames and I look away. "No! I just wondered, that's all. It's not something I've ever thought about before. It's more the kind of thing my friend Lydia would ask, I suppose. She's into the whole vampire thing."

"You haven't spoken about this to… this girl Lydia, have you? Or to anyone else, Maddie? Tell me the truth? Have you told her what I am?"

I hesitate. Technically, I have. I have told her, but she didn't get it. She didn't understand. So I feel I can honestly tell him that I have kept his secret, for now.

"No one knows but me. Does that mean you have to kill me?"

"You are right to be wary of me, Maddie. But like I said, I have vowed to protect you and I am a man of my word."

I lean back on the couch and let go a bit of a sigh. He hasn't told me everything by any means. I don't want to seem rude or push him too far. I don't want to seem needy, either, and yet I yearn for the comfort that only he can give. Oh, why does he make me feel so guilty all the time? Is it all about what we want from each other? My blood longs for him, and he longs for my blood. Is that how it is?

"Time for supper?" he asks mildly.

"What, exactly, did you have in mind?"

"I mean for you, not for me, I'm alright for the time being. I'll ring down to the front desk and they will place an order with a local restaurant, and eventually it will be delivered to my door."

"That wouldn't be so bad, I suppose," I say, with a weak sort of smile.

"What sort of food do you like? Italian, Mexican, French?"

"Normally I'd say I like them all. But today… I… why don't you just choose something for me, Johnny? Make it easy for me?"

"Then I will ask for chicken in a wine sauce, with damsons and almonds. I know you'll love that." He speaks wistfully, and touches my hand.

While we are waiting for the food, we broach the topic of me running away from the tour. My phone has been turned off ever since I sent those messages to Johnny in the train. I'm afraid to look now, in case there are a thousand voicemails from Mrs. Bertorelli.

"You can't leave people worrying about you, Maddie. You have to let them know you're okay."

"If I tell them where I am, they'll come and get me. I can't go back now and stand around looking at Roman artifacts and stuff. I can't. I've promised Edward and Richard I'll go back."

"Yes. You have. Against my better judgment, I must say, but the deed is done now. You must come with me to the Tower tonight."

"You'll let me?"

"I have no choice. It is my duty to protect the River of Time. Your conversation with Edward and Richard will have… repercussions… if we don't return and sort this muddle out."

"Has the council met to decide what must happen to the boys? Do they live or do they die?"

"Maddie. Don't ask me questions to which I do not know the answer!"

"Then how will we know what to do when we get back to 1483? Do we go ahead with a rescue or not?"

"You tell me. This was your idea."

I look up at him in disbelief. I feel uneasy and short of breath. He would never entrust such an important decision to an outsider. Never. The other Patrons wouldn't hear of it for a start.

I shoot him a troubled, frowning glance. "You're asking me to *guess* what will happen, when and if we get back to the Tower?"

He returns with an equally intense, questioning stare. After a long pause spent eyeballing each other awkwardly, I burst out and break the silence.

"Johnny, stop that! If you're hoping I'll break down and admit I've got some master plan, you're going to be disappointed, okay? I'm not psychic, you know. All I know is that my heart tells me to go back and try to get those kids out before it's too late!"

As the words come out of my mouth there is another voice in my head, and it mocks me.

*Madeleine, it's already too late.*

# Chapter Sixteen

Johnny drives me to the Tower after dark. The Lamborghini glides through the streets like a silver ghost. There is a lot less traffic on the roads at this time of night, and I realize that it's no distance from Johnny's place to the Tower. I suppose he chose it for that very reason. Proximity to the scene of the crime.

Johnny takes me in through the staff car park, warning me not to go anywhere or do anything without him. We go upstairs and he leads me through a door marked 'Patrons Only' into a large room lined with racks and racks of clothing – outlandish costumes from every era imaginable. There is a woman sitting at a polished wood table. She's sewing something, stitching away by hand with a needle and thread, under the light from an old Anglepoise lamp. She has a little pincushion strapped to her wrist, and her needle darts in and out of the object she's mending. An old felt hat, by the look of it.

Johnny waves his hand at me, and gives the woman an imploring smile. "Please, Rachel, do what you can. We have to go through the portal in about fifteen minutes."

"Anything for you, Mr. De Vere." Then the woman smiles at me over the top of her specs.

"I'll leave you here," Johnny says to me. "Rachel will look after you."

I lower my voice, anxious not to be overheard. "Can't you wait for me? After what happened last time I was here, I don't really want to be alone with anyone but you."

"I have to go and change my clothes, Maddie. There isn't much time," he says quietly. "Don't worry. You'll be alright with Rachel."

I glance over to where I can see her, she's pulling some clothes off the racks for me to try on. "You mean she's not a… "

"Oh, she is. But you'll be quite safe with her. She's very… self-controlled."

I gulp. Rachel? In the beige twin set and the fake pearls? A… person who thirsts for human blood? I glance nervously in her direction, and she looks up and gives me a knowing smile.

*They're everywhere.*

I'm left standing there with Rachel.

"Not much meat on you, lovey, is there?"

I swallow, nervously. "What?"

"You can't be more than a size eight or ten."

"I have no idea," I say, apologetically. "Is the sizing the same here as in the US?"

"No, love, but I can judge it by eye."

She gets up, and starts rummaging through the racks of clothing while I stand there and wait. I run my eyes over the desk. There is an old family photograph taken in the twenties, with Rachel in the middle looking exactly as she does today. Taken before she turned, maybe.

She finds me a blue dress that laces up the front, and a white petticoat thing that goes underneath. She's also found some leather shoes, and a cloak and a hood – red, like in a kid's nursery rhyme.

I go behind a screen and put them on, fingers fumbling in my haste not to delay things any more than is necessary.

When I've got the gown on, Rachel laces the bodice up tight so it shows off my waist. Then I pick up the red cloak, twirl it around my shoulders and fasten it at the neck. I push it back so you can still see the pretty blue dress. Rachel adds the hood, letting it hang down my back for now. I take a peek in the long cheval mirror that stands in the gloom in the corner of the room. I smile. "I knew it. A cross between Little Bo Peep and Little Red Riding Hood."

"All ready for the big bad wolf," says Rachel, with a smile that shows small, pointed teeth. Then she glances up at the doorway, where a lone figure stands like a statue in the shadows. I hadn't realized until then that he was back.

"She'll do, won't she, Johnny?"

I look up seeking his approval and see that his face is ashen white.

"Is *that* what you found for her to wear?"

Rachel looks up, surprised. "Yes. Fits her nice, I thought. I'm sorry if you don't approve."

Johnny clenches a fist, apparently without even realizing he's doing it. His knuckles are very white. "That blue dress. It… it has been hanging up in here all along?"

"No. It's new. It came in last week." Rachel's beady dark eyes stare up at him, searching his face, trying to understand her mistake. "It's bang-on for the time period, Johnny – and it fits her just lovely. What's wrong with it?"

He passes a hand over his face. "Nothing."

"You sure about that?" Rachel asks, peering at him over the top of her half-rimmed glasses. You look like you've seen a ghost."

"It's… perfect."

I give him a shy, coy look. "You don't like it?"

"I loved it."

"What?" His form of words surprises me.

He moves closer and puts his hand on my cheek. "It's a very pretty dress."

"Look, I hate to break up this little love scene," Rachel says, with a glance at the old classroom clock that adorns the wall, "but if you don't get up there pronto – you'll miss the moment."

"Yes. Indeed." Johnny turns on his heel, and strides away down the corridor with his own cloak billowing out behind him. "Come on, Maddie. This was your idea."

Yeah. Right. Like I even have a clue what I'm supposed to do when I get back there – to 1483. But I do as I'm told and make for the door.

"Thanks, Rachel. Were you the one who made my black velvet dress for me?"

"Yes, lovey."

"That gown was beautiful. A real work of art."

"Thank you, dear. Now go on, off you go."

It's my third time through the door – portal – whatever you care to call it. The doorway that leads to the past. I brace myself for the falling sensation and the nausea and dizziness. I close my eyes so I don't get blinded by the white flash, but to my surprise it's much easier this time. I land on the rampart – kind of crouching, but on two feet.

Okay, that wasn't so bad.

My fingertips feel in the darkness for the smooth stone beneath my feet. There is a heavy thud, followed by a jingling sound. Johnny curses softly in the dark, letting me know that he's here too.

"What's the matter?" I say, my voice a low whisper in the dark.

"My coin purse. I think it spilt as I landed."

He starts searching for the coins, feeling with his fingertips across the cold stone floor. We can't manage in Medieval London without money, so we both spend the next few moments groveling around, searching for the small, unfamiliar coins that people used back then. My fingers bump into his in the dark, and he stops looking for the coins as he takes my hand in his. Cool, smooth fingers. His skin is always cool.

He curses quietly, caressing my fingers. "It's madness to bring you here."

"It was my choice, Johnny."

"It was a hard choice," he says, reaching out and touching my face, in the dark. "I fear there will be harder choices for you to make, my sweet, before our time is through."

His hand is cool against my flushed cheek. Refreshingly cool. "You're starting to sound like you belong here, Johnny."

"I do. I did. I was born here, remember? This is the year I was twenty-one."

My eyes are growing more accustomed to my surroundings now, and I can make out the angles of his masculine face, moving closer to mine.

He touches my cheek and pulls me towards him. "I will follow thee always, my love."

He brings his lips down onto mine forcefully, and for a moment I am lost in the passion of his kiss. This is the man I want. No matter what.

Only my fear about what we must do tonight helps to bring me back to reality.

"Come on – we must hurry. Do not make a sound as we go down through Brackenbury's chambers."

He leads me by the hand, down the spiral staircase and into the room. It is deserted – thank heavens it's the middle of the night. We go out into the grounds of the Tower, and slip across the wet grass towards the place where the Princes are kept.

I notice we go a slightly different route from the one that I took just yesterday when I did this on my own. Johnny leads me to a small arched doorway, almost hidden in the gloom. He finds the key, undoes the lock, and we slip inside.

"Johnny, will the King be here at the Tower? If this really is the night that those children are meant to die?"

"No, he will not."

"Does that mean that… the killings… have nothing to do with him?"

"In my opinion, they have everything to do with him." Johnny says, with a dark look. "But he will distance himself from it. The whole affair is a tangled web of deceit, with Richard sitting in the middle of it like a great, greedy spider."

"You believe he is behind it all?"

"Yes." Johnny's voice is a whisper in the half-dark. "But that smooth-tongued rogue will make sure that there are several degrees of separation between him and the Princes tonight. He will distance himself from the killings. Scholars will squabble for five hundred years about tonight."

Suddenly I'm wishing I'd read up on all this medieval stuff – if only to see if I could find some weak spot, some gap, where I could jump right in. But it's too late for that now. I'm here. I'm taking cautious, silent steps on ancient flagstones, with the cold striking up through the soles of my thin leather shoes.

Then he puts a finger on his lips. "Hush now, we are getting close."

We move as silently as we can. Up the stairs, around the corner, deeper into the darkness. The whole place is quiet, like a graveyard. The only light comes from burning wicks placed in sconces high on the wall.

What a dreadful place for two fatherless boys to end their days.

Just as I am about to round the next corner, Johnny pulls me back.

"Guards," he whispers. "Two of them."

I press my back against the wall and try not to make a sound. Johnny goes round there to confront them, alone.

I hear sounds of hand-to-hand combat, small grunts of effort and stifled cries of pain. One pale cold creature against two guards – with all their human failings. An unfair fight, some might say. I listen to the sound of the skirmish, trying to decode each sound.

He has to overcome them. He has to get the key.

I can't look. Don't want to look. I don't want to see what Johnny has to do to those guys in order to get that key.

All goes quiet. Moments later Johnny emerges, dusting himself off. He sheathes his knife in the leather pouch that hangs from his belt. I notice that there appears to be no blood on his clothing, and though I promised myself I would ask no questions I find that I have to ask one.

"Did you kill them?"

"No," he says, with a rueful smile. "I have bound them up like a pair of trussed chickens."

I breathe a sigh of relief.

"Good. I'm glad. I have to say that it wouldn't seem right – to take two lives in order to spare two."

"Even if those men are the devil's henchmen?"

"Yes."

"I cannot promise that the King will spare them, Maddie, when he learns that they have allowed his prisoners to break free."

* * *

This time I'm determined not to frighten the boys as we enter the room, so I call out before I open the door. But of course, when we go inside, they are nowhere to be seen.

"Hey guys! It's me. Maddie. I told you I'd be back."

No answer. Hiding again, I guess. They can probably see that I've brought someone with me. A strong, well-built young man. Perhaps they fear that tonight they meet their murderer.

"It's okay. He's a friend. He's here to help you."

Edward comes out first from behind the tapestry on the wall. He approaches us slowly, staring at Johnny with large, frightened eyes.

Johnny bends down on one knee and bows his head to Edward. "God save the king."

The boy flushes with embarrassment. "Get up, man, get up!"

Johnny lifts his head, but he doesn't get up. "You are Edward Quintus, are you not?"

"I am he that once signed his name Edward Quintus. But no longer. I cannot claim to be the master of my own fate, and I am certainly not the King of England anymore. My place has been taken."

"Yes, Your Grace, by a vile, usurping boar."

The other boy creeps out from behind a wall-hanging on the far side of the room.

Johnny bows his head again. "Richard, Duke of York."

I clear my throat and try to make things a little less formal. "This is Johnny De Vere, guys, he's here to help get you out."

Johnny rises to his feet. He's taller than Edward, and much broader. To my eyes, he looks every inch the sort of man we need for this mad scheme of ours, but I can see that poor frightened Edward is not so sure. Tentatively, he reaches out to shake Johnny's hand, but the moment the boy makes contact with Johnny's cold fingers he recoils in horror and dismay.

"You're one of them!"

A pang of fear goes through me. "No!" I protest. "He's with me."

Edward looks aghast and he searches my face for answers. "He's one of those unnatural beings – with the cold hands and the evil eyes! Madeleine, you are deceived!"

"He's a friend," I insist, with my voice rising to match the panic I feel inside. "he's helping us to bust out of here tonight. He's just fought and disarmed the guards, to give us half a chance to escape. We must go while the coast is clear."

"I am not going anywhere with that… creature! We are safer here than surrendering ourselves to someone – some*thing* – like him. He's one of them. Are you so blind that you cannot see?"

"One of… what, exactly?"

"I suppose they must have a name, but I do not know it. I know what they are though, and what they do."

"You do?"

"Yes! I do. I've lived here for weeks and watched them come and go. There's a whole group of them, and they haunt this place. Pale, cold, unnatural creatures – every one of them. The very incarnation of evil. They prey on the blood of innocent people."

Gee, for a kid who's been locked up for the last six months he's pretty well-informed. But Johnny's all we've got.

So I lie.

"He's not like that. He's just like you and me!" Unfortunately, the faint tremor in my voice betrays me, and Edward looks even more distrustful than before.

Johnny gives a short, impatient sigh. "Tell the boy the truth, Madeleine."

I glance up at Johnny, the… person I have come to care about so much, and I see the pain in his dark eyes. He is used this. He is used to people reacting with fear. He lives with this every day of his… *life*, if you can call it that.

Slowly he repeats his command. "Tell… the boy… the truth."

I swallow, and turn back to Edward. "Yes. This man is… a vampire. He must feed on human blood or else he will die."

Both boys take a visible step back as I utter those awful, awful words.

"But he is also my friend, and he will be your friend too if you try and trust him. When I couldn't bear to stand by and leave you two here to face the fate that your enemies had in store for you, he was the only person who would help me. If you won't come with me and Johnny tonight, then you are done for, you understand? He's your only hope. If you can't bring yourself to trust him, you *will* face death in just a few short hours."

The younger boy gasps and buries his face against his brother's chest. "No! Not tonight. Let me live to see just one more day!"

"Hush, brother, I will guard thee. I will not let them hurt us."

I turn on Johnny, feeling bad that I've upset the boys. "Now look what you made me do. I've scared the crap out of them. Why did you make me do that?"

"Do you think I should have allowed you to stand there and lie to them instead?"

"Guess not."

"They have to accept my help," Johnny says, folding his arms "Things cannot move forward until they do."

So we stand there, the four us, glancing nervously at one another. Each one of us trying to assess the risks. More than one of us failing, dismally. How can anyone be expected to know the future in a situation like this?

"Perhaps we *should* trust him," Edward says quietly. "Maybe you need a monster, to fight a monster. Is that right, Madeleine, do you think?"

I frown at him. "I'm not sure you should call my boyfriend a monster, but yes, I suppose you might be right."

"Boyfriend?" repeats Richard, with a perplexed look on his face.

"Boyfriend?" says Johnny, raising an eyebrow, and giving me just a hint of a smile.

"Look. Can we get going?" I say hastily, "because if we're still here when one of those lowlifes outside gets his ropes off, we're in deep trouble."

Richard gathers up a few of his belongings – some childish things. We step over the trussed-up bodies of the guards, who are writhing about on the floor struggling and chafing against the ropes that bind their hands and feet.

The Constable of the Tower – the man who prayed in the chapel that he wanted nothing to do with all this – shows us a safe way through the grounds and out to the gate.

I realize as we go out into the dark street, that I have no plan beyond what has already taken place. I have no idea where to from here.

"The place we went that night we spent together," Johnny murmurs in a low voice, as if he reads my thoughts.

"You mean the inn? The R—"

"Don't say the name," he warns. "Someone might hear."

So in silence we make our way through the dark streets, down cobbled alleyways and across courtyards. Johnny takes us the long way, to throw anyone who might be following us off the scent. He even makes for the river at one point and then doubles back over a wall and through a little yard behind a shop.

"Isn't this private property?" I say, tripping over some bits of wood leaning up against the back wall of the house.

"Yes, but the owner is a friend."

"Is he a carpenter or something?"

"A coffin-maker."

I am holding Richard's hand, and I feel him shudder.

"A friend? Or a vampire?"

"Both."

"Come on," says Johnny. "We need to go this way, to cover our tracks."

The little boy tugs at me, reluctant to go in to an undertaker's yard. "Maddie, are you sure that it's safe to go in there?"

I don't say what I really feel – of course I don't. "Absolutely."


Johnny leads us in and out of the back streets of London until he's sure that we've thrown any potential stalkers off the scent. Part of me feels like he's being over-cautious, and part feels he's not being careful enough. I'm beginning to think this guy is almost as reckless as me.

We get to the Rose and Crown, and the publican's wife is waiting in the doorway with a lantern. It is one of those old, old lanterns, with horn instead of glass in the panes so you can't see the wick that burns inside, but it casts a warm yellow light onto the cobblestones. A welcoming light.

"Inside, the lot of you. I hope they don't hang me for this, Johnny boy."

"You're an angel of mercy, Annie."

Taking no chances, she leads us through to the private rooms at the back of the pub where guests aren't normally allowed.

Dark rooms, with low ceilings, where she and her husband and their children live. They don't seem to have 'bedrooms' as such – just little beds recessed into the walls and covered with warm curtains.

"Come in, come in. It's modest, but it's home. Kitchen's through there. It's the biggest room we've got. We do all the cooking for the inn out there."

The rest of the family are asleep with the bed curtains drawn, but we sit around the kitchen table and make our plans for tomorrow.

Mrs. Atkins says a messenger has told her there's a ship lying at anchor in the harbor that will take the boys to France. We must wait for word that she's ready to sail, and then take the boys down to the wharf and get them safely on board.

To me this seems like great news, but Johnny remains aloof. "Who gave you this message, Annie? What type of man was he?"

"One of your lot, of course. A traveler."

"Yes, Annie, but which one?"

"Tall one, with the yellow teeth. He's not as nice as you."

Johnny smiles. "Ah, that one. Randolph, I think you mean."

I frown. Randolph organized the escape? I suppose he had to. If the boys fate *is* to live, then he must protect the River of Time.

Mrs. Atkins stretches and yawns. "Well, I'm ready for me bed. Make yourself at home. There's ale in the larder, and a piss-house out the back."

Her crude choice of words surprises me, but I guess that's what they call it, here in 1483. The boys stretch out in front of the hearth, on mattresses filled with hay. The fire's out now but the whole room still feels warm.

Mrs. Atkins turns, just before she gets to the door. "The girl comes in early to start baking the bread. But I've told her not to disturb you."

There is an old upright 'settle' in the corner – a bench seat made of oak – with lots of homemade pillows on it to make it more comfortable. Johnny and I sit there together, and after a while I get real sleepy lying against his chest.

Several hours later, I'm woken with a jolt. Someone's opening the shutters in the kitchen and the sunlight comes streaming right in.

In an instant there is chaos and confusion. Johnny's howling in pain, trying to shield his face with his hands. Grabbing his cloak – hauling it over himself, but his hand is still exposed, and it burns.

I'm on my feet and I'm yelling "The light – block out the light!"

Behind me, Johnny is screaming in pain. I've never heard a grown man scream before, and it sure is a frightening sound. The maid and I fumble to close the shutters again, while behind me Johnny falls to the floor, moaning in agony.

More haste less speed, but at last the light is gone.

I turn around to see how bad the damage is.

He is lying on the couch, gasping, weak with the shock of being exposed to the light. One side of his beautiful face has a painful red mark slicing down from his forehead to his jaw. The skin blisters right before my eyes.

His right hand and forearm are much worse. The skin is badly burned. Charred, almost. An ugly weal of flesh has risen in a jagged line from his forefinger all the way up his arm – almost to the elbow, where his rolled up shirt sleeve gave him some protection from the sun's rays.

I kneel down to comfort him, unable to take my eyes off his horrible injuries, and feel overwhelmed with sadness and pity. A splash of mild English sunshine – a warm friend to the rest of us – is a vicious enemy to him.

The boys are awake and on their feet, watching with wide-eyed fear.

Gwen, the maid, is beside herself with guilt and shock. "What must I do, sir? Shall I fetch water? Or will that make it worse?"

Johnny struggles to regain his composure. He holds his arm against his chest, as if nursing it in a sling. "No water, thank you."

"What then?" says Gwen, desperate to right her wrongs. "Can I put a salve on it? Ma makes a good salve or I can run to the apothecary's shop if you like?'

"No… It will heal. But I'll need… oh, Maddie, this could not have come at a worse time… "

"What do you need? Johnny?"

"I need to bathe it."

Gwen leaps up and hurries to the hearth. "I'll get this fire going and heat some water right away!"

"No, no. Gwen, I can't use water."

Edward comes across the room and inspects the arm as if he planned to enter the medical profession one day. "Your kind don't benefit from water, do they? I suppose you must use blood."

"Blood, sir?" says Gwen "You want to put blood on his arm?"

Johnny shivers. "Yes. Blood is what I must have. But it's not a very convenient time to go and find some, when the safety of our friends is at stake."

Mrs. Atkins appears in the doorway, in a tent-like white nightgown and an old brown shawl. Woken up by all the noise.

"Oh my Gawd, you've singed him!" she comes and kneels with me in front of Johnny and inspects the bad arm. She tuts under her breath. "Gwen, you stupid girl. I told you that you had to leave them shutters closed."

Gwen is distraught. "Yes, but you didn't tell me why, Ma, did you? I might have taken notice if you'd said! Oh, saints, I can't look at him. It's horrible!" She picks up the front of her pinny and hides her face in it, sobbing guilty tears.

Mrs. Atkins sighs. "I told you he was one of them, didn't I? Well, 'tis done now. We've got to concentrate on putting it right. Johnny-boy, listen to me. How bad is it? How long will it take to heal?"

Johnny struggles to get the words out through the pain. "It… will mend," he says, through gritted teeth. "It will mend in a matter of days… but I do need to bathe it… in blood."

The ever practical Mrs. Atkins is the first to come up with a possible solution. "Would pig's blood be any good, do you think?"

Johnny looks up, gasping with the pain. "Pig's blood?"

"Well, that's all I've got, sonny. We don't go in for a lot of human sacrifice round here."

"But you have pig's blood?"

"Yes, as it happens, I do. We slaughtered a pig yesterday. I was going to make black pudding. Will it work?"

"We could try."

"Gwen – stop your fussing and go get the bucket with the lid, that's standing in the corner of the pantry. See if you can fetch it without spilling it, there's a love."

Gwen gives her mother a dirty look and goes to fetch the blood.

"I'm sorry… about the pudding," Johnny says, without looking up.

"Don't be worrying about that, Johnny-boy. We've got plenty of food here. The Pub's doing ever so well, what with all the fuss over the coronation. Ever since then, every night of the week – we've been packed."

"Nevertheless, you must allow me to recompense you for your loss."

"Don't be silly, sir. It was Gwen's mistake.

"Shut up, Ma!"

Edward stretches out his hand and touches Gwen on the arm. "It was just an accident. An innocent mistake. John doesn't blame you, and neither do I."

She blushes up prettily and seems mollified by that.

"It should have been *your* coronation, shouldn't it?' she says.

He puts a finger to her lips. "Walls have ears."

I smile. They like each other, and that's how it's meant to be. I pretend to ignore them and concentrate on what is happening with Johnny's arm. He dips his hand into the bucket and douses his arm with pig's blood. Over and over again.

"Are you all right, watching this?" he says to me. "You look a little pale"

He continues the rhythmic sloshing of the dark red fluid over his arm.

"I don't like the idea of the blood much, but if it's helping with the pain then you must do it. I hate to see you in pain."

He gives me the strangest look.


Later on, Johnny starts acting really weird. We put his bad arm in a sling to try and immobilize it, but he won't sit still. He paces to and fro across the room, complaining about the pain. His breathing becomes rapid, almost like he's short of breath. Beads of sweat keep forming on his brow – which is odd – I've never seen him show any signs of reacting to temperature before.

He murmurs to himself. Speaks in French. Cries out angrily and gesticulates with his good arm at imaginary enemies all around. Then he rests, exhausted, with his back against the wall. He lets his body go slack and slide to the floor.

Gwen speaks to me in a hoarse whisper. "He's gone mad, hasn't he?"

I stare helplessly at him, wondering what to say and what to do. "I've never seen him like this before. The one person we need to get us through this – and he seems to be falling apart."

"It's all my fault," she says. "I swear I meant no harm!"

Finally, there is an outburst.

"I cannot let this happen!" Johnny leaps to his feet and snatches his cloak. "I cannot endure the pain. He's on his way to London, I could warn him! I could stop it all from unfolding before it begins."

I am frightened by his words. "What's going on, Johnny?"

Edward is on his feet, touching Johnny's good arm. "Yes, sir, what do you mean?"

Johnny shoves everyone away and puts on his cloak. "I can't. Not again. I must warn him… "

"Who are you talking about? Who is it that you wish you could warn?"

"In just a matter of hours… it all happens again, Maddie. The river – the hateful, evil river. It washes all my bright hopes away."

He's determined to go. There's no way anyone's going to stop him. He has the strength of ten men.

"But, Johnny, you promise you'll be back before we have to get the boys on the ship, right?"

His reply is gruff. "If I'm not, you will let it sail. But I will try to return in time, and help you take the boys to a place of safety."

Richard looks so frightened that I suspect he's about to start hiding behind the furniture again.

Edward's eyes are bright with fear, too. "If Madeleine is required to do this alone – to negotiate with your… allies on our behalf – you must leave her some token of your authority so they know that she's been sent from you."

"Must I?" says Johnny, rather bitterly.

"Yes, please, I think it might help. What about your ring. It has your seal on it, does it not?"

Johnny laughs. A hollow, empty laugh. "So that's how it goes, is it?'

Edward sighs. "Will you just give her the ring?"

Johnny strips the ring from his finger. He approaches me, eyes dark and glowering, and takes hold of my left hand.

"Just remember, Madeleine, time is like a wedding band."

"What?"

But he says no more. With a strange, soulful look in his eyes he slips the ring onto the third finger of my left hand, and kisses my fingers.

He bows curtly to Edward, and to Richard, and then he is gone.

The one person we need to get us through this is no longer here.

# Chapter Seventeen

Gwen is at the door. She's just run down to the wharf, to find out the state of play. She's breathless and her eyes are bright.

She comes in and goes straight to Edward.

"Sire. The ship's making ready to sail."

Edward looks up at me. His eyes beseech me to make a decision.

"He made me promise," I say, but it sounds lame. Edward and Richard are two kids with a hell of a lot of enemies. If they miss this chance to get to France, there may not be another. I feel the agitation in the air. The desperation.

I could take them down to the quayside. I could get them on board and wave goodbye. All we have to do is time it right and get the right ship.

But this is not a moment to be reckless with the young lives we have risked so much to save. I look out of the window so I don't have to keep seeing the wild-eyed fear in Edward's eyes. Blue eyes, just like my brother's. Young Richard's are the same – only his are brimming with tears.

I turn to Gwen. "You spoke to the sailors? How long have we got?"

"Not long. They want to catch the tide."

Time and tide wait for no man.

"I say we go."

Edward's face shows an emotion I can't begin to describe. His eyes glimmer with bright hope. Freedom waits in France, and I have said yes.

"Madeleine. I have not the eloquence to express my gratitude to you."

"Then don't. I haven't gotten you out of the country yet."

We all look around for our cloaks and hoods. We prepare to walk down to the quayside, in broad daylight. If we are seen I can easily imagine what our fate will be. I will be executed for treason. Swiftly. Publicly, no doubt. And the boys will meet the fate that Time has planned for them.

Gwen speaks up, standing by the doorway. "I'll lead you. I know the quickest way."

"No," says Edward, with a surprising note of authority in his unbroken, twelve-year-old voice. "There is no need to put another life at risk. Dear Gwen. You have helped us enough."

She nods, relief tangible on her pale, worried face. "Oh, Sire, it was my pleasure and my privilege." Her voice cracks. "Good luck. God speed."

Edward takes her hand and presses it to his youthful lips, a rather adult gesture he must have learned at court. "Tell your mother I owe her an enormous debt."

Gwen looks like she's going to swoon.

"G'bye, Gwen," says Richard. The younger boy looks small and slight beside his brother. A tear rolls down his face and he swipes it away and tries to look like the man he may yet become. If this crazy scheme comes off.

I swallow back my fear. I have to stop all this. Emotion doesn't mix well with secrecy and stealth.

"Okay. No more goodbyes." I herd them all towards the door. "Put your hood up, Richard, and keep your head down."

He obeys me instantly, and we file through the door and go one by one down the rickety wooden steps that lead into the courtyard of the inn. I lead the way and we head for the archway of bright light that leads us out into the main street.

We have only gone a short distance when I hear Gwen running to catch us up. She's carrying a large basket covered with a linen cloth. The type of thing the baker might carry on his rounds. She reaches us, panting, and thrusts the basket at me.

"Take this! It's pies, baked this morning. We were going to sell them in the pub come lunchtime. Act like you're hawking them, Maddie. Then it gives you a reason to be abroad in the street."

I smile. She's right. The three of us all walking along like we have no right to be there might draw unwelcome attention upon us.

I take the basket from her. "Thank you. That's a great idea, Gwen."

"Wait 'til you get close to the docks before you start selling, or them pies will all be gone."

She gives Edward one last apologetic glance and tries to turn away. "Fare thee well! I'll never forget you, sire, never in all my life."

"Nor will I forget you, Gwen. Fare thee well."

She goes to curtsey again, but he puts a warning hand on her arm. It is not safe for such displays of respect in the street. She bites her lip and turns her head away, and then she makes a bolt for it and runs back towards the inn.

Edward gives me a puzzled look. I can see the confusion on his young face, inside his hood. "What is *wrong* with Gwen, do you think?"

He's twelve. I guess he doesn't know. So I decide to enlighten him.

"She likes you."

There is a pause while the tall boy processes this piece of information. He frowns and looks dubious. I'm guessing that either he can't believe it, or else they use another word for it here in Medieval England. I've no idea which one.

A blush seeps into his youthful cheeks. "She does?"

I nod. "She does. Now keep walking. We got a ship to catch, remember."

We start walking along, dodging other people and bits of refuse all the way along the street. But the exchange with Gwen still bothers Edward. I can tell.

Richard almost laughs. "It's a good thing she picked you, brother, for I am already married."

"Is that the truth?' I say incredulously, as we turn a corner and catch sight of the murky waters of the Thames. *Married at nine?*

"No," says Edward. "He was married, but is no longer. It was a diplomatic alliance, but the little girl died two years ago."

I will never understand this place. Child marriages. Executions without trial. Disease and poverty. But beyond all that harsh ugliness, there is something more. Something beautiful and unspoiled about this crazy place. This place they call Merry England, that has long since slipped from memory.

We head down to what they call the Pool of London, where all the big ships are moored. It isn't actually a 'pool' at all, just a stretch of the river where all the vessels from far and wide come to deliver their cargoes. We must be getting very close, for I see masts up ahead.

At last we reach the quayside, and I gasp in amazement and delight. It is unlike any port I have seen before, or ever will see again. The wharf is full of people. A chaotic, jostling place. But it is what lies beyond that surprises me and causes me to blink. The river is almost log-jammed with ships of every kind. Full-bellied sailing ships with bright colors flying from their masts. Pirate-style ships with men swarming all over the rigging. Treasure ships built of rich golden timber, with sails furled tight.

The whole place is thronging with sound and color and the scent of faraway places. Orders are sung out from one man to another. Barrels are hoisted up and onto the quay, handcarts of merchandise rattle past me, while I just stand and stare.

"Never in my wildest dreams… " I murmur.

"Don't stare, Maddie." Edward glances nervously left and right, as if at any moment one of his enemies will seize him and drag him back to the Tower again.

"But it's… beautiful! It's like nothing I've ever… "

"Watch out!"

A wooden chest sways dangerously close and Edward pulls me out of the way as it is hoisted onto the quay. Everywhere I look there is a new sight to see. Men walk by with that unmistakable staggering gait – sailors, they must be. Swarming round me, people in bright colored tunics are at work, loading and unloading cargo. Buying and selling is going on right here by the side of the river. I breathe in, as I gaze around in wonder, and the air is perfumed with scents of places far from here

"Concentrate, Maddie."

With difficulty, I tear myself away from what is going on all around me. I glance down at my basket and remove the white linen cloth that covers my wares. I sell a few pies to a man in a bright blue tunic. Edward – struggling not to sound too well-bred – asks him if he can tell us where our ship is moored.

The man stuffs his pie into his mouth and uses his work-weathered hand to show us the way. He swallows much too fast and adds "That's the *Fleur de Lys*, over there."

"Thank you," Edward says, gazing at the little round-bellied boat that will deliver him to freedom, if all goes well.

The man wipes his mouth with the back of his hand. "Bad luck on board, if you ask me."

Edward turns back to him, and frowns in surprise. "Why do you say that?"

"She got in three days ago, but the crew, they've none of them been near the tavern. Did you ever hear of such a thing?"

Edward and I glance at one another, but after a moment he shrugs it off.

"She's from France. They do things differently."

The man who bought the pie just laughs. "I've met plenty of foreigners before, sir. They like their grog, the same as you and me."

Edward smiles. He puts an extra pie in the man's hand. 'Thank you. Thank you kindly for pointing her out.'

We make our way along the wharf, rather slowly, for Mistress Atkin's pies prove to be quite a hit with the crowd who populate the quay.

Richard tugs at my hand. "So you think he was right, Maddie? About the bad luck on board the *Fleur de Lys*."

"No. Of course not. All will be well. Johnny wouldn't have arranged this if he didn't think it was the right thing to do."

"But Johnny said don't go down to the ship without me."

Edward and I exchange a glance. We've made our decision – to go against Johnny's instructions and try to board the vessel before it sails. We must stick by it.

We approach the gangplank and Edward speaks a few words in French to the man on duty. The sailor's face shows surprise, but then he beckons for us to come on board.

Richard clutches my arm. "Is it safe to go on board, Maddie? Will they look after us?"

"I hope so."

The man seems friendly enough. He takes hold of Edward's arm, encouraging him to board the ship. He speaks rapidly, in French.

"He wants us to go below and speak to the Captain," Edward says. "He says that the Captain will decide."

I stand there biting my lip. This is the moment of vulnerable truth. We are about to meet the man who holds us in his power. If he double-crosses us, then all is lost. My heart pounds inside me – so loud that I swear it must be audible to everyone nearby. But it is almost as if the decision is already made.

We cross the gangplank, with our hearts thundering, and step onto the warm, well-scrubbed deck of the *Fleur de Lys*. I feel the gentle movement of the water under the boat, and it comforts me. The rhythmic ebb and flow of the Thames lulls my fears for a moment.

"A fine ship," Edward says, glancing nervously up at the furled sails of the *Fleur de Lys*. "Dear Lord, she looks sturdy enough, doesn't she?"

"She does." I marvel at the smooth timbers, golden in the sunshine, that form the body of this amazing little ship. One strong mast rises from the middle of the deck. On board sailors work steadily, making ready to put her to sea.

We descend into the belly of the ship, by way of a wooden ladder, that leads us down through a pitch dark hatch cut into the deck of the ship.

"Ah, Bonjour!" The captain arrives, and like so many of the people around us, he is small, and stocky and dark. Edward speaks furtively to him, in French, explaining who we are.

"I 'ave been… expecting you," the Captain says, speaking in English for my benefit, I guess.

I look up and smile, hearing words I can understand at last.

The Captain turns back to speak to Edward. He points to a place where two hammocks have been slung, partitioned for privacy from the rest of the crew. "You'll sleep here, and your young brother alongside you."

"My gratitude knows no bounds," Edward says, and bows.

Then, emotion overtakes him, and he passes a trembling hand over his face.

"And you will take your meals with me." The captain's lips quirk into a tiny private smile, and I am struck by the glint in his eye.

"Well, it seems you have everything prepared for us," Edward says. "Madeline, we will escort you back on deck and bid you farewell."

The Captain shakes his head. "Say your goodbyes here, sir. We must leave immediately."

I find myself staring into Edward's blue eyes as if I could communicate my fears to him that way. "I don't want to leave you just yet, I—"

"All is well, Maddie. You have saved our lives."

"I don't know… "

My words trail away. There's nothing I can say with the Captain standing right beside me. But I turn to Edward and give him a meaningful look. "Why don't we say goodbye *on the quay*?"

"He will be taken care of," says the Captain, in a brusque tone of voice. He murmurs something in French and it sounds like an impatient curse.

Edward gives a discreet, rather regal cough. "We must delay these good people no longer, Madeline. The Captain wants to catch the tide."

That brings me to my senses. I don't suppose there's any chance I can get back inside the Tower in time to catch *this* tide, and I'm afraid to go there alone, anyhow. *Johnny, why did you have to abandon me – just when I needed you most?*

I must set my fears aside and leave the boys to their fate on board the *Fleur de Lys*. I turn to Richard and embrace him like a brother.

"Gee I'm going to miss you!" I say, kissing the top of his head.

He clings to me rather too tightly, whispering in my ear. "Don't go."

"I have to go. Johnny will be wondering where I am." At least, I *hope* he will.

"Or the other way around," Edward observes with a worried frown. But then he takes my hand and kisses it. "Madeleine, I will never forget your courage."

"Nor will I forget yours." With hot tears stinging my eyes, I turn away and follow the Captain toward the ladder. I look up at the bright square of light above me. It seems to beckon me back up to the deck of the ship. I've done what I came here to do.

The Captain extends his hand to help me onto the ladder.

I take hold of his hand gratefully, but the sensation strikes fear in my soul. *His hand is icy cold.* Like Randolph's was. Like… they all are.

He pushes me forward, and I glance at him in alarm. Yes. His eyes are dark and glittering. His flesh is cold. A smile plays on his lips, and I fear that he knows that I know.

"You are a friend, of… Monsieur De Vere?" I say, playing for time, while my thoughts race ahead.

"Yes, yes," he says impatiently, hustling me to leave. "A great friend."

*Friend or foe? Friend or foe?* My mind keeps asking me, but I don't have the answers. Instead I try to rationalize it all. After all, most of Johnny's friends must be… icy cold. But there is something not right about this guy. If only I could test him in some way.

One of the other sailors appears and leans down into the hold to haul me up. But I still have questions for the Captain.

"You are French?" I say desperately, looking back down into the dark hold.

The Captain says, "I am."

"Perhaps you have visited De Vere's beautiful house, in Normandy?"

"But of course," he says, with a throaty laugh. "Finest in the region. Goodbye. Au revoir."

A pang of terror crosses my heart. Because he fell into my trap, just as surely as I fell into his. Johnny is from Champagne, not Normandy, and the Captain is no friend of his or mine.

The sailor grabs hold of my arm and hauls me away, propelling me roughly towards the gangplank.

"No!" I say, but it's no use.

He practically carries me off the ship. He shoves me onto the quay and steps back aboard the ship. He pulls up the plank, and in an instant it is done. He whistles to the other men to tell them that the ship is ready to leave.

The last link between me and the Princes is severed. I gaze down in despair at the swirling, eddying waters of the Thames that now separate me from my goal. The boys are on a ship bound for hell, and I have led them to it.

# Chapter Eighteen

I stand on the quayside, watching the ship easing away from the place where she was moored. I feel so helpless. So alone. Inside my head I rage at him. At Johnny.

*Why, why, why do you keep secrets from me? If you knew it wasn't safe, you could have warned me! But all you said was 'Don't go down to the ship without me'. You didn't tell me not to go at all!*

The ship glides further from me, widening the expanse of water between me and the boys. I drop my basket onto the quayside and spill the rest of Mrs. Atkin's pies. "NO! WAIT!"

The sailor raises his hand in a mock salute. Then he shrugs, as if to say 'too late'. He turns his back on me and gets on with his work. The sailors swarm all over the ship, all working together to ease *The Fleur* out into the middle of the River.

It is almost as much of a surprise to me as it is to them when I hit the water with a loud splash.

Jump right in, my heart told me. Jump in and swim out to the boat.

Easier said than done. My skirts will kill me first. My sky blue gown billows around me as I plunge into the water. I am blinded by my skirts and by the dirty brown water that rushes past my ears. I struggle. I fight. I kick with all my might.

I surface and gasp the air – sucking it in desperately. Wet hair covers my eyes and I push it roughly away.

"Edward! Richard!" I scream, at the top of my voice. "Get off the goddamn boat!"

I thrash my arms desperately in the water, as the ship slides further away.

"Maddie!"

Do I imagine it – or is that Richard's voice I can hear?

The weight of the water in my skirts hauls me under. I try to scream but the water drowns the sound. I try to recall what I just heard. What I just saw.

*A face leaning anxiously out from the side of the ship. A flash of incomprehension and fear.*

I surface again, gasping like a fish out of water, sucking the air into my starving lungs.

"Get off the ship!"

I'm fighting to stay afloat just long enough to warn them. I'm flailing my arms and struggling to see.

Yes. The boys are up and over the side, Richard first leaping nimbly through the air. His hood has fallen back from his anxious little face and his golden hair catches the light.

*Good boy! Now, where's your brother?*

The water threatens to take me again, though I flail my arms and try to swim with all my might. I push my face upwards and out of the water, and fight for a glimpse of the ship.

Edward makes ready to leap the rail this time, as the sailors shout and race along the deck to try to snatch him back.

But he is too quick for them. I see rather than hear the splash as he hits the water. For some reason, the phrase 'the quick and the dead' keeps ringing in my waterlogged ears.

I catch snatches of shouts and curses – people on other boats all rushing to see. I see a gruff-looking man on a river barge leaning down and hauling one of the boys out of the water. I can't see from this distance which one it is – just a boy with long, pale arms, all dripping wet, being dragged like a piece of seaweed onto the barge.

A third time, I'm under the water and I'm running out of strength, but I'm not quite ready to let the River take me just yet. I push myself up and get my next breath, trying to look and see how far I am from the quay.

That's when I'm sure I see him.

Johnny.

In broad daylight. Standing on the quayside. He throws off his plumed hat and his cloak, and in one athletic movement he dives in a graceful arc into the river.

I feel a surge of jubilation, though my body is ready to give in.

He's here. He's coming to get me.

In an instant he is with me, holding me, and I cling to him deliriously, pressing myself against his body in the water.

I'm so frantic that I clutch at him and pull him under the water with me. But his arms are strong, and he hauls me to the surface again.

"Don't struggle," he says. "You're safe now."

He flicks the water from his dark hair and starts to make for the shore, dragging me along with him like a heavy net full of fish. Slowly but surely, we get closer and closer to the quay.

I cling to his powerful shoulders and let him do all the work. I'm way too exhausted even to try. My body struggles just to breathe.

We have drawn quite a crowd and so there are many hands ready to drag us out of the water. Next thing I know, I'm lying on the wharf like a dead fish, with all my sodden skirts sticking to my body.

Only I'm not dead, I'm alive and I'm gasping and shivering.

"Johnny!"

He is kneeling beside me, close to me. He is holding my wet shoulders in his large square hands and staring in bewilderment at my face. He smiles and his breath is warm on my face.

"Dear lady, my name is John, but how do you know me?"

My mind lurches. *His breath is warm?*

"But I thought… you were… Johnny De Vere!"

"I am," the young man says. "I am John De Vere."

He frowns at me, in confusion. The dark locks of hair drip water onto his face, and his cheeks are flushed from his exertions in the river. He swipes the water away with his hand, and I am struck by the realization that I have never, ever seen Johnny redden with color. The Johnny I know is always pale.

There's a whole bunch of people staring down at us. Their faces show everything from amusement to concern. All the colors of their outlandish clothes seem to dance before my eyes. I see them all fractured – like a cubist painting – their beards and their faces are a confusion of images in front of me.

I clutch Johnny's hand, but it is warm and strong and… unfamiliar.

I begin to feel dizzy, as if I am falling. "You're not him."

He frowns. "Lady – what say you?"

"You're not him!" It comes out like an accusation – harsh and ugly and raw.

He stares down at me, looking as bewildered and confused as I feel. "Good lady, you gaze at me as if I were a monster. Pray, tell me your name?"

"*My* name?" I say, in surprise.

"Yes. You must have a name?"

It's all becoming painfully clear. I gasp, like I'm going to need oxygen soon. I stare at the kind face of the young man who jumped into the filthy waters of the River Thames to help a total stranger.

"You're not him. Or rather you are… only… *before…* " My voice trails off. I glance around wild-eyed, trying to get some kind of grip on the situation.

I'm soaking wet, I've lost the boys, and despite the crowd of anxious faces all around me, including the face of the man I thought I knew, I am alone.

I stare at the familiar angles of Johnny's handsome young face, but I see no recognition there at all. He shakes my shoulders again and tries to rouse me.

"What say you, dear lady? Your meaning eludes me."

"If you're Johnny," I say, in a desperate whisper, "then… I am so screwed."

# Chapter Nineteen

"Do you think she hit her head when she fell?"

The question comes from a large woman holding a dirty-looking child in her arms. "She talks like she's got the devil in her."

A man in a bright red tunic leans over me, peering down. "Or too much drink, more like."

"I'm perfectly alright, thank you." I'd like to stand up, or at least sit up, but my soaking skirts slow me down. The guy I thought was Johnny tries to help.

"She's not from London, is she?" says the woman with the baby.

"No. I am not. Look, thank you, for everything, guys, but—"

"She was with them youngsters that jumped off that ship just gone."

"Yes, I was. And I have to find them. Please! Will you just let me through and let me see—"

I stagger to my feet and crane my neck to see what's happening on the river.

"What the hell happened to the boys?" I say, in tones of deep dismay. I push through the crowd and make my way to the water's edge again.

"Look out. Watch she don't throw herself in again!"

"I have no intention of doing that."

I stand, dripping wet, scanning the water. The river is alive with activity – just as it was before, but it has changed, it has all moved on, in those few moments it took to get me safely out of the water. The boys are nowhere to be seen. The barge seems to have disappeared too – or else it has slipped under London Bridge and is now hidden from view. I turn my head and see that the *Fleur de Lys* is almost out of sight, making for the open water of the sea.

Johnny – or the man I thought was Johnny – comes up behind me and touches my arm. "Who are these boys that you seek? Are they kinsmen of yours? Brothers?"

Not knowing what else to say, I nod. "Yes. They were in the water, but they got onto one of the river barges. I think."

As if he can't trust a girl like me to have a clear idea of what just went on, Johnny turns to the other bystanders and asks them what they saw.

The woman with the baby speaks first. "There *was* a couple of lads – they was on board the *Fleur*. They jumped over the side when the silly girl threw herself in."

"I saw them too, sir," says another woman. "Maybe they was meaning to help."

"Meaning to help?" says a guy with the weather-beaten face of a sailor. "Looked like they was jumping ship to me!"

Then they all start haggling about what went on and whether or not the boys got back on the *Fleur de Lys*.

"Well, they're gone now," the sailor says. To indicate that he thinks the show is definitely over, he picks up his heavy canvas bag and leaves.

The new 'Johnny' is more concerned. He turns to me and touches my arm. "I'll help you find your brothers."

I turn around and look up at his handsome face, surprised by the generosity of his offer. "Would you?"

He smiles and gives me a courteous little bow. "You are obviously in distress. You should not be left alone in a... place like this. I feel it is my duty to help you find your kinsmen before I take my leave."

The woman with the baby grins, revealing a missing tooth. "You two can't go wandering around like that all day, you know. That water's filthy and you both stink like a pair of drowned rats."

She's right. I look down at my sodden skirts – all stained and dirty now. I didn't even stop to consider all the revolting stuff that gets tossed into the Thames when I made my decision to jump right in.

The woman glances respectfully at Johnny. "My sister's husband runs the Chandler's shop at the end of the street. Why don't you go in there and dry off for a while. He'll see you right, if you spare him a coin or two."

"I'm staying here," I say resolutely. I turn to Johnny. "You go if you like, but I'm waiting to see if they come back."

But even as I say the words I'm starting to shiver. In the UK, September is not a great month to go swimming, that's for sure.

Johnny touches my arm again gently. "The Chandler's shop is within sight of this place. If the boys are able to make their way back here, someone will surely tell them where you are."

"Course they will, you silly goose," the woman insists. She leans in close and speaks to me in a low voice. Her breath smells of ale. "Your dress is all stuck to your bosom, dearie. You're leading men's thoughts astray."

I frown at her in disbelief, but as I look up, I notice Johnny standing there, and I catch the merest hint of a blush creeping up the side of his face.

"Get over there and make yourself decent, girl! What are you waiting for?" The woman laughs and gives me a shove.

"I can't... I can't leave them... " But I barely resist, as they lead me away.

The shop is a narrow, half-timbered building with an open front so you can walk straight in off the street. A couple of wizened old men sit guarding the merchandise, which is displayed in old barrels cut in half. We walk in past all the coils of new rope, and breathe in the strong scent of pitch and tar. There is an apprentice working with some hot tar over in one corner, applying it to a piece of heavy canvas – I guess to make it waterproof. Another man chisels at a lump of wood, patiently working away at it, and as I draw closer I see that it is beginning to take the shape of a ship's block.

The woman with the baby calls out for her sister, and she comes running out into the shop with her sleeves rolled up and her apron on, to see what all the fuss is about.

"This gel's just had a bath in the River. Nearly drowned before me very eyes, she did. But this lovely young gent was so gallant – he jumped right in and saved her. Should a seen it, Thora, he was ever so brave."

Thora – the Chandler's wife – starts clucking and fussing about my wet clothes. She takes me through to her own part of the house at the back, apologizing for the mess.

"It's washday for me, so I don't mind laundering your clothes for you along with all the rest."

Gratefully, I start stripping off the wet, stinking garments, until I look up and see that Johnny has followed us through – and he's gazing, wide-eyed, at me.

"By my troth, I've seen few women so generously blessed —"

"Out!" says Thora. "Go stand in the shop, sir, until I'm ready for you. I must attend to the lady first."

After he's gone, I give Thora an embarrassed glance. "I can't think why he said I was generously blessed."

"He said it himself, lovey. He ain't seen *many* women."

She hands me a large linen sheet to wrap up in, and I follow her out to the backyard, where the efficient lady has her wash tubs set out just behind the back door. A sort of awning has been rigged up out of a bit of sailcloth to protect her from showers of rain. Beyond that, the yard is full of mud and bits of unwanted ships' chandlery, which the children are playing with. To my left, I hear an unmistakable 'oinking' noise, which, coupled with the smell, tells me the family keeps a pig.

Thora dumps my filthy clothing into one of the barrels, and goes off to speak to Johnny. She takes him a bucket of water.

I could kill for a long, hot shower right now.

Thora returns with Johnny's clothing and makes a start on laundering them, while I stand there wondering what kind of small talk it would be safe to make in a situation like this.

"Get into the tub with the rinsing water, if you care to, my dear," says Thora. "That's how I keep my children clean."

I consider this for a moment. I glance around and hope that no sailors are peering over the fence – a definite possibility in a place as busy as the port of London – and then I shed my sheet and step into the tub. My need to wash away the dirty waters of the Thames wins out and I sink gratefully into the water.

Later, Thora shows me through to her kitchen, where Johnny – dressed in a darned shirt and some shabby looking hose – is already enjoying a tankard of ale.

My gaze flutters over him – taking in every contour – enjoying the arresting sight. He leans back in his chair with his long legs stretched out in front of him. His face is flushed with the heat of the fire. He hasn't bothered to do up his shirt, and a sliver of his beautiful torso is revealed. Not surprisingly, every detail of his physical appearance is heart-achingly familiar.

So, here we are again. Me and Johnny. Or someone who looks exactly like him. In London. In trouble. Relying on the kindness of strangers. Again.

It is as if nothing at all has changed – except Johnny. Oh, yeah, that guy is definitely *not* the same. It's as if the understudy was playing the part today, or something.

For a start, he's behaving like the goofy new kid at school. He sits up straight when he notices me, and sloshes some of his ale onto his knees. He's awkward in my presence. Bashful even. Embarrassed about catching a glimpse of me earlier, I guess. He seems to be trying, and failing, to stop himself from staring at me.

There isn't much to see now, that's for sure. I'm wrapped up in an old linen sheet and I have a moth-eaten shawl around my shoulders. I sit down by the fire and accept a bowl of broth from Thora, who insists that I need something 'to warm me through'.

I don't tell her that the sight of Johnny in that shirt, with his dark hair gleaming in the firelight, is doing that job just fine. Instead I take cautious sips from my bowl of broth, while he sits opposite me nursing the tankard of ale.

Thora arranges our clothes in front of the fire so they will dry out quicker, and then she leaves us alone.

I glance up and catch Johnny's eye. He's looking at me like he's never seen a woman before – well, not an American one, anyhow. Which isn't surprising. Columbus hasn't been there yet.

"You must have a name?' he says.

He speaks as if he's trying to coax a secret from me.

I pause, reluctant to supply him with either my real name or the one I seem to have acquired by accident, but I can see I have no choice.

"People round here call me Madeleine," I tell him.

"Ah, Madeleine," he repeats, savoring the word. "A very pretty name."

He seems very pleased that I've finally been induced to part with a crumb of (highly inaccurate) information. And I can see that although he claims to like the name, it means nothing to him. This guy has no issues with a girl named Madeleine. No resentments and no history.

Not yet.

He takes a sip from his tankard and the pewter gleams in the firelight. "The way you speak – it's unusual. I have never heard cadences quite like it."

I stare into my broth and wish he would stop pursuing this line of inquiry. No use telling *this* guy I'm from Champany. He'd know I was a fake straight away.

"I presume, Madeleine, that you are in some kind of trouble, and that is why you're afraid to tell me your story?"

"I'm kind of… in the middle of something right now."

"In the middle of something?" he says, as if I'm speaking a foreign language.

But I pause and can't begin to tell him what it is.

There is a long pause and we both take cautious glances at each other now and then. Okay. I'm not stupid. This is Johnny from the past. This is Johnny before he changed.

He sets his tankard down on the hearth and leans forward to speak to me urgently. "Madeleine. How can I help you, if you refuse to trust me? I assure you I am a man of honor. A man of good family, with estates in both England and France."

I lift up my spoon to take another sip of my soup, more out of a sense of duty than hunger, and Johnny gazes at me, thoughtfully. Wistfully, almost.

This is embarrassing.

Then something about me seems to catch his eye and I look down to see if the sheet I'm wearing has slipped. But no, I'm still hanging on to my modesty.

Johnny keeps staring at me – like he was mesmerized or something. He utters what sounds a lot like a swearword – in French. "Where did you get that?"

"What?"

I realize that he's staring at the ring – the one that the other Johnny gave me just before he went crazy and left me to deal with all this stuff on my own.

"Oh… the ring?"

"Yes, yes. The ring."

"It was given to me."

"By a man named De Vere?"

"Yes. By a man named De Vere." I sort of sigh wearily. This is getting way too complicated. Johnny leans forward and insists on taking my soup and putting it down on the hearth so he can have a closer look at the ring. He catches hold of my hand and starts examining the ring on my finger.

"It is just as I thought," he says in amazement. "It bears my family crest. Just like this one!"

He starts comparing the ring that he's wearing with my ring, and finds that they are identical in every detail – except that his ring looks a lot newer than mine. His fingers keep touching mine, and they are disconcertingly warm.

"I don't understand." He keeps lining his hand up with mine so the rings are side by side. "This one could be its twin!"

"Yep, they are kind of similar."

"But this ring was commissioned especially for me by my father. It was given to me on the occasion of my twenty-first birthday – just a few weeks ago."

*Yeah, and where the hell are the laws of physics when you need them!*

The ring is the same one, of course. Only now there are two. There's the one he's wearing– the brand new ring given to Johnny in 1462 before he became a vampire. And there's the one I'm wearing– the ring that has been sitting on Johnny's ice cold finger for the last five hundred years getting more and more 'vintage' every day.

Oh. My. Godfather. This is horrible.

"I am beginning to understand," says Johnny, which gives me a real start.

I stare at him in dismay. "You do?" I do not add, *I sure hope not.*

"Clearly, you are betrothed to one of my kinsmen. But which? I have heard no happy tidings from anyone."

"Er… no! I mean… it hasn't been announced." *Oh my gosh – now I'm telling him I'm marrying some guy who doesn't even exist.*

"So… who is the lucky man?"

"Um… " I adjust my ring self-consciously, playing for time. This is another fine mess you've gotten me into, Johnny De Vere. "Look – his name's John, the same as you. I can't quite explain how, but… "

"I had a cousin named John. He lived in Champany, but I believe he was killed in the War of the Roses. "

"No. He wasn't. That's the guy – the one from Champagne," I say. Clutching at straws.

The new Johnny doesn't look entirely convinced. "But he has been mourned dead for a long time. We were told he perished at the Battle of Losecoat Field. It was in the year of Our Lord fourteen hundred and seventy, I believe."

"Reports of his death were… false."

"I see."

I realize I'm flushing now, with the heat of the fire and the strain of making up all these lies I have to tell him, I guess. Johnny looks uncomfortable, too.

"Look. It's gotta be the truth, hasn't it?" I say, inspiration hitting me like the kick from an alcoholic drink. "And I can prove it."

"Oh yes? How?"

"Well, you see. I know all this stuff about your family, don't I? I know that you've lived in France the last couple of years – managing your father's estate."

He nods. "That's true, but I admitted as much myself."

"I know that you were born in Kent."

"I was."

"And I know that you have no sisters, and no wife, as yet."

He smiles. "I do not."

"I even know where your political loyalties lie, Mr. De Vere."

His face grows serious and his dark eyes show suspicion – even fear. He leans forward. "You do?"

"Yes, and although you *say* you've come to London to pay your respects to the new King, he does not, in fact, command your respect."

"Shhhh," he says, suddenly worried about eavesdroppers.

"So there you go. I couldn't know all that stuff unless a member of the De Vere family had told me, could I?"

Suddenly his expression changes. He smiles apologetically and looks very sincere, and very, *very*, attractive. "Forgive me, Madeleine, for ever doubting you. You are practically my own kinswoman – you wear my cousin's ring."

*What can I say? The damage is already done.*

He clears his throat and then, oh my goodness, he goes down on his knees in front of me. "I place myself at your service, dear lady. I'm sure that my cousin would want me to offer you my protection. I'm convinced that if he were me, he would do the same."

I listen to his little speech and the irony of what he is saying almost makes me laugh, but this whole thing is getting way too serious for that. "Yep. I'm pretty sure he would too."

"Madeleine, will you please accept my help in reuniting you with your – *our* – kinsfolk?"

I look up and catch the seriousness in his dark eyes. "Okay."

He frowns at this unfamiliar utterance. "I beg your pardon?"

"I meant yes. Thank you. I accept."

He sighs, apparently with relief. He begins to talk about ways we can try to track down my 'brothers' as soon as our clothes are dry.

"Look. Johnny. If we are going to try to trust each other – there are a couple of things you need to get up to speed on. So listen up."

He frowns, struggling to follow my meaning. "Your cadences are very unfamiliar .."

"These brothers we're looking for. They're not my brothers. Okay?"

"They're not?"

"No. They *are* brothers. But not mine." I take a deep breath and tell him *exactly* who they are, and I see his dark eyes go wide with alarm and astonishment.

"You… you are involved in a plot to free the rightful heirs to the throne?"

"Yes. So you can see why I'm so worried, can't you?" I rake a hand through my long hair, which is drying out now in the warmth from the hearth. "I know I saw Richard getting pulled up onto that river barge, but I'm not so sure about Edward. After he jumped, I don't remember seeing Edward at all."

Johnny's face flashes with anxiety. "You are saying… that you have *lost* the King of England in the Thames?"

"Sounds a whole lot more serious when you put it like that."

"Madeleine, it is far, far worse than you seem to appreciate. Whoever gets his hands on those boys will use them to snatch power. It could lead us into civil war. Even now that a new King has been crowned, there are those who would rise against him at a moment's notice."

"But… I had to try to help those kids. Richard's only nine and he was scared out of his mind. And Edward – you should have seen him when he was a prisoner at the Tower – he knew he was under threat of death and he was in misery – I had to try to set them free."

Johnny whistles, under his breath. "You are either guilty of high treason or great bravery. Fate will decide."

Then the chandler's wife pokes her head round the door, which makes us both jump, since we've been discussing high treason.

"You're not letting them clothes get scorched are you? We don't want you to have to go home with a hole burnt through to your bum."

She comes and clucks around the clothing, turning it, fussing over it. My dress is drying out well and so she takes it away and says she'll finish it off under the flat iron.

Later, when I am dressed again, with my hair brushed out and lying loose down my back, Johnny is permitted to come back into the room.

He sees me and stares at me with that intense, brooding look all over again.

"What's up with you?" I ask.

"That blue gown… "

Here we go again. "It's all I've got."

"Oh, it's delightful," he says, with a shy cough. He tries to avert his eyes, but I realize, with a pang, that he can't.

He gazes at me, feasting his eyes on me. "I once saw a painting – in Italy – in the house of a very rich man. It was a depiction of our Lady, the Virgin Mary, and she was wearing a bright blue gown. It was spectacular in its beauty. But you, in that gown, with your golden hair around your shoulders… " his voice falters. He is blushing. His handsome face reddens delicately. For me.

"You loved it," I say, in a whisper. Now I understand.

"Yes, but you are a such a vision of loveliness that you outshine every other I have ever seen before." His eyes are bright, now that he's made this bold admission.

"Thanks," I say, inadequately. Then I struggle to lighten the atmosphere a little – to shrug it off, like I get called a 'vision of loveliness' ever other day. "You sure now how to turn on the compliments, don't you? My father warned me about guys like you."

Johnny smiles and rubs his chin, like I've put him in his place and he deserved it. "Your father gives you sound advice."

I'm glad he doesn't mind being rebuffed – but I don't really want to encourage him. This is crazy. I feel like I'm being disloyal to Johnny, flirting with this guy. But this guy *is* Johnny.

We went into the chandler's shop as strangers and we come out as partners in crime. United in our wish to find the princes. We head over to the water's edge and scan the horizon.

"That barge could have gone for miles by now. I knew I shouldn't have wasted time just waiting around here. Heaven knows where they are now."

"Look. Think about what you would do if you were the master of the barge," he says, scanning the busy river all the time as he speaks. "He's a boatman. He's seen plenty of people fall in the river in his time. He stops and hauls the boys out."

"He hauled Richard out, that's all I saw."

"Yes. So he's got a drenched boy sitting on his boat catching his breath, what's he going to do next?"

"I don't know. I have no idea where he was headed, do I?"

"That depends on what was on board. But that's not the point. He's not going to want to take the boys with him, is he? He has no idea who they are, and they are wily enough not to tell him, one would hope?"

"Yes, I think so. Their time in the Tower has made them both very wary of strangers."

"Good. Let us hope they had the presence of mind to tell him some story about high spirits and leaping into the river as a dare. If so, the barge-master is going to think they are a right pair of young scallywags and stop at the first convenient place to drop them off."

"Sounds logical, I suppose."

"Yes. So it follows that he dropped them off on the South Side of the river, at a landing place further along on that side."

"I guess you're right. He was kind of nearer to the other side of the river, wasn't he?"

"Exactly." He smiles at me, glad to see I can follow his reasoning.

"Where's the next possible place he could drop them off?"

"There's a set of waterman's stairs, right by London Bridge."

"Then, that's where we start looking. Come on!"

* * *

Johnny-come-lately says we ought to hire a small boat and cross the river that way, but I've had my fill of the water for today. I insist that we head for the bridge so there can be no further danger of getting my feet wet. I figure it'll be quicker anyway.

Soon as we set foot on the bridge I can see that I'm going to be proved wrong. London Bridge is not what I was expecting at all. For a start it, it is so overloaded with shops – some of them several stories high – that you can't even see the water. It's a busy shopping precinct – full of people touting their wares and customers holding stuff up to the light and haggling and bargaining about the price. It's a wonder the bridge stays up at all with all of that on top of it. No clear expanse for people to travel across in a calm orderly fashion – No.

Worst of all, up on the parapet, there are some dreadful gruesome lumps of smelly flesh that turn out to be the heads of people recently executed.

I clutch Johnny's arm when I realize what they are.

"Oh! Jeez! That's disgusting!"

"That's what happens to the enemies of the King. I did suggest going the other way," he says, with only a mild hint of 'I told you so' in his voice.

"I don't want to see," I say, closing my eyes and letting him lead me along.

"Alright, hold onto my arm," Johnny says, steering me along with all the other people wanting to use the bridge today.

I can feel the strength – and the warmth – of his arm inside his shirt sleeve. It feels oddly familiar, and yet unfamiliar. The arm of a stranger. A stranger I have already met – five hundred years from now.

"It's alright," he says gently, "we are through the gate now. You can open your eyes again."

I look up at him, apologetically. "I wish I hadn't seen that."

"They are displayed here as an awful warning. How can a young lady so brave in some ways be so innocent and silly in others?"

I notice that he doesn't release me from his protective hold. He seems to prefer to walk along with our arms linked.

A little way further on, the traffic on the bridge comes to a complete halt. A cart up ahead has lost a wheel and collapsed in the middle of the road – all the produce it was carrying has spilled all over the street.

We stand and watch as the people fall upon the spoils of the accident, while the man who was driving the cart struggles to reattach the wheel and the horse gobbles apples from a nearby stand.

"Is it safe to have so much weight on the bridge, Johnny? I mean look at those shops and dwellings – layer upon layer of them – built as high as they can go. And all these people and animals. It's a wonder the bridge doesn't fall down."

"Occasionally one of the archways does give way," he says, "and everything tumbles into the river. But it hasn't happened for a year or two."

"Jeez, Johnny, if you'd told me that, I would definitely have agreed to get the boat."

He smiles and squeezes my hand. "Perhaps you will trust my judgment a little better next time. Come on, the people are going through."

We shuffle forward with everyone else, but it takes us an hour to reach the other side.

The boys are sitting on the steps playing knuckle jacks, using a set made of real little knuckle bones. Their muddy clothes have dried out, more or less, all stuck to their bodies. Good quality garments made of velvet and silk are now darkened by river slime and hardened in unattractive wrinkles down their skinny arms and legs. The princes could not have disguised themselves more effectively if they had tried. The river has made them look exactly like a pair of London mud larks.

Richard looks up and sees me first.

"Maddie!"

I run ahead and embrace them. "I'm sorry. I'm sorry! I didn't know the captain was a bad guy, I swear! Not until it was too late, anyhow."

Edward leaps to his feet, and hugs me. "You risked your life to warn us."

"I was almost too late. Forgive me."

"There is nothing to forgive," Edward says, ever the gentleman. "We wanted to come across the river right away and find you, but neither of us has any money."

"We tried to use the bridge but we got turned back because we couldn't pay the toll," Richard says, in the plaintive voice of a child who has never had to deal with a desperate shortage of cash. Until today. "I'll die soon if I don't get something to eat."

Edward sighs ruefully. "Everything of value got left on board the *Fleur de Lys* unfortunately."

"No," I say, with tears brimming in my eyes. "Everything of value is right here." I pull the embarrassed boy into another fierce embrace, wetting his neck with my tears. "I… I'm just so thankful you're okay!"

Finally, realizing there is only so much female emotion that a lanky twelve-year-old can stand, I step back and dry my eyes.

Johnny is standing a little way away, watching us all. He takes the opportunity to come forward now, and to my surprise, snatches off his hat and plunges down on one knee in front of Edward.

"Your Grace, I know I have the honor of bowing to my King, for I have seen a portrait of you at the home of your uncle, Earl Rivers."

"Good grief, man, get up!" Edward's face pales. "We had the discussion about not bowing just yesterday, did we not?"

That's when I realize, with a stab, that Edward is not aware that Johnny has… um… *changed.*

I tug at Johnny's shoulder. "Get up already! Edward's under cover, okay?"

Johnny rises to his feet, slightly shamefaced. Perhaps perceiving that he has acted unwisely. Meanwhile, Edward's looking questioningly at me, and then at Johnny, and then at me again.

I sigh, and clutch at the first plausible excuse I can come up with for the new state of affairs. "Johnny has no recollection of what went on before we all jumped in the river," I announce desperately. "I reckon he must have hit his head."

"I can assure you, dear lady, I did not!" Johnny says hotly, as if I was insulting his male pride.

"You do not remember us?" Edward says, in astonishment. "What about all the plans we laid just yesterday?"

"Your good grace," Johnny almost bows down before the boy again, but I put a warning hand on his arm. "I am at your service, but I am not aware of any *plans.*"

"You are not?"

We all glance nervously at one another for a full minute.

"I was on my way to Westminster. I was about to procure a boat for the last leg of my journey when I saw the lady jump – I mean fall – into the river and I heard her cries for help. A gentleman cannot stand by and watch a lady drown, so I leapt in and swam out to lend my assistance."

"That was gallant," Richard observes. "Specially as the river smells like rotting fish and chamber pots." The boy raises his own arm up to his nose and sniffs it suspiciously.

Johnny steps closer so he doesn't have to speak so loud. "The lady has told me about the involvement of my kinsman in your flight from… the place where you were lodged."

Edward frowns, and it strikes me he's not satisfied with that explanation. His curiosity is naturally aroused. He opens his mouth to speak, but I'd rather *not* have a discussion about the Tower, or the King, or anything like that right now, so I try to change the subject.

"Well, anyway," I say, gazing meaningfully into Edward's confused blue eyes. "*This* Johnny De Vere is every bit as friendly as the other one, and he has *also* offered to help."

"I see," says Edward, but the perplexed look on his face makes me pretty sure that he doesn't.

I shoot him an agonized glance and mercifully, he doesn't argue.

Richard approaches shyly, and stands beside Johnny. "I'm glad you're back, sir. Madeleine did her very best but… "

Johnny smiles, frowning only slightly when the boy said the bit about being 'back'.

I give an apologetic shrug. "But my best didn't turn out so well."

"So I'm glad you are around to take charge of things again."

Johnny's face shows bewilderment too. "Again?" he repeats.

Richard looks up at Johnny. "Why does the sun not burn thee today?"

Johnny smiles down at him. "This sunshine isn't strong enough to burn me," he says. "And I do not burn easily. I have the olive skin of a Frenchman – do I not?"

The child stares at the place on Johnny's hand which was burnt only this morning. Only there's no mark there now, at all. Too curious to be fobbed off with an explanation that does not fit the facts, Richard reaches out, and touches Johnny's hand. He touches the warm human fingers of the man he thought he already knew, and I see the look of surprise on the boy's face.

Shock. Recoil. Confusion.

Richard turns to me, round-eyed with surprise and stares up at me with worried incomprehension.

"Let's not ask any hard questions, shall we?" I say, borrowing a phrase that was once said to me. Richard bites the soft flesh of his bottom lip, as if in a physical effort to prevent himself asking those questions.

So off we go, the four of us.

Two of us are clean and respectable, two of us are filthy dirty. I guess that to an outsider, we might look like a pair of do-gooders taking pity on a couple of urchins. Johnny says we'll go to his father's house in Westminster, which is not far away. None of us are completely comfortable with the arrangement, but we definitely need somewhere to go.

Somewhere they won't come looking for us.

This time, Johnny insists that we hire a boat, and we all get in to a funny little rowing boat, and we make our way along old Father Thames.

And yes, it is much more civilized being rowed across the river with the soothing sound of the oars stirring the water, instead of the jangling raucous crowd of people swarming across the bridge. I glance up at Johnny and he seems to read my thoughts. The look on his face says 'I told you so'.

We reach the other side, and while Johnny is preoccupied paying the boatman, Richard leans across and tugs my arm.

"It's not him, is it?" he whispers.

"Not exactly," I say, knowing my reply sounds lame. "He has no memory of us, but he wants to help, just as before."

Richard's face is perplexed. "Has he been bewitched or something?"

"Something like that."

Richard scowls. "I know it isn't him – his hand is completely healed."

Edward overhears us, and joins in our low, secretive conversation. "Those creatures heal fast."

"But brother, he is as warm as you and me!" Richard says urgently, his voice rising dangerously. "I touched his hand and he—"

"Shhhh!" I say, sending them my best 'beseeching' look and willing them to be silent. "He's on our side. That's all that matters."

Johnny calls for us to hurry up. "My father's house is not far from this landing spot. Just a short walk."

"Good thing too," says Richard a little disconsolately. "For I am as hungry as a bear."

Johnny laughs. "Well, young sir, we keep a pair of servants at the house all year – an old couple, but very faithful – and the wife is a most excellent cook. She will be honored to offer you food and wine."

"Thank you for opening your house to us," says Edward, apologetically. "It's kind of you to receive us there."

Johnny looks respectfully at the mud-stained boy. "It is quite a modest place."

Edward smiles. "After the Tower – it will be paradise, I'm sure."

# Chapter Twenty

He's right. It is like paradise. A beautiful old house, standing apart from its neighbors, surrounded by a walled garden full of fruit trees. Apples, pears, and dark red plums. The luscious fruit hangs glistening from their boughs. The house has the sun upon it, and it looks safe and inviting – a plump, cozy-looking place with a freshly-thatched roof.

Incredible – to find something like this, in the very heart of the city.

"It's beautiful."

"Isn't it? " Johnny says, with warm affection in his voice.

"You love this place."

"I do. I've loved it since I was a child. When my father acquired this house, it became a pleasure to come up to town. Come inside!"

He leads the way through the gate and up towards the gabled door. Inside, we encounter a woman – a plump, cheerful lady with gray hair escaping in wisps from under a white linen bonnet.

"My stars – what have we here!" she says. She stares at Richard and Edward, with their filthy clothes and muddy faces, as if they might carry the plague.

"Two young rascals, Ursula, who have fallen into the river."

"And… you have brought them home, sir?"

"Yes. May I ask you to heat some water, and find fresh clothing for them both?"

"As you wish, sir," she says with a curtsey, but I can see she thinks this is an unusual request.

Richard tugs at my hand, and turns puppy dog eyes on me. "Can't we have food, first, Maddie. We haven't eaten for *days*."

"Now, that's not true," I murmur, but I look up at Ursula and give her a pleading smile. "Could we sit them outside on the steps, maybe, and give them a bit of bread?"

Johnny places a hand on my back. "This is Madeleine, I met her down by the docks."

Ursula blanches. Quite clearly, when she looks at me, she's not seeing the Virgin Mary. "Did you indeed, sir? Well, that's not like you, I must say."

"Be careful what you say, woman. This lady is virtuous and respectable. She is no dockside whore. She's betrothed to a kinsman of mine."

"My apologies, Master John. I must send Alfred out to get something to cook for your supper. I'm right glad to see you, sir. It's been so long. Was it a warm summer in France?"

"Yes. I swam naked in the lake most days," he replies, shucking his cloak from his shoulders, "but I'm very glad to be home."

The next hour is spent attending to the needs of the two youngsters, which Ursula, to her credit, does with great care and attention. She heats a tub of water and finds clean linen towels, scented with rosewater. She runs around searching out old clothes to put them in, and before long they are fed, bathed, dressed and contented.

They occupy themselves for a while in the garden behind the house, with some of John's old playthings. Wooden swords and hoops.

But after only a short time they tire of this and lie sprawled on some cushions in the sun. They watch the insects crawling about in the grass and before long they are fast asleep.

"Would you look at that?" I say, with a smile. "They must have been so tired!"

"Not surprising really," says Johnny, with a surprisingly tender look on his face as he looks down at the sleeping children. "What kind of rest can they have had – all these months they've been living in fear?"

The housekeeper comes out into the yard to empty a pail of grubby water, and when she has done this, she comes and joins us. "Ah bless them! Look at those two, fast asleep in the sun like a couple of village lads after haymaking."

"They haven't slept properly for weeks, Ursula. They've been through quite an ordeal."

Ursula's face clouds with concern, and she touches Johnny on the arm. "If I may so, sir, they are very nicely-spoken for London urchins."

Johnny looks at her, and frowns. "They have fallen on hard times, Ursula. Their father has but lately passed away."

"Yes, they told me. Quite a gentleman, by all accounts. Kept horses… and hounds… and hawks. It's a very fine household that has all that."

"Ursula. Don't."

"Don't what?" she says, peevishly. "I'm just wondering out loud."

I turn my head away and try to act like I'm not listening.

Johnny sighs. "You can wonder all you like, Ursula, but you *must* accept my explanation. They are a pair of paupers who have lately lost their father. Madeleine has a kind heart and she has asked me to help find a place for them."

"Master John," she says, "Don't you lie to me. Those boys speak like royalty, and if they be who I think they might be, then every soul in this house is in danger. Mortal danger."

A guilty look flashes across Johnny's beautiful face. "Indeed. Now we must say no more about it. Someone might overhear. Tell old Alfred we will require three horses. We leave on the morrow – before dawn."

The housekeeper's face looks troubled, but she returns to the kitchen. I can see her through the open door, tending to some aromatic dish she's making in an iron pot over the fire.

Johnny asks me to stroll around the garden to while away the time. He places a hand upon my back and guides me through a simple trellis gate that leads to the orchard beyond.

I think of the other Johnny, guiding me through Traitors' Gate. He touched me in the exact same way. Right before we enjoyed our first kiss.

This young man beside me is so achingly familiar, but he's acting like we only just met – smiling and making small talk with a twinkle in his eye.

"The plums are ripe," he says, and I turn to watch the birds pecking the moist fallen fruit that lies all over the grass.

Johnny glances up at the tree where more of the rich, glossy fruit hang heavy on every bough. "They are juicy and very, very, sweet, shall I pick one for you?"

I smile, perhaps a little coquettishly. "Thank you kindly, sir."

He reaches up and shakes the tree and I scream with laughter as a volley of ripe plums falls down around me. I dodge them and he makes a grab for me, grasping the chance to encircle my waist.

I only allow him a moment of stolen intimacy, and then I push him away playfully. "Keep your hands to yourself, you naughty boy!"

"Forgive me. I couldn't resist." He reaches up, and plucks another fruit. "Here. A lovely ripe plum for thee."

I take it, grazing my fingers against his, while he lowers his lashes seductively. He watches me as I raise it to my lips, savoring its sweet scent and color. I know that I'm teasing him. But that doesn't stop me. I kiss its deep red skin.

His eyes glint dangerously. "Lucky, lucky plum."

*Oh, this guy knows all the lines, doesn't he?*

It's like I'm the pretty girl at the party and he's hoping to take me home.

"Taste it." He dares, with a smile upon his lips.

I bite into the sweet flesh and the plum oozes juice. "Mmmmm!"

I know what I'm doing. Acting all provocative on purpose. But he doesn't object – far from it. He smiles and sighs contentedly.

Raising his angel's face to heaven, he murmurs, "Madeleine, you have bewitched me!"

We spread a cloth upon the ground and sit soaking up the afternoon sun. Johnny stretches out his length beside me, and for the first time in days I feel safe and secure. He calls for Ursula to bring him his lute, and he plucks gentle melodies for me. His fingers caress the strings with a skill and proficiency I can only admire. I've never had a gift for music. I love the gentle sound that he brings forth, it's seductive and sweet and charming. Before long, I become as indolent and drowsy as the bees.

Later, when the sun has set, and the boys have gone to lie down in a proper bed, Johnny and I sit down to eat, and make plans for the day that lies ahead. Ursula stands at the old oak dresser polishing up the silver.

"There. That's better," she says, holding a knife up to the light so it winks in the candlelight. "We haven't used the good stuff since your father was here, Master John."

Johnny smiles. "I'd be happy with a dish and a spoon, eating by the hearth like I did when I was little."

"I dare say. But we have a lady in the house, and it's nice to use the silver for a change." She lays it down on the table for us. "Doesn't that look nice?"

The food is even better. My tentative first taste almost makes me swoon.

"You like it, then?" he says.

"It's great."

"Chicken, with damsons and almonds," he says, dipping his bread in the sauce. "Ursula knows it's one of my favorites."

I feel a kind of pang when he says that, recalling that time at Johnny's ultra-modern apartment by the Thames. This is the same man who sits with me now – before his life was changed forever.

I glance shyly at him. His linen shirt is loose, split almost to the waist. The scent of his oh-so-human masculinity, the perfume of fresh sweat on his body. His face is flushed with color. His lips are full and warm, with crumbs of bread upon them. He licks them away and smiles at me.

"Eat up!" he says. "For it will not be easy to get a good meal when we are on the road tomorrow."

Seeing him eat is extraordinary. Ripping off bits of bread and biting into it, seeing him chewing hungrily and swallowing with real enjoyment, wiping his mouth with the back of his hand once, when he didn't think I was looking.

He pushes the wooden platter towards me, but I shake my head. I don't want more bread. In my heart of hearts, I know exactly what I want. To taste his lips and feel their warmth. To press my own mouth against his and savor his human kiss. To lay my cheek against his living, breathing body and lose myself forever in his arms.

"Madeleine. We must talk about tomorrow. I have asked my groom to prepare our horses. But in which direction do you think we should ride?"

I am stricken for a moment. My plans went as far as getting the boys out, that's all. Beyond that, I don't know. I guess I was hoping he'd come up with something.

"Johnny… I thought they'd be on their way to France by now. I don't know where else to take them. I have no friends here, except for you."

"And my cousin," he corrects, with a frown.

I look down at my plate. I push the last morsels of my dinner around and wish he wouldn't talk about the cousin. I have gotten myself into a real mess, but how else could I explain away the ring?

Johnny's dark eyes meet mine. "Where has the man gone, do you think?"

"I don't know."

"Has the man lost his sense of gentleness and chivalry? If I was betrothed to you I would not leave you wandering around London on your own!"

I am surprised by the force of the emotion behind his words. He gazes at me with an intensity that floods me with heat and confusion.

"You have been more than kind," I say inadequately.

He takes my hand across the table, and holds it like he'll never let me go.

"So," he says. "Do we make for the coast then? Or would it be safer to head for Scotland, and get them over the border?"

But then the answer hits me. "Johnny. I know where we should go. In fact, I believe we *must* go there."

# Chapter Twenty-One

His eyes shine, as he leans urgently towards me. "Where is this place? Name it, and I shall see thee safely there."

"It's your house near Swanley. Where you… I mean, your cousin… took me to visit once before."

"But, Madeleine. I have no house in Swanley."

My heart almost stops inside my chest. "What?"

"My father's estate is further south, my sweet, and I own no property in Swanley. It's a tiny place in Kent, is it not?"

"Yes," I say heavily. "It's definitely in Kent."

His curiosity roused, he squeezes my hand. "So, this house you speak of—"

"The Grange. It's called the Grange."

"Why did you think it belonged to me?"

*Because it will belong to you in the future, and I have already been there.*

"Um… I must have gotten mixed up. But… all the same… that's where we've got to go." I realize that I'm clinging on to hope. The kind of hope that is born out of desperation. I have no idea who or what we'll find at The Grange. But Johnny from the future seemed certain that I'd been there before.

So it *must* be the place we're meant to go.

"Right," says Johnny, all courage and bravado. "We ride for Swanley."


We're both too agitated to sleep. We plan the route. We count the hours.

We run round the house looking for things that may be useful to us on the journey. Knives, blankets, and small things of value we can use to barter on the way.

We wake the children an hour before the break of day, and prepare them for the ride. Richard complains bitterly when I toss him a cloak and hood.

"It's too early, Maddie. Can we run away another day, please?"

"It's now or never, I'm afraid. Be a good boy and do as I say."

"I must say, I did quite like it here," says Edward.

"It's dangerous to stay so close to London. Lots of people saw what happened down at the river, when you two jumped ship. If they work out who Johnny is, they will soon come here."

After that, they get ready without a word, and I see Edward's lips moving in silent prayer.

Johnny says he'll gather up the bags and pouches, and I run out to the stables to see how Alfred is getting on with the horses.

Struggling to work as fast as he can, Alfred throws a saddle upon the back of a fine brown mare. "She's a lovely palfrey, this one, she'll serve you well if you treat her right."

"She's perfect."

The horse whinnies softly, seeming to sense my fear. Alfred soothes her with a firm, reassuring hand. If only my fears could so easily be brushed away.

Johnny appears in the doorway, followed by the two boys.

"Are we ready?"

"Yes sir," says Alfred, touching the place on his forehead where his forelock used to be. He leads the horses out into the yard, where the first signs of daybreak can be seen.

"Edward," he says. "You have the black one, it's a fine horse for a young man like you."

Edward makes an agile leap into the saddle – obviously an experienced horseman. Thinking that I'd better hurry, I do the same. I hitch my skirts and mount the gentle brown mare.

"What in heaven's name do you think you are doing?"

Johnny stands beside the horse, looking at me as if I've lost my mind. His gaze rests not on my face, but on the expanse of thigh I am revealing in order to ride astride.

"I'm preparing to ride to Swanley. What do you think I'm doing?"

With his gaze apparently glued to my leg, he swears under his breath. "I thought you would sit behind me, Madeleine. I thought Richard would ride the mare."

"Oh. Sorry. But hey, he's small and light, he could sit behind his brother on the black one, couldn't he?"

*I'm not giving up my mount that easily, Johnny-boy.*

Finally managing to tear his attention from my thighs, Johnny looks up and catches my eye. I guess he must see determination on my face because he sighs and shakes his head.

"Have it your own way then, woman, but for heaven's sake cover yourself up."

He plucks at my skirts and tries to arrange them into some semblance of modesty. I must confess, the touch of his warm hands upon my body feels good in so many ways.

Then Johnny leaps onto the back of his own horse, and I feast my eyes on him. There is nothing like the sight of a good-looking guy on the back of a spirited horse.

I can't resist calling out. "You're a knight on a milk-white steed – all you need now is the armor."

He frowns. "You think I shall require a breast-plate?"

"I'm only kidding. Let's hope so, anyhow. Come on! Let's hit the road!"

Edward hauls his brother up to ride with him and we wheel our horses round and out of the yard.

We ride first in the direction of Canterbury, planning to say –
if we are stopped – that we are joining the hordes of people who
go on pilgrimage there every year. All along the route we see
returning pilgrims on their way back to London. Many of them
have made quite a holiday out of their pilgrimage – traveling
with friends, staying at pleasant places all along the way.

Some of them hail us and exchange a few words as we pass.

"You must kiss the tomb of Saint Thomas," one man says
cheerily. "He has chased my backache away!"

We learn to spot the pilgrims at quite a distance, riding or
walking slowly into view. When they get closer we can soon tell
if we are right, for most of them wear a metal medallion bearing
an image of the Saint.

As the sun rises in the sky the day becomes quite warm.
Johnny removes his cloak and tucks it away in his pack.
"Nothing like a ride through the countryside on a bright
September morn."

"You are happier, now we are well away from London?"

"Yes. Though I know we are not out of the woods yet."

I smile. Since leaving Southwark, we have ridden through
pleasant countryside the whole way. When I did this journey
with Johnny in the Lamborghini, it was houses nearly all the
way.

This Johnny smiles across at me as we ride along, He's
enjoying the adventure, I can tell.

On the brow of a hill we turn back to take in the view. We see four horsemen riding fast, the hooves of their mounts tearing up the earth as they speed their way towards us.

"No," says Edward in dismay. "No."

The sight of them chills my blood. "Come on! Nobody's in that much of a hurry to see St. Thomas! Ride!"

We wheel our horses round in a violent hurry, and Johnny's rears in fright. I hardly even look to see if he stays in the saddle.

"Yah! Come on, girl. Let's show 'em what you've got!"

She obeys me, and we tear across the hillside. The thunder of hooves tells me that the others follow. We ride like devils possessed. A wild, desperate ride.

We will not surrender when freedom is only a gallop away.

I hear Edward's voice behind me, the cultured tones of our displaced young King. "Hang on Richard! Hold tight and we shall have our victory!"

My confidence soars, charging ahead like I was leading the light brigade. When we are well down into the valley where our enemies cannot see us, I hear Johnny yell at me.

"Turn by those trees up ahead! Turn away from the Canterbury road."

Yes, I know he's right, but we are going at such great speed that I struggle to make the turn. My horse rears as we approach the hawthorn hedge, and I am thrown to the ground with a sickening, bone-jarring thump.

"Madeleine!" Johnny wheels his horse around and comes toward me, stretching out his arm to try to lift me to my feet.

"Go. Go without me!"

"Never."

"Take my horse with you. I'll say I saw you ride on to Canterbury."

"No! It's too dangerous!"

I ignore Johnny and turn to Edward instead. "Ride on without me! I have not come this far to see you captured! Please!"

He nods, his pale blue eyes full of gratitude and fear. He commands his horse to ride on and soon sets a fine pace. His brother clings tight to his back. I watch them go, with relief in my heart.

"Take that horse and ride, Johnny-boy, or you will live to regret it." I narrow my eyes and speak through barred teeth.

He looks like he's going to refuse again, but then he rides over to my horse and picks up the dangling reins.

"Zounds, woman! By my troth, this is the hardest thing you've ever asked me to do!"

I struggle to my feet, though my whole body is throbbing with pain. With shaking fingers I undo the clasp of my red cloak and pass it up to him.

"Go!"

I don't stay to watch him ride away. I turn and run into the field of wheat stubble beside the lane, shedding my shoes as I go. I splash through every puddle I see, hoping to muddy my feet. I *must* make myself look like a peasant to have any chance of pulling this off. All the way along the journey I've seen them – local farm girls. I hitch my blue dress up around my thighs, tucking it out of the way, as they do when they are working in the fields.

As the horsemen come tearing down the valley, I bend down and dig into the dirt with my fingers. I don't even know what I'm pretending to do. Weeding, maybe?

My knowledge of medieval agriculture is pretty minimal.

I'm not sure whether to look up as they ride by, or pretend I'm so absorbed in my work that I haven't seen them. I opt for keeping my head down.

I stare at the clods of earth in my fingers. I struggle to quiet my breathing, and pray that the beating of my heart – so audible to me – can't be heard by the men as they approach.

"Woman! Did you see the fugitives! Answer me in the name of the King!"

He doesn't dismount, which is a mercy. The further away he stays, the more likely I am to get away with this.

Their horses paw the ground, skittish and nervy. One of them is so hyped that it tries to bolt, but the rider pulls it back into line and it stands there, nostrils flaring.

"Woman have you lost your tongue? Or do you want to lose it?"

"They took the Canterbury road, sir," I say, hoping like hell I don't sound too American.

"All of them?"

I nod. Not wanting to say more than I have to.

One of the men looks anxiously up the highway. "They could claim sanctuary if they reach Canterbury. We cannot touch them then."

"Cannot touch them!" The first man almost spits the scornful words. "King Richard does not always respect sanctuary, and we must do what the King desires."

"What if she speaks false?" says the third guy, much to my dismay. "She may have been bribed to lie."

*Here we go.*

"Shall we send two riders one way, and two the other?"

I almost sink to my knees in fear. "They… rode by… in great haste," I say, mentally checking every word before I utter it, in case I say something dumb or modern. "They have given me nothing."

The first man turns to his friends. "Canterbury is the most likely road – from there they could ride to Dover."

"And you will break the news to the King, if we return without them?"

"I will reap the glory, you mean, when we bring back their heads upon a spike."

"Let us waste no more time, men. Onward, to Canterbury!"

After they've gone, I do sink to my knees. The adrenalin rush dies away and the pain from my fall seems worse than ever.

But I'm the luckiest girl alive. I know that.

I limp over the furrows in the field, searching for my shoes. I sit on the ground and put them on, inspecting my aching legs for cuts and bruises.

I walk along the road towards Swanley, with the sun low behind me. Eventually I am offered a ride in a two-wheeled oxcart, that is going along the road the same way. I let my aching body sink back against the sacks of grain and lie there as we rumble along, looking at the sky above.

The Grange. I still have to get to the Grange – it's my best chance of meeting up with Johnny. I know it seems crazy to cling to that, but I have to. It's the one place I know of, that I can be sure exists here in 1483. And the only reason I knew it existed was because the other Johnny took me there in his Lamborghini. That other visit seems like eons ago, but in fact it was only last week.

*Yesterday and tomorrow, it's all the same, he said.*

"Will you let me know when we get to Swanley?" I ask the kind man who stopped and let me ride on his cart.

He gives me a wheezy laugh. "Certainly. But there's not much to see!"

Swanley turns out to be not much more than a crossroads and some dirt tracks leading away to three cattle-farms in the distance.

I ask to be dropped off here, and stand in the middle of nowhere with the wind rustling through the sycamore trees. As the oxcart rumbles away I feel a pang of loneliness and fear. But then from behind the trees, they appear.

The two boys come running out of hiding to greet me, and Johnny leads his white steed into the sunlight. The other horses are hidden among the trees.

"They fell for it!" I say proudly. "They'll be halfway to Canterbury by now."

His face is stern. "You must never, ever, do anything like that again. I have been in misery waiting for you. Cursing myself for leaving you there. I was trying to decide just how long we should wait before I could go back, and I cannot even *tell* you what I feared I would find."

"I'm sorry."

"Madeleine, everything you do sears my heart. That day I met you by the river, I was slain – by thy fatal glance."

*Slain by my fatal glance, huh?* I haven't heard that one before.

"Yeah, well. Sorry about that. Let's get on and find this barn, shall we?"

"Yes," he says, with a short sigh. "Where is this wretched place?"

# Chapter Twenty-Two

The sun sets and we walk on through the twilight until I find the turning.

I almost miss it because it doesn't have the smart sign bearing the name "The Grange". But the rise of the hill and the curve of the road tell me that this is the one.

"There it is!" I say and hurry towards it, happy that we're finally here.

Johnny from the past and I stand together in front of the brand new barn.

*So this is when it happened.*

"This is it, then?" he says, staring up at the building, unsure what to do next.

"Yes," I murmur. "This is it."

It is a much younger version of the barn I saw with the other Johnny. Its brickwork is sharp and its roof is new and doesn't sag. But in every other way, it is just the same. He was so sure I had been here with him. He remembered standing here with me.

The doorway at the Tower has given me the chance to join him in that memory, at last.

"It's just a barn," says Edward. "What's so special about this place?"

I don't answer. I'm lost in thought, gazing at the barn. Wondering why fate wants me here.

"Maddie?" Richard shakes my arm violently, breaking my reverie. "Stop staring! Tell us what we must do next!"

"Sorry. I was thinking about some… hard stuff."

"Well?" Johnny says. "We've arrived at your chosen destination. What now?"

"Um. I don't know. I guess we go inside."

So we push open the heavy door that still smells of newly milled wood and we go inside.

Hay. The barn is full of hay.

Not even grain, as you might expect with a name like 'The Grange'. I guess they keep that someplace else – there are several other buildings on the site. I gaze around the massive oak-frame building. On one side there is a wooden platform for winnowing – separating the wheat from the chaff. On the other side some tools are leaned up against the wall.

I don't really know what I was expecting. I wasn't silly enough to think I was going to see Johnny's fine collection of vintage cars. I know they don't get here for another few hundred years.

Johnny from the past looks around, a little disconsolately. "Maybe we can rest here until daybreak and then move on. At least there's no shortage of hay to lie down on."

"I like it here," says Edward, flopping down in the hay. His brother spies the ladder that leads up to the hayloft and can't resist scampering up it to explore.

Johnny and I are more wary, well aware that we trespass here. Outside in the yard a dog barks, having heard or smelt our presence.

"I can see the farmhouse from here," Richard says, peering out of a small unglazed window – high up in the wall of the barn. Then he gasps and ducks his head. "The mistress of the house approaches! She's got a lantern… and a pitchfork, if I am not mistaken."

"Quick, boys, dive into the hay!" Johnny commands.

"Where do you want me to hide?" I say, glancing nervously at the ladder, wondering if there's still time.

Johnny catches hold of my arm, and pulls me towards him. "Stay by my side. We will act like lovers – then she may think we have reason to be here."

I hear someone just outside now, struggling with the latch and cursing the weight of the heavy door.

Johnny reaches for me, pulling me into a theatrical – and rather lusty – kiss. I can't help but give a little squeal of protest, as I'm assailed by the rough texture of his face. A hot, male chin

– definitely in need of a shave. But soon I am silenced by the warmth of his lips, and the arousing pressure of his tongue.

I melt against him – melding my body into his. A frisson of sensation goes through me. He's so… warm and male and real.

His heat ignites the flame within me, and I relish his fiery kiss.

Oh, yes. The pretence is over. Johnny and me, making out like it's our one and only chance. Yeah. Doing what we've wanted to do – in fevered moments of imagination – for most of the last two days. His mouth is on mine, his hands are on my body, holding me tightly against him. And I just ride it out, relishing the moment, enjoying his wild, sexy kiss.

"Fine night for it and no mistake," says a sarcastic voice nearby. "Anyone would think it was May Day the way you two are carrying on."

We separate shyly, but we can't stop gazing at each other. Johnny's holding my hand and he doesn't let go. His dark eyes stay with me for a long moment. My heart's thundering, and not only because I'm afraid.

I realize that for him, what just happened was our very first kiss.

"Very nice. A pair of turtle doves, a-cooing in the barn."

A woman stands in the doorway, holding her lantern up high as she squints at us through the gloom. I'm guessing she's glad to have arrested our attention. Finally.

She hobbles into the barn, and I put her at about fifty or sixty. No more than that. She's crabbed with infirmity more than with age, I'd say, but it's difficult to tell. Her face and hands are lined, but perhaps it's from weather and work.

"I suppose you couldn't wait for December and the sprig of mistletoe."

Johnny clears his throat. "Good woman, I beg your pardon for our trespass."

The lady holds up her light so she can have a better look at him.

"You're a gentleman," she says, in an accusing tone. "Don't you have a barn of your own to go courting in?"

"I do indeed, Madam. Fine estates in France and another here in England."

"Well then, what are you doing in mine?"

"We are travelers and could go no further when the light began to fade."

"Never heard of knocking, then? Just made yourself at home?"

Johnny looks a little shame-faced and seems to be lost for words.

The woman sniffs. "Where are you from? And where do you think you're going – apart from up the primrose path?"

At this point Johnny and I both make the mistake of answering. Unfortunately he says Canterbury and I say London, right at the exact same time.

"Make up your minds!"

"Canterbury!" I say, changing my tune.

"From London," Johnny adds. Speaking rather fast.

The woman glances around, holding up her lantern and peering into the darkness. "Where's the other one?"

I try to sound as innocent as I can. "Other what?"

She sighs sharply. "Your companion. You must have one."

"Why do you say that, good lady?" Johnny says, with a jovial smile. "As you see, we thought we were alone."

"Yes, yes. You was making hay alright. I'm not blind. Not yet, anyway. But neither am I a fool, sir. I've just counted *three* horses, trampling around in my herb garden outside."

There is an awkward pause.

"That is indeed unfortunate," Johnny says. "We should have come up to the farmhouse directly and requested assistance tethering our mounts. In the failing light, we seem to have stumbled upon the wrong building."

"I see," she says, in a suspicious tone. Then she looks beyond us, and addresses the quietness of the dark corners of the barn. "Come out, wherever you are! Come out and show yourself to me! You will have seen by now that I'm an old woman. You could do me more harm than I could do you, I'll wager."

That makes me smile.

Perhaps she's not so bad, though she's a tough old bird.

"Come out!" She starts poking about in the hay with her pitchfork. Very energetically.

"Ow! That was my leg!" yelps Edward, in tones of rather aristocratic annoyance. "Maddie! Stop her! She's hurting me and she made a hole in my hose, look at that!"

I turn and look, but I can't actually see any wound or the hole or anything much else in the shadowy gloom inside the barn.

"Get inside the house, the lot of you. My husband will want to know what's going on out here."

"You have a husband?" says Johnny, remembering his manners. "I must introduce myself to him, at once."

I stand there wondering for a moment why it was that she came out of the house alone. Why wasn't it the guy who came out, with the pitchfork? The old lady seems to understand our curiosity, and answers the question that neither of us liked to ask.

"He's old before his time, with pains in all his joints. He sits beside the fire all day, because it hurts him to move. Come along now, I don't want to stand here all night and I won't have it said that I'm not a proper hostess. I've got ale in the cooler and honey and oatcakes in the larder."

Richard's head emerges from the hay, an elfin face anxious not to be overlooked. "I like oatcakes."

The woman's eyes light up in surprise. "Another one! A little nipper, this time. Pray tell me, is that all of you? Or are there any more beneath the hay?"

We all head for the house, and I troop in after Johnny, who has to bow his head to get in through the door. My eyes rest for a moment on his strong shoulders and I feel another pang – I can't stop reliving that kiss.

The old lady crosses the low room. "Giles. We've got company."

The man looks up from his place by the fire and peers round at us suspiciously. In his arthritic hand he holds an empty tankard. He attempts to put it down on the oak table beside him, but he misses and it falls on the floor.

The old man swears and Johnny steps forward and picks the tankard up, setting it carefully on the table. "My apologies for the late hour, sir. We are travelers en route to Canterbury."

The man snorts. "You're well off the beaten track in that case, sir. We don't get many pilgrims down here."

"Yes," says his wife darkly. "There's none so careless about taking the wrong road as them that don't want to go there."

The old man frowns and they exchange knowing glances.

The two boys exchange glances too. Edward looks nervously round at the door, as if he might need to make a run for it soon.

Johnny starts acting all jovial and friendly, to defuse the tension. "This is a fine farm, sir, a splendid place."

"Yes, it is, but it don't belong to me. It belongs to the Abbey, nearly fifteen mile away. They used to have monks here looking after the grange, but they lease to us now. We give a portion of our crops to them as rent."

"You are the grange-master, then?"

"Have been for twenty years." The man rubs his painful hands.

"It's a wonderful spot," Johnny says. "I should like to own a place like this, one day."

*And one day you will, I'm thinking. Many years from now.*

The farmer shrugs. "Wife and I do our best, but it's a big place and we are not as young as we used to be."

"You have a son to take it over, and look after you in your old age?"

The woman shakes her head. "We were not blessed with children."

Giles hauls himself up out of his comfortable seat and limps over to the table.

"Sit down, sit down. Wife will bring us some food."

Gratefully, we all sit down. It's a huge, long table – fashioned out of the heart of the oak. Giles takes his place at the top.

"What news from London then? Is it true that the Princes are dead?"

Johnny looks up. "Where did you hear that?"

"Everywhere, or so the wife tells me. She said they was talking about it in the village. It's a bad business and no mistake. Are they dead, do you think, or did someone steal them away, somehow?"

The woman sets the cakes on the table and invites us to take one and share the honey. "They was just babes, weren't they? Little boys."

"Not that little," says Richard, rather unwisely.

Everyone at the table freezes.

Giles frowns. "What ages were they, boy, since you're so well informed?"

Edward gives Richard a none-too surreptitious kick.

Johnny helps himself to another cake, and keeps his voice casual. "I believe they were about twelve and nine. What other news of our great city interests you? The coronation, perhaps?"

"Twelve and nine, did you say?" The old lady asks, glancing nervously at the golden head of the younger boy.

This time, Richard looks down at his plate and says nothing.

"The coronation, I'm told, was a most magnificent spectacle," Johnny says. "The king wore blue cloth of gold, with a long purple mantle trimmed with ermine."

Edward chews his food, and refuses to meet anyone's eye.

The old lady shakes her head. "He was never meant to be crowned, that man. He's a bad lot, and he'll come to a bad end."

Edward looks up at her and gives her a warm smile.

She smiles back and ruffles the boy's hair. "Do you have a name, boy?"

I bite my lip. We should have decided on some aliases.

"No," he says quietly. "You can call me what you like."

"You look like an Edward to me," she says with a meaningful look. "Though you're awful tall for twelve."

"He's not twelve," Johnny says, firmly. "He's fourteen at least."

"Good strapping lad," the old man observes. "Soft hands, though."

"Hush, Giles. He's no laborer, and he's certainly not for hire."

"I am," says Edward, to everyone's surprise. "I'm looking for a place, and so is my younger brother. Good lady, do you need help here?"

Johnny looks alarmed. "This farm is rather near to London… " he murmurs, though everyone can hear.

"Too near to London, eh?" Giles shifts uneasily in his seat. "Are you in some kind of trouble, boy?"

Richard sighs. "We didn't even get through the oatcakes this time. And it was all my fault."

I turn to the old lady, and touch her hand. "Can you keep a secret?"


We talk for several hours after that – late into the night.

The woman wants to offer the boys shelter, but her husband shakes his head.

"If anyone finds out they're here we'll be seen as traitors, harboring the king's enemies."

"Oh, fie! We could say we knew nothing about it."

"If we keep our lives we'll lose our living," he protests.

"We'll lose it anyway, Giles. You said yourself we can't keep going another year without getting more help."

"You think they'll plough and sow for you? And shoulder sacks of grain?

"Why not? The older boy's got a good pair of shoulders on him."

"He knows nothing of farming!"

"I'm an exceptionally quick learner," says Edward, keen to put a good word in for himself, if no one else will. "All my tutors said so."

The woman leans forward and looks him in the eye. "Well lad, what you must learn most quickly, is how to tell a good lie."

"Then teach me," the boy says eagerly. "For my life depends upon it."

"You're not from London, for a start," says the old lady. "You were born in… Yorkshire, but you've spent your life in Kent – that's why you've lost the accent. Your name is… Tom, maybe, or something similar—"

Edward nods. "I like Tom."

"You're fourteen – no less – like the gentleman said. Which means you were born in… let me see… "

"Fourteen hundred and sixty eight," Edward says breathlessly. "I was always very good at reckoning."

"Aye, well, you'll need that if you're going to become the grange-master," she says, with a pleading look at her husband. "Giles. He's keen. And they've nowhere else to go. What do you say?"

"I say you're a soft old fool and you're married to an even bigger one."

Edward beams. "Good lady, I will serve you well." He hastens across the old man to shake his hand warmly. "Kind sir, you will not regret this decision. Thank you. Thank you so much for giving me this chance." Then he turns to me. "What do you think, Maddie. Tom the Grange-master, instead of Edward Quintus?"

"Sounds good."

"A gentleman farmer. A life of my own. A safe place for me and my brother."

Richard raises his head from the table. He's full of oatcakes now, and he looks very sleepy. "Shall I be called Tom as well?"

Edward laughs. "Find your own name, scallywag. I have taken Tom."

Not long after, Johnny turns to me, and takes my hand. "We must go. If we leave under cover of darkness, then no one will know we've been here."

I am tired and I'm sleepy, but I nod and say that I will.

The old lady protests. "You can't go blundering around them country lanes in the dark, sir. It's not safe."

"It's not safe to stay either. If this is to succeed, we must confuse the enemy. We won't ride, we'll take the horses and lead them away on foot as far as we can go. If we get tired we will curl up under a hedge somewhere."

"Fine gentleman like yourself, sleeping under a hedge? And the lady too?'

"Desperate times. Desperate measures."

The woman snorts. "You won't be able to see where you're going and you'll fall into a ditch."

Giles shouts out from the chair. "Wife, you must let them go. They mean it for your own good."

Reluctantly, she shows us to the door.

"I suppose it's for the best. We can keep quiet about the lads for a week or two, until the fuss has all died down. Later on, I'll say they are my nephews and their mother was taken by a fever."

Johnny nods his head. "You're a good woman, with a stout and noble heart."

When we are fastening up our hoods and preparing to go out into the night, the old woman notices something.

"How charming that you and your lady love wear those matching rings."

Johnny flushes. A handsome red color rises in his cheeks and he turns his head away. "Oh, we're not… I mean she's not… "

"No?" say the old woman, raising an enquiring brow. "That's not the way it looked when you were kissing in the barn."

# Chapter Twenty-Three

I wake up shivering. I peer out from our little hiding place and see two hares bounding across a meadow covered in dew. It's a cold, still dawn and there is a hint of morning mist. Above us, birds swoop across a dove gray sky, making soft calling noises. Down here, in our nest in the lee of the hedge, I'm aware of the rough texture of the horse blanket we slept on, and the scent of crushed grass underneath our bodies.

We did not get far, last night. We led our horses up the cart track and back on to the road, heading west as if we were making for the next town. There wasn't much moon, and we didn't dare ride. It was so dark we could barely see more than a pace or two ahead. After what seemed to me like ten miles – though Johnny said it was two – we gave up the struggle and tethered the three horses to some young trees.

Johnny made us a little bed under a hedge and I spent the night in his arms.

Now, in the early dawn, I turn my head cautiously to see if he's still asleep. He looks like a fallen angel, even though we've been sleeping rough. His handsome jaw is dark with stubble and there is a smudge of dirt on his cheek. His linen shirt is rumpled, and where it falls open I see a scattering of curled hairs. Masculine perfection, lying right beside me.

Good thing I have no mirror. I probably look like I've slept under a hedge. I sit up and try to smooth my hair down around my face, but as soon as the covers fall from my shoulders I am shivering convulsively.

"Come back to bed," he says tenderly.

I must have woken him when I stirred. He reaches out and pulls me close, hauling his cloak up around us both. His body heat soon warms me, and I nestle against him, feeling completely safe and secure.

Last night we were too tired to think of anything but sleep. This morning, my thoughts turn all too quickly in another direction. He strokes my hair, and his breath is warm on my forehead. I feel sure that if he keeps doing that I'll shiver again, and this time not with cold.

His whole body is pressed against mine, and I'm keenly aware that yes, he is a man. A red-blooded, warm-blooded one.

*Must I really say goodbye to him, today?*

"Johnny?"

"Yes?"

"Will I stay at your house, when we get to back to London?"

He turns his intense dark eyes upon me. "I'll take you wherever you want, sweet lady."

I try not to let my thoughts linger on the words, *I'll take you*, though they resonate through my whole body, searing me with their double meaning.

Tentatively, I reach up and put my hand behind his head, letting my fingers tangle in his dark, unruly hair. His eyes flare with surprise, but he doesn't ask me to stop. I pull him towards me. His mouth is on mine in an instant, and I savor his hot, sweet kiss. His intensity shocks and thrills me and he rolls me onto my back, fierce in his response. His lips ransack mine, and leave me breathless.

"Oh, Madeleine," he murmurs, "if thou were not promised to my cousin... I'd beg thee to be mine, and cleave to thee forever!"

I hear his strange words, and my mind tries to remind me that he and I do not belong together, we are from two worlds that were never meant to collide, but my heart and my body do not listen.

"I want to belong to you, Johnny!"

We kiss again and again, and he wraps his arms around me so tightly that I think I'll die of pleasure. There is no way I could fight free of his fierce embrace, even if I wanted to.

But it is him who breaks away. "Have mercy," he breathes, and pulls away from me. I try to hold him close but he twists in my arms, and I feel him struggle to regain some control over his own body.

We separate, reluctantly. We are both flushed with sensation and with shame.

"I don't understand," I say.

"I am nobly born and gently bred, Madeleine. I'm well aware of what is right and what is wrong. You are promised to my kinsman."

This was all my own fault. Why did I make up that stupid story in the first place. I swallow. I can't let him go. My heart yearns for him. I know that if I try to undo it all now, I'll only make things worse. But foolishly, I set out on some kind of lame explanation of it all.

"Johnny. You are probably going to hate me for saying this, but… what if I were to tell you that your cousin *did* die on the battlefield at Losecoat Field, and that it was all a story so that you would help me save Richard and Edward? It would change things between us, wouldn't it?"

"Madeleine. I know the temptations of the flesh are very sweet, but think carefully now, before you make so free with the truth."

"This is the truth, Johnny!"

"It cannot be. You told me otherwise just the day before yesterday—"

"I know you didn't believe me, when I told you the story about the cousin in France. Now you treat it like some sacred marriage vow."

"You swore to me that the tale about my cousin was true! Yet you would cast him off so lightly? Another comes along and you would offer yourself to him without a second thought? A promise is a promise. And if it is not, then you are a deceiver."

"I needed your help. The person who brought me to London told me to tell that tale – for my own safety!"

"And now you say you played false? Either you deceive me now, or you deceived me then. My cousin is either alive or he is dead! What is it to be?"

"There is no cousin! It was always you, Johnny! Everything I said about him. It was all about you."

"You have his ring!"

"I have YOUR ring! You said so yourself when you saw it."

"This is my ring," he said, angrily brandishing his finger. "And much as I would have liked to have placed it on your finger, I never did. You appear to have its twin, that's all."

"Appearances can be very deceptive."

"And women, too, it seems."

"Johnny. When you mentioned twins… you *could* say it's a bit like that with you and your cousin. It's very complicated but… let me try to explain… it's like you and he are twins, only… "

Anger erupts across his face. "My cousin is my twin now! My twin! Lady, you have taken leave of your senses! Whatever the truth is, I'm glad I am *not* this other De Vere, for he is betrothed to a most fickle young woman, who would tempt every single man she meets!"

There is a noise – the sound of laughter, carrying across the meadow. A group of field workers have arrived to start the day's work. Five or six men, carrying hoes and pitchforks on their shoulders, just across the field. They've seen us, but they point and laugh and go on their merry way.

"Why were they laughing? Is it because we were having a fight?"

"They think I've been swiving you. What other conclusion would they come to, finding a man and a woman half naked under a hedge?"

"Swiving?"

"Ending your maidenhood."

"Well, they couldn't be further from the truth," I say, with undisguised regret. I resolve to try and get him to take me back to London with him. Maybe he'll let me stay in his house to wait for the cousin to turn up, which he never will – for we have altered the course of time and there may not be a modern world for me to go back to. Maybe. The other Johnny may have evaporated, too. Leaving me with this man… this man who is flesh and blood and human just like me.

After they've gone we set about breaking camp and preparing to go back to London. Johnny saddles up the horses, while I roll up our bedding.

Then, with hardly a word, he helps me to buckle our luggage onto the backs of our horses. As he lifts up the leather pouch that I've been using for my things, it emits a small, but unmistakable, electronic beep.

Johnny looks up. "What is that curious sound?"

"Nothing. Here – hand the bag to me. I'll fix it."

He stares down at it with sudden fascination. "What do you hide in there?"

To my horror, he goes right ahead and flips open the leather pouch. He roots around inside to see if he can find what is making the noise.

"Hey, you can't do that. A girl's purse is *not* open to the public, you know!"

But it's too late. He has it in his hand.

My cell phone. Bleeping intermittently, because the battery's almost dead.

I sigh. That thing has already gotten me into so much trouble.

"What, in heaven's name, is this?"

"It's nothing. A trinket from where I come from, that's all. Please give it to me."

He opens it up. He sees the blue screen and his eyes widen. "What strange place are you from, Madeleine?"

He's no fool. He wants an explanation, and I must give him one. He's looking at the picture of me and Lydia that has appeared on the screen. He's frowning down at it, curiously. Two teenage girls – best friends – grinning at the camera like a pair of Hollywood wannabes.

He looks up at me, searching for answers.

"That's me," I explain, rather superfluously, "with my friend, Lydia. She's like a sister to me."

He nods, staring at the unfamiliar image. "It is so tiny – this portrait – and yet so lifelike… "

"Please. Give it to me."

Reluctantly, he hands it over. His face is clouded with confusion.

"Look, I can't show you how it works. It doesn't work around here," I hesitate, not knowing how best to explain it. "It's… a token of home, that's all. A way of keeping in touch. You weren't meant to see it."

"It must be a wondrous place – your homeland."

"Yes, it is. But I'm going to miss *this* place… and you… so much."

"You're going back home?" he says, with pain in his eyes.

"I think I have to… "

How can I tell him that I don't have a clue how this works? I don't know what waits for me beyond that stupid door! Maybe there is no modern world to go back to now that we have altered things forever. How can I even begin to explain!

Johnny mounts his horse, and we ride on in awkward silence. It reminds me so strongly of that *other* return journey – when the other Johnny drove me back London in silence after visiting the Grange –it almost brings tears to my eyes.

"I'm in love with you," he says, as if it pains him to admit it and yet he needs to say the words.

"I know."


It is almost sundown when we arrive back at Johnny's house in Westminster. We ride round to the stables to deliver the horses to the groom – but strangely, he is nowhere to be found. Johnny says he'll stable them himself, and fetch them food and water.

"Go inside," he says, helping me down off the lovely brown mare. "You must be very weary." Then he frowns in surprise, as he looks across at the house, bathed in evening sunlight. "Ask Ursula why she has closed all the shutters."

I let go his hand, and head towards the house.

The door is ajar, and I assume it's okay to walk right in – I am Johnny's guest after all.

The kitchen is deserted. The fire is cold and dead.

I tell myself that there's a rational explanation, while the goose bumps rise on my skin. I gaze across the flagstone floor, towards the other doorway. I am drawn by the sight of three small splashes of… something spilt over there…

I go over to get a closer look, and when I get there, I shiver in fear.

It's blood.

# Chapter Twenty-Four

My heart runs cold.

Blood.

On the floor.

Whose blood?

That nice old man, Alfred, who tends the horses? Or Ursula – plump, rosy-cheeked Ursula – who only lived to make people comfortable and content? I see now that the splashes of blood form a line on the floor, and with horror in my heart I follow them – dreading what I will find at the end of the trail. First they lead me to the place in the corner where Ursula kept her shoes – rough wooden clogs that she used to slip on whenever she went outside. She called them her pattens.

Hope flickers inside me when I see that the shoes aren't there. If she put them on and ran for her life, maybe she got away.

But the blood? Someone didn't get away.

I am almost sick with fear.

I have to get out of here – but not without Johnny. I have to warn him. Perhaps if we have not yet been seen, there's still time to escape. Our horses, though tired, are very loyal. We could gallop away from here.

But in my heart of hearts I know that whoever is here – waiting for us – already knows we are here. They will have been watching and waiting, listening for the sound of the horses hooves as we approached. Watching us dismount. Waiting for the right moment.

I turn and make for the oak door that leads out to the garden. I put my hand on the heavy iron latch and try to lift it as quietly as I can. The door begins to open towards me, and I can see Johnny outside in the sunlight, rubbing down the flanks of his chestnut mare.

"Not so fast."

The chilling, familiar voice comes from behind me.

Right behind me. Close enough for me to sense the cool chill of his breath beside my ear. He breathes like a bitter winter breeze.

In vain I try to snatch open the door, pulling it desperately towards me, but it's too late.

A gnarled white hand slams it shut.

My mouth is dry, and my eyes dread what they will see when I turn around.

I turn, with my heart shrieking inside me.

*Randolph.*

He is dressed as a fifteenth century nobleman. Black silk, like an undertaker, trimmed with crimson, like a king. A heavy gold chain hangs around his withered neck. His cloak is very heavy for September, being lined with the pelts of a dozen little creatures who might have preferred to keep the skin on their backs. It is fastened at his throat, with a blood-red cord.

He smiles at me. A hideous parody of a smile. "Your time has run out, I'm afraid."

"No." I try to take a step back, but the solid timber door is right behind me.

"Ever the little rebel, aren't you?" he says, reaching out to take hold of my shoulders, curling his icy claws around them like some demonic bird of prey.

"Get away from me!"

"Ah, my sweet little morsel of human frailty. When will you ever learn? You think you have been so clever, don't you? But you cannot defeat Time."

My mind is racing. I'm going to die, I can see that.

All I can think of is Johnny. It is the hour of my death, and my thoughts are all for him. I want to warn him. I want to tell him to run away.

But Randolph holds me tight in a grotesque lover's embrace. Close enough to see the lines on his face. Close enough to appreciate that his yellowed teeth are very sharp. Closer still, so

I am forced to inhale the sickly sweet scent of his breath, a bewildering, frightening smell that almost numbs my senses.

Desperate not to succumb, I try to focus on his eyes.

He has the eyes of a murderous, rabid dog.

"You, young woman, are a pestilence and a plague! If you had allowed me to carry out the King's wishes, untold wealth would soon be mine."

Suddenly it becomes clear. "You! You're the maverick?"

"What?"

"The one who wanted to use this situation for his own personal gain – kill the Princes and collect the reward, huh?"

"That is indeed my intention."

I hear Johnny's footsteps just outside, on the other side of the door. I struggle like an animal caught in a trap, but Randolph claps a cold, claw-like hand over my face and pulls me aside to wait behind the door.

Johnny turns the handle and pushes open the door, calling out to me.

"Alfred's not there, Maddie. It's beyond my understanding what can have happened to him—"

I bite hard on the frozen fingers that muzzle me. "Johnny… Don't!"

But it's too late.

Johnny wheels round in surprise as he comes into the room. Randolph kicks shut the door with his foot, all the time maintaining his iron grip on me.

Johnny's face changes, as he sees me held hostage.

"Come one step closer and you'll watch her die!" Randolph tightens his grip on my throat. His cold claw forcing my head up, until I whimper in humiliation and pain.

"I'm dead already, Johnny. Run for your life, while there's still time."

Johnny raises his chin, proudly, courageously, and looks back into Randolph's eyes. "Unhand her, you ugly dog. What the devil do you think you are doing, invading my house like this?"

*He doesn't understand. He thinks he can win.*

I try to tell him – with eyes alone – that Randolph cannot be defeated. He's not some bully in the schoolyard or a bad guy in the street.

Randolph's long curved fingernails caress my neck. He is playing with me. He is a cruel, tormenting cat, toying with a mouse. When he speaks, he croons like a lover.

"She will die," he says, stroking my neck. "But first she will tell me where she has hidden those boys."

"Never!" I say, almost spitting the word at him.

"Oh, but you will, my sweet."

To my dismay, I see Johnny reaching for his dagger. I shake my head and try to beg him, silently, not to make that mistake. Randolph tips my head back, exposing my neck. He bares his teeth in a hideous parody of a smile and then flexes his jaw – open and shut.

Johnny approaches, looking more surprised than afraid. "What vile, bestial creature are you?"

"Don't come any closer, Johnny. He's a vampire!"

"A vampire?"

*He doesn't know. He doesn't understand.*

Johnny advances another step, fingers curling around the dagger. "Looks more like a mad old fool to me. A deranged, *diseased* old fool."

Randolph hisses. "In time you will respect me, boy!"

"Don't take another step! He'll kill us both!"

"But… I can see that the man is unarmed," Johnny says, "What harm can he do me, Madeleine?"

His confidence is high and I know we are both doomed.

He takes a third step towards us, and this time, it's almost a swagger. The ice-cold points of Randolph's teeth press against my neck. Time is running out for me.

"Get back, Johnny. Get away from here! He's going to… devour me… suck the lifeblood out me… "

Johnny almost laughs. "He is not!"

"No?" Randolph says, lifting up his head for a moment. "Then tell me the name of the place where they are hid!"

Johnny's patience ends and he lunges forward.

In one swift movement he stabs his dagger into Randolph's arm and knocks his head back with his left fist, to prevent the man from sinking his teeth into me. There is a resounding clanging noise, like a man's fist hitting a door made of iron.

Johnny yelps in pain and reels backwards, clutching his hand.

The dagger falls with a metallic clang onto the flagstone floor, accompanied by a thin stream of greenish fluid that I can only assume is Randolph's blood. Johnny's eyes flare as he sees the blade of his dagger, covered in the mysterious green stuff, fizzling and hissing as it lies there on the ground.

Johnny gasps in bewildered surprise. "What in heaven's name?"

I watch helplessly, as the blade on the dagger corrodes before our very eyes.

Randolph whirls me around, releasing me and throwing me against the timber door that leads from the kitchen to the hall. I cry out in pain as soft flesh collides with medieval wood, but Randolph only laughs.

"Time to change places!" he says merrily, snatching Johnny as his new hostage. Randolph leers at me from over the top of

Johnny's shoulder. My beloved man gives a cry of pain and anguish as his arms are pinned behind his back.

"Yes," says Randolph, with a cruel leer. "Let's try it this way around, shall we? Perhaps we'll meet with more success."

The creature grasps a handful of Johnny's thick dark hair, pulling his head back so I can no longer see his frightened eyes. I feel his fear though. I feel it more keenly than my own. Johnny gulps and tries to swallow – his Adam's apple moving as he does. This time, I must watch while the creature nuzzles his evil face against my lover's neck. I see – with perfect clarity – the yellow teeth preparing to descend and bite into the warm, inviting flesh. Johnny's neck, though strong and male, seems vulnerable in the monster's hands.

"Time for a taste of Champagne?" Randolph says.

"NO!" I scream out the word. "No! You can't!"

Randolph sniggers, eyeing me with amusement. He places a teasing kiss on the neck of the man I love. "Then tell me the name of the place, Madeleine."

"What place?"

"The place of safety – where you took the boys."

"You'll kill him anyway."

"Yes, I will. But you will tell me, just to delay it."

Yes. He's right. I will tell him. Because every moment that he does not kill Johnny is a moment that is precious to me.

"Don't tell him, Maddie. I would gladly die for thee, and for my King. There is no shame in dying like that – for love and loyalty. Get away from here as fast as you can. Let the beast gorge itself on me."

"I can't! I can't do that!"

"The name of the place, Madeleine? Or shall I bite, as the foolish boy invites me to."

"Release him and I will tell you everything you want to know." I glance nervously at the door, wondering if there will be a chance to make a bolt for it.

"*If you tell me…* then I will release him."

Johnny struggles in the creature's arms. "He lies! Can't you see that he lies!"

I go over and open the door. A shaft of bright light falls into the room. A band of hope across the flagstone floor. I turn to the creature who stands in the shadows beyond. "Let him walk free and you'll get what you want. Just let him walk away from here."

Johnny tries to protest. "I'll not leave you here alone, Madeleine."

Randolph sighs impatiently. "An impasse, then? Let's do something that will speed things up a little, shall we?"

Making a low guttural noise like an animal, he leans down and takes his first bite.

A ripping, tearing sound follows – a flash of white – and I'm screaming "No! I'll tell you! I'll tell you! Swanley! Kent! A house called The Grange!"

He's torn a piece of the shirt from Johnny's body. That's all he's done. Evil trickster that he is. He turns his head and spits it out, as if it disgusts him.

Gasping with shock and horror, I gaze at Johnny, who is cursing me under his breath. His shirt hangs off him in rags, revealing the curve of his shoulder and swell of his bicep below, but his skin is perfect. Golden brown and completely smooth.

He shakes his head, sorrowfully. "Everything we've worked for – tossed away. Oh, Madeleine… "

I tremble, as I gaze at Johnny's smooth, unblemished flesh. The glorious masculine curves rise and fall softly as he takes each breath. He is still whole and unharmed. Angrily, I address myself to the creature. "You've got what you want, now let him go!"

Randolph laughs. "And now for the real thing."

Sick at heart, I know I have been duped. I turn away, blundering towards the window in helpless, hopeless despair. Almost blinded by tears, I pull back one of the drapes, wanting to see the light of day.

A howl of pain and anger makes me turn back and take a look.

Of course! The creature burns! Blistering and burning, it scrabbles to keep a grip on Johnny. But with its flesh reddening with anger and agony, it fights frantically to escape the light at the same time.

"Get free of him, Johnny! If we can get outside into the sunlight, he can't follow us there!"

Johnny struggles to break free, valiantly wrestling with the strong arms that coil around him. They move around the room in a wild dance – crashing against furniture, sending shelves full of earthenware jars cascading to the floor. Wooden plates, pewter tankards – down it all comes – noisy chaos and dancing objects everywhere. Randolph wrestles Johnny across to the side of the room that is still in shadow.

I run to another window to let in more light. I snatch the fabric away, ripping it down in my haste. Sunlight streams into the room and there is another howl of pain.

At last, Johnny succeeds in breaking free. He shoves the blistered creature away from him and onto the floor.

"Come on!"

We both run for the door, not daring to turn and see if the creature rises to its feet. Knowing that it does.

We almost collide in the doorway.

I shove Johnny forward through the door, almost knocking him off his feet. He lurches but he just about keeps his balance and sprints out into the light.

I hurry – too fast – trying to follow him, and I almost make it.

Almost, but not quite.

The door lintel is raised just an inch or two, and in my haste to get outside, I trip on my long skirt and fall headlong onto the floor.

Bruised and cursing, I lie on the path with one foot not quite out of the door. I see Johnny sprinting ahead, and I'm glad. I'm glad he got away.

I push myself up on my grazed palms and tear with stinging fingers at the skirts that bind my legs. I hear Johnny calling out in anguish when he realizes I'm not there. He turns back and starts running towards me.

"Maddie, come on!"

But it's too late. The vampire hauls me back.

He hauls me into the house, dragging me across the floor by my feet, like a bird being dragged inside by a cat. He pulls me into a patch of the deepest shadow he can find, and rolls me over onto my back.

"At last. I have you in my clutches again, and this time there is no reason on earth not to satisfy my appetite!"

I whimper as he rips the blue dress apart at the front so he can see me – exposed and naked. He leans over me, baring his yellow teeth, salivating at the thought of tasting my blood. I close my eyes. I think of Johnny. Only of Johnny.

Smash! The sound of breaking glass. Shards of glittering glass fall all around me, flying into the room. The vampire looks up in dismay. Johnny is right outside, smashing the shutters off the rest of the windows.

Letting the light flood in.

Johnny vaults into the room, boots first. He lands like an athlete on the flagstone floor, fingertips resting lightly on the floor, glass shards under his feet. He launches himself onto Randolph's back, grasping the folds of his rich clothing, hauling him off me.

I roll over and try to struggle to my feet, while Johnny wrestles valiantly with that salivating monster. Randolph drags him down, down onto the ground, rolling him into the shadows. The smell of seared skin is nauseating.

My shredded dress impedes me, but I find a heavy pewter candlestick and pick it up. I thwack Randolph's bony back just as hard as I can, but it makes a horrible resonating sound like a lump of iron hitting a rusty ship's bell, and that's about it.

The men fight on.

I rush wildly to where the knives have all spilled out onto the floor.

I think of Ursula polishing them – holding each one up to the light. *This one's real silver*, she said. My hands sift through them in desperation.

Why can't I remember? This one? That one? I need to know which one!

I see a knife lying under the table. Gold chasing on the handle, and a long, pointed blade. I'm not certain it's the one, but I make a grab for it all the same.

The men are wrestling on the floor, first Randolph on top, then Johnny. Randolph is desperate to avoid falling into a shaft of sunlight, and Johnny fights to put him there. Even though he's burnt, Randolph has the strength of an angry lion.

If I don't do something, I will see Johnny vanquished in seconds. The men roll one last time, and Randolph gains the advantage. He's snarling like a wild animal about to tear apart its helpless prey.

*His heart, I must strike through the heart. But does he even have one in there?*

Randolph's back is curved and bony. I raise the knife high above my head and pray that I will have the courage to see this through.

"Time to die, Randolph!"

"What?" He raises his head and looks around wildly at me, giving Johnny just enough opportunity to push him away.

Flat on his back, Randolph sees the silver dagger.

His face takes on a look of angry surprise. "No!" he shrieks and raises his hands to ward me off.

"Too late for mercy now!" I scream.

I lunge down towards the creature. I sink the knife hard into his chest, investing every emotion into one sharp thrust. All my hatred, all my anger, all my longing to be free. Everything. All there in the force behind the knife.

I drive the blade home with the fury of a hellcat.

Randolph makes a wheezing noise like he's winded and can't get his breath. His face is contorted. He writhes in angry agony on the floor. His bony hands clutch at the blade, but his strength is failing. His fingers are weak and ineffectual, plucking pathetically at the knife that spears him to the ground. Greenish fluid pours from the wound.

I realize I am watching him die. He tries to speak, but at first all that comes out is a horrible wheezing sound. He struggles to utter his last words, and finally he finds some remnant of his voice.

"Murderer… " he whispers.

"It was self-defense."

"Swanley… in Kent… "

"Yes, and the secret dies with you."

His evil black eyes turn on Johnny, who kneels beside me in his torn and bloody shirt. "But not with you."

Then, the creature sighs his last cold breath. His jaw goes slack, and slimy fluid trickles from his mouth. The unpleasant grimace of death settles on his face, making me shudder and turn away.

When I look back, the eyes are open and staring. Staring at me, or so it seems. The grimace is still there.

It almost looks like a smile.

# Chapter Twenty-Five

Johnny kisses me, pulling me into his arms.

Kneeling beside the silent monster, we embrace and for a moment the sweetness of victory is ours. Johnny is breathless with happiness. Delirious almost.

"You did it! You vanquished him and we are free!"

I nod slowly. "He's dead."

"Brave girl! Clever girl!" he says, cupping my face with his bruised, bloodied hand. "My only love and the champion of my heart."

I let my gaze travel slowly over his body. I see small gashes and wounds everywhere, on his chest, across his cheek, and on his brow.

"Johnny… you're injured."

He smiles, and shrugs it off. "It's nothing. A few scratches, that's all. No broken bones. It will heal."

I try to nod and force myself to agree with him, but perhaps he sees the fear in my eyes. He touches one of the wounds and frowns.

"It stings a little."

"Let me bathe it for you. Maybe that will help."

I get up and go over to where Ursula keeps a big tub of water, covered with a linen sheet. I pull back the cover, and look into the tub. The water looks pure and clear. I tear up the linen into smaller pieces, wet them and bring them back to Johnny.

I kneel down beside him and with infinite care and gentleness, I wash each and every wound. He sits patiently, letting me work. Every now and then he smiles and strokes back the strands of hair that fall in front of my eyes.

"Marry me."

It doesn't sound like a question somehow. My gaze meets his, and my heart is pierced by the look in his warm, brown eyes. He frowns, and raises an eyebrow questioningly, waiting for my reply.

"You want to, don't you, Maddie?"

"Yes."

His face bursts into a triumphant smile. A handsome, male grin. "We'll make it right somehow with my cousin. I promise you – all will be well."

I shake my head. "You're cousin is not the problem."

"No? Then, Madeleine, tell me what is?"

I pause, with the bloodstained wet rag in my hands. My fingers are trembling, and my voice cracks when I try to speak.

"The problem… is… time. I don't know how much time we've got left."

Johnny's face changes. Clouding with anxiety as he begins to see my fear. He takes the rag out of my hand and tosses it aside. "What do you mean?"

I put my hand on the side of his beautiful face, and kiss his lips. They are still warm. The tears come brimming into my eyes, and trickle down my face, even as I try to kiss him. To savor that last sweet taste.

Then, urgently, he takes hold of my shoulders. He pulls me back so he can study my face. "Madeleine. Tell me. You knew that creature, didn't you? You knew what kind of demon he was. Does he have friends who will come after us? Tell me, is that what you fear?"

I shake my head. "Forgive me. It was all my fault. You should have let me drown in the river. You should have walked away."

Shaking and sobbing, I let fresh tears fall down my face. I don't even bother to try and wipe them away. I catch sight of the grinning face of the corpse, just there beside me. Randolph's last laugh. Or so it seems. I cover my eyes and rock myself to and fro.

"Don't cry," says Johnny. "Please, don't cry."

He gets up. He fetches Randolph's cloak, shakes the broken glass from it, and drapes it carefully over the corpse.

He pulls me to my feet. "Come away. We will forget what has happened here today. It's draughty in here now. Let's go into another room – one that still has glass in the windowpanes. We will be happy together for a while."

"For a while, yes."

He leads me away. Away from Randolph's body. He leads me into the next room, which is still as spick and span as Ursula could make it. He encourages me to sit on the old oak settle, and fetches an extra pillow to make it more comfortable.

"It's cold," he observes. "Even in here."

A fire is already laid in the grate, and he kneels down and reaches for the tinder box to set light to the kindling.

Before long, it is burning merrily.

Johnny reaches for his lute and sits down and starts to play. I listen to the beautiful sound he makes. He plucks at my heart. He wants to lull my fear away.

But soon, he is shivering.

Beads of sweat form on his brow. He tries to play on, ignoring the signs of fever that plague him, but before long they cannot be ignored. He shudders and shakes. He grips the lute fiercely for a moment, and then lets it slip and fall to the floor. It makes a hollow, discordant sound.

"Maddie?" he gasps. "What's happening to me?"

"Do you feel pain?"

"Yes. In my head, in my body. Everywhere."

I don't know what to do. I don't know how to help him.

"This is what you feared, isn't it. Maddie, speak true! Tell me what will happen!"

"I don't know. I've never seen it before.'

He cries out in pain as the spasms begin to take him. I leap out of the way as his whole body convulses. I'm transfixed by his agony, I stand there, helpless while he is wracked with pain.

"The creature," he gasps. "He did this? He did this to me?"

"Yes."

Another spasm. And another. I snatch the lute out of the way as Johnny rolls off the settle and crashes onto the floor.

Sprawled there, he looks up at me. Pleading, questioning eyes.

"What will happen, Madeleine? Will I die?"

*I can't. I can't say it.*

"Help me!" he moans, reaching out to clutch my hand. "Oh, my love, please help me!"

I hold his hand tight in mine. "I will do anything I can."

Before long, he complains of the heat of the fire, even though he seems to be shivering.

"If you can walk, I'll help you get to your room." I hoist him up onto his feet and duck my head under his arm. "But you've got to cooperate with me, you hear?"

We climb the wooden staircase, with difficulty, as it's barely wide enough for one.

"My room is the one on the right," he murmurs.

I smile. He sounds almost bashful. "Okay."

I steer him in there, swaying under the weight. It's a spacious room, paneled in dark wood, dominated by an old canopied bed. I head straight for the bed, anxious to get him down before he falls. I'm glad to see that the curtains are pulled back already. He falls like a felled oak onto the bed, collapsing onto the pillows. I fuss round trying to get him under the covers and make him as comfortable as I can.

He looks like he's dying. His healthy color is gone – replaced by hues of gray and hints of blue. He's sweating, but he's cold and clammy.

I sit beside him on the bed, holding his hand.

He squeezes it gratefully, and gazes up at me. "My love, I did not imagine it would be anything like this, when I brought thee to my bed."

I smile sadly. "You will get better."

He gives me an unhappy, regretful smile. "There is no shame in dying… for love and loyalty."

For several hours I am at his bedside, watching the poison taking over his body. He believes he will die, and I do not disillusion him.

He complains about the pain and yet he refuses to blame me. He touches my face and says he is glad that I live and that I must return to the place I came from and remember him kindly.

But then the convulsions come back. Agonizing spasms grip him and torture him, again and again and again. His body thrashes and writhes upon the bed, while I watch on in helpless misery. Seeing his terrible pain – I even start to wish, for his sake, that he *could* die.

I try to comfort him, but he seems to stare past me at some imagined horror that he sees in his mind. "No! It cannot be!"

"It's alright Johnny. There's nothing there."

I clutch his hand, and try to calm him, but he is beyond comfort. He stares and points wildly at something, *someone*, that he sees standing in the doorway.

"What sorcery is this? What witchcraft!"

"Hush." I try to blot away the sheen of perspiration from his forehead.

*Then a voice speaks behind me, a third person in the room.*

"He must drink this."

I know the voice.

I loved it – I love it still.

I turn, slowly, and there is Johnny. Johnny from the Tower. The man I met that night at Heathrow airport. He comes into the room and sets a tankard full of liquid on the table. I look up at his face, and see there is no trace of the terrible burn that marked his skin. He looks in every way as perfect as the first day I set eyes upon him.

The poor injured boy lying on the bed clutches my hand in fright. "Is it a vision, Madeleine? Or can you see him standing there?"

"It's only a dream," I murmur, deciding, yet again, that a lie serves me better than the truth.

He turns his pallid cheek against the pillow in despair. "Now I know that I will die. It's a bad omen to see one's own soul, standing in the corner of the room. It means the angel of death is upon me."

The other Johnny lifts up the tankard and brings it over to me. "He needs this. You must get him to drink it."

I take the tankard from him and gaze down at the dark red liquid it contains. It is still warm, judging by the temperature of the metal that holds it.

I shudder. "Where did you get it?"

"Don't ask. Give it to him."

I put one arm around my patient – my beloved man – I kiss his forehead and encourage him to sit up just enough to take a sip.

"No, Maddie, I can't! It looks like… it smells like blood!"

"Please, John. For me."

He struggles to take a sip, spitting most of it out. Splashes of blood fall onto his pale cold chest and onto the linen sheets. "No… I can't… The idea reviles me!"

"You must. It will make you strong again. Please. I don't want to watch you die."

He glances dubiously into the red depths of the tankard. "What madman told you to try this remedy?"

I nod my head at the other Johnny, standing tall and awkward in his dark clothing on the other side of the room. "Him."

Johnny looks up at the apparition of himself, and then he looks at me and whispers in fear, "I thought only I could see… "

But he is too weak to protest. The malady has him, body and soul. He lets me put the tankard of blood up to his lips and he drinks.

He drinks it all.

He collapses back on the pillow and closes his eyes as if to sleep. At the leaded window a light flickers, just for a second, as if someone out there had a torch. Lightning. A thunderstorm coming our way. I wait for the sound of thunder, but there is a long pause before it rolls.

"You must come with me now, Maddie," the other Johnny says. "You don't belong here. It's time to leave."

Johnny's eyes flutter open, and he gives a feeble cry from the bed. "Don't go. Don't leave me!"

"I'm staying," I murmur. I twist the ring on my finger – the ring that is over five hundred years old.

The other Johnny shakes his head. "You think you can stay, in this place, with a monster? You think I would leave you here, knowing what he will do?"

"I'll be alright."

"I have seen it, Maddie. I've known his rage and his fury at what he has become. I've seen how he tries to starve himself to death rather than take life to sustain his own. How he suffers – in abject misery – until the savage desire to taste blood overtakes him and he runs into the street and murders the first person he sees!"

I shake my head in disbelief. "No… he wouldn't do that!

"He has to quench his thirst. He knows no other way!"

"He wouldn't hurt innocent people. I know he wouldn't."

"He will. He does. Until he learns."

It begins to sink in. Johnny knows what happens next. Johnny *always* knew what happened next.

Anger flashes inside me, matching the thunderstorm outside. "If you knew this was going to happen, why didn't you kill Randolph, while you had the chance? You said you met him after the Great Fire of London. If that's true, you've had three hundred years to sort this out!"

"It was not his fate. I am a Patron. I protect the River of Time."

"Don't give me that. You said you couldn't bear the idea of it happening all over again. You went to warn your younger self not to be so foolish! You wanted to change things so this didn't happen!"

"Yes. But when it came to it, I just couldn't do it."

"Why not? Are you afraid of Randolph?"

"No."

"Then why? Why didn't you kill him and save your mortal life?"

"Because… unless everything happened the way it was meant to happen… you and I could never meet. I wanted to find you again. To forget the past. To have a future, with you."

I am trembling. "I did this. To him. To you."

"Yes. He gave his mortal life for you. And now you must leave. Don't waste the sacrifice he has made."

"No. I can't let him face this alone. You don't walk out on the people you love!"

"No, you don't. That's why I'm not leaving without you, not this time."

But I'm still mad at him. "Johnny, if you weren't trying to change what happened, then where the hell *have* you been?"

"I've been back to our time. Talking to the police. There's quite a search going on for you, you know."

*I don't even want to think about that.*

"Madison," he says, and it shakes me to hear my real name. "They've been searching for you for days. Your mother is exhausted with worry and your step-dad, Jake, he's out of his mind. Your friend Lydia seems to think it's all her fault for telling you where your father works, and your teacher reckons she's about to get fired."

I almost weaken, hearing the names of the people I care about. But I stare at the anguished face of the man I love and wish, desperately, that things were different.

Then I hear his cry – the man who lies in torment, on the bed.

"Madeleine! The pain comes again! Help me!"

I rush back to him, to soothe him and to kiss his cold, clammy skin.

When the spasm is over I turn to the other one, the one who has seen it all. "How can you ask me to leave him?"

"I have died for you once, Madison. Don't ask me to exist without you… for even one minute more. Take my hand. Come back through the door with me."

Leave Johnny to be with Johnny? My mind lurches.

I turn back to the man lying on the bed. "Johnny? Do you hear me? We will find each other again."

But he's slipping in and out of consciousness. He's delirious with pain, and I am in despair.

I look up at the other one, searching his face for answers. "What can I do? How can I tell him that I love him?"

"You could try leaving him a note." There is a resonating bitterness in the voice of the man who has suffered all this long ago.

Yes! Of course! A note!

I run to the desk – no paper – so I tear a leaf from the bible that lies on the table. Vellum parchment, of the finest quality. I take a fresh quill and dip it into the ink. I agonize, only for a moment, and then I write "Forgive me."

I freeze when I realize what I'm doing.

I am writing *the letter*.

I look up, and into Johnny's eyes. Dark eyes filled with tenderness and regret. The same as the warm brown eyes of my medieval lover, but filled with sadness from waiting for so long.

"No!" I lay my quill feather down on the table, marking it with ink. I shake my head. "I won't write it."

"You must."

"NO! I can't do this to him. This letter will send him searching for me for five hundred years."

He nods. "Do it."

I shake my head, but I remember the words he once told me and they echo like a mocking curse in my head. "Time is like a circle – a wedding band, you said!"

"It is."

"It wasn't the whole truth."

"What should I have told you? That time is like a hangman's noose? And mostly we are the victims of a harsh, cruel fate? Would you rather I had told you that? Would you have believed me if I had told you that I've waited for you for five hundred years – and would wait a thousand more, if I had to?"

A tear rolls down my cheek. "No."

On the bed the young man – who saved my life that day I fell into the river – lies in agony, moaning and crying out for me. There is nothing I can do for him. Except this.

I have to write the note.

At least one thing is easy. I know exactly what to say.

"In time you will forgive me" I write, going as fast as my inexperience with quill pen and ink will allow. The tears run down my face, but I do not stop to swipe them away. "I'll be waiting for you," I write, "at Heathrow, last Wednesday in August."

"Come on! We will miss the tide!"

I will finish it. I will tell him the year. I will.

I scratch the words but my quill runs out of ink.

"Come on, Maddie. We have to catch the tide!"

Lightning flashes outside and illuminates the haggard face of my poor injured lover. The man whose mortal life I have destroyed.

"There's no more time!" Johnny yells. "Leave it!"

"Let me finish it!"

I dip my pen again, and struggle to form the words 'in the year', only I remember that Johnny always used that old fashioned form of words – *in the year of Our Lord* – should I try and write that, maybe?

It's my own fault. For hesitating.

"Now!" Johnny pulls me from the desk. I fight to keep writing, but he hauls me away. The tip of the quill pen leaves an ugly black line on the paper.

A flash of white lightning illuminates the room. Thunder breaks, rolling like gunfire over the house, as time almost rends in two.

Two broken hearts, mine and his.

Five hundred years of heartache in between.

"It's a choice, Maddie. A hard choice – and it must be made now!"

I take Johnny's hand and follow him into the future.